STANDING OUTSIDE THE FIRE

A Holder County Novel

JILLIAN NEAL

Photography by

GOLDEN CZERMAK / FURIOUS FOTOG

Edited by

HAPPILY EDITING ANNS

Published by Realm Press

ISBN: 978-1-940174-53-2

Library of Congress Control Number: 2020906301

First Edition

First Printing – April 2020

Occupational Therapists help make all of the pieces of daily life work the way they're supposed to. They help their patients live their lives to the fullest. I could never have written this book without the help of my dear friend, Mary Jo. The pieces would never have worked.

To Mary Jo--

Thanks for always helping me live my life to the fullest.

CONTENTS

PROLOGUE

It was Jamie Holder's twelfth birthday, and he stared at what had to be the most beautiful girl he'd ever seen in all of his years of life. He had a problem. The boner he'd just sprung in the middle of algebra wasn't going away. He tried to remember what his big brother Ford had told him about getting rid of them, something about turnip greens and Sunday preaching, but he couldn't think of anything but how pretty she was and how much he wanted to know what her lips tasted like. Cotton candy from the fair, he bet. Not that crap they sold in bags at the feed store on Saturdays. No. She was the real deal, the melt in your mouth, candy-sweet, spun sugar that turned your tongue bright pink.

The girl with a halo of messy red curls and freckles scattered across her wind-pricked cheeks attempted to smile at him as she stood dutifully beside the teacher. Ms. Hendrix needed to get on with this stupid introduction so that Jamie could get to asking this girl to marry him.

He shook himself. What the hell was wrong with him? Obviously, he couldn't get married until his daddy gave him his parcel of Holder Ranch, so Jamie would be able to take good care of her.

She was wearing a dress that he knew she was gonna get teased for. It wasn't at all what the rest of the girls in the school wore, mostly Wranglers and T-shirts. But she looked so pretty. Jamie couldn't stand to think about the other girls teasing her for her clothes. It looked homemade, and that wasn't cool in Holder County, but it probably had been back wherever she came from. It was also several sizes too large for her small frame. He'd just make sure no one was a bitch to her. That would be his mission from now on—to protect her.

"Class," Ms. Hendrix announced, "I want to introduce you to our new student, Charlotte Tilson. She's just moved here from Oklahoma City. I'm sure you'll all make her feel very welcomed." She said that the way teachers do that thing where you know it's a threat even if the words aren't necessarily threatening.

Jamie raised his hand. Ms. Hendrix made no effort to hide her eye roll. He knew she hated him. He sucked at math. It was boring and when he got bored, he tended to run his mouth. He didn't mean to. It just always seemed to happen. "Yes, Jamie. What is it?"

"Charlotte can sit here." He pointed to the desk right beside his, thankful for once that no one had taken the seat on the first day of school. Maybe algebra would somehow magically turn into his favorite class.

"Thank you," Charlotte whispered. She headed his direction, and he prayed she wouldn't notice his...problem. He scooted himself further under his desk trying to conceal his Wranglers.

There'd been a bunch of talking between Ms. Hendrix and the principal and the counselors before they'd brought Charlotte in. He wondered what that was all about. Almost nobody ever moved to Holder County unless they decided to give cattle ranching a try and there happened to be a ranch for sale. That occurred next to never, so a new kid in school was rare. The school had been named after some relative of Jamie's just like everything else in Holder County. He couldn't remember which one, and he really didn't care. All he knew was that it was a pain in his ass that everyone knew everything there was to know about him, his brothers, and all his cousins just because they were Holders.

But this new girl wouldn't know anything about him yet, now would she?

Smiling at that, he turned to study her again as she sank slowly down in the cold metal seat beside his. Her backside was as pretty as her front. Ford was gonna have to come up with some better plans for the whole boner deal because things were not improving.

Suddenly, an ear-piercing screech blared through the classroom, piped in through the intercom. Fire drill. Jamie promptly panicked. Now was not a good time for him to have to stand up. He mentally practiced a few of his uncles' favorite curse words and then, switching tactics, prayed everything in his pants would return to normal size and hardness levels.

Squeaks and clanks of chairs and backpacks sliding along the floor signaled his classmates standing to file outside. Everyone was thrilled for a fire drill on a warm spring day. No algebra, beautiful girl, and getting to go outside. This day was pretty awesome if you didn't count the whole hard-on thing.

But when Jamie forced himself to stand and willed his dick to cut him a break, he saw Charlotte still sitting frozen in her seat. Tears threatened to escape from her long eyelashes.

His problem went away. "Hey, it's okay. It's just a drill. Nothing exciting ever really happens here. I promise. Come on," he offered her his hand, "I'll show you where we go."

Charlotte placed a timid, shaking hand in his. She was freezing despite the warm day and the windows being opened. He closed the warmth of his own hand around hers and eased her toward the classroom door.

She moved stiffly like one of those zombies from that movie he and Ford had snuck in to see when their dad had taken them into the new theater out in Odell last weekend. The alarm must've frightened her. Poor thing.

His heart ached, and he couldn't breathe even thinking of her crying. He'd seen his mama crying once a few months ago, and it had nearly ended him. He didn't know what to do when girls cried, and mamas shouldn't ever cry. They're too good to ever have to go through anything that made them sad enough to shed tears. His daddy had finally told him and Ford that their mama had lost a baby.

Jamie had seen that happen with a few of their cows, but never his own mother. He didn't really think they needed any more brothers. Plus, his Aunt Ruth and his Aunt Leigh had just had babies and he figured his mama could just love up on them since they were always together, but that seemed the wrong thing to say just then.

He refocused on Charlotte. If he could remember to focus on anything for any length of time, he'd probably do better in school, but it was trying. However, he'd bet the ten-dollar bill in his back pocket, the one that his Uncle Gentry had given him for putting out the fire that had gotten away from them when they were burning the fields last month, that he could focus on Charlotte for a long, long time and never get bored. "It's okay. I promise. I won't leave you. I'll stay right with you. They'll take roll when we get outside and then maybe they'll let us go play out on the field. It's just a drill." He wasn't certain what else to say that might reassure her. Maybe they didn't have fire drills at her old school. That would suck.

Despite Charlotte's fear, Jamie still felt that same sense of adrenaline bursting through him at the sound of the alarm. He didn't want her to be afraid of anything ever, but as far as he was concerned, answering the call of the alarm, rushing into the things other people ran away from, saving anyone who might still be inside—that was the stuff his wet dreams were made of. Although, he suspected they'd be starring Miss Charlotte Tilson from now on.

He guided her out the doors, through the covered drop off where the buses normally parked, and onto the field. There was no sign of smoke anywhere, and there weren't any firetrucks coming. He hated that he was disappointed in that, but he was. Somehow, he'd figure out a way to be a cowboy like his daddy and also how to be a firefighter too.

"See, it's okay. Told ya it was just a drill." He tried again to get Charlotte to talk or to even look like she knew where she was. She managed a timid nod, and he took that as a good sign.

As they stood out in the practice field, Jamie was still holding her hand. He sure as hell wasn't going to drop it even though he could hear that punk, Sid Ridgeland, making snide remarks about it to his lackeys, Denton Cooper and Clinton Rivers.

"Finally get yourself a girlfriend, Holder," Denton chanted.

Charlotte seemed to suddenly realize that she was still clinging fast to Jamie's hand. Panic lit in those emerald-green eyes of hers.

Jamie tightened his grip. She didn't seem to mind. "Did you finally figure out how to piss without Sid holding your member, Dent?" he came right back. He wasn't taking shit off of either of them. If they teased Charlotte, he'd deck them. He didn't even care if he got in-school suspension for it. His daddy wouldn't care either. His mama, on the other hand, well, he'd just have to explain it to her real careful like.

It was at that moment that Jamie heard an angel, or what he thought must've been one. Charlotte was giggling. His heart lurched and then began to fly inside his rib cage. Damn thing was going to bust through.

Her giggles sent Denton back Sid's way which was fine by Jamie.

"Only my father calls me Charlotte," she whispered when her laughter had dissipated.

"Oh," Jamie considered that, "well, what do you want me to call you?"

"Charlie," she urged. "That's what all my old friends used to call me. Mama used to say Charlotte's too formal for me. She called me Charlie too."

"Okay," Jamie grinned. "I'll call you that too. Hey," he couldn't stop himself even though he knew he should, "do you wanna be my girlfriend like they said?" He gestured back toward the resident middle school stooges even though that was not what he should've done. Dumbass. He cringed. "I mean not like that but...kinda like that...but not really...because they're fuckers."

She was laughing again. Jaysus, if she kept that up he had no chance of not sounding like a dumbass.

"Maybe," she shrugged. "Could we be just friends first?"

"Sure. Yeah. That's...yeah." Defeat shredded through his chest.

Charlie glanced back at the school. "I hate fire alarms," she offered cautiously.

"How come?"

She shrugged again. "I just do."

But the universe was definitely on his side that day because the bell rang just as the fire alarm ceased its constant blare. He grinned. "Wanna go hide out in the tube on the elementary playground? Now nobody's gonna know where anyone is 'cause half the kids are gonna go on to their next class. We can just hang out. No more fire alarms."

Charlie looked at him like he was officially her hero. Oh yeah, he needed more of that. A harsh swallow contracted his throat and if she didn't stop beaming at him, he was gonna have another problem. Damn thing. She sank her teeth into her bottom lip as kids scattered all around them. Finally, she squeezed his hand even tighter and nodded. "Are you sure we won't get in trouble?"

"I promise." They took off at a run.

She'd eventually coaxed him into going back inside after skipping one class. They'd eaten lunch together, and Jamie didn't like that she didn't have ice cream money. "You can have mine." He offered her his ice cream sandwich.

"No, thank you." But the way she eyed the treat made it seem like she really did want to say yes. He broke it in half.

"I don't want all of it anyway." That wasn't exactly true, but he didn't want it as much as he wanted her to have some. She looked like she didn't get to have things like ice cream all that often. He intended to change that.

CHAPTER ONE

"Fuck," Jamie grunted as he forced his body to lean upwards in his bed. Bad plan. He collapsed back down. His muscles ached from fighting the demons of sleep. Christ, his tongue felt like the Sahara complete with tumbleweeds piercing the roof of his mouth. This was the hangover to end all hangovers. After all, that had been his goal when he'd started drinking at noon the day before.

Slapping at the bedside table, he knocked his watch on the floor. He had no idea when he'd gotten around to taking that off, and it didn't really matter. Finally, he located the bottle of Crown that he'd tried to drown his sorrows in the night before. Making another attempt at sitting upright, he managed to unscrew the bottle. His head spun right along with the lid.

Drunk was the only possible way he was going to get through this day, and likely the rest of his stupid life, so he'd deal.

Another low curse growled from his chest when he upended the bottle and not a single drop of liquid sanity poured out. He tossed it on the floor. The resulting thunk ricocheted through his head.

As more and more of the reasons he'd gotten shitfaced the night before filtered through his whisky-laden brain, panic bolted him up out of the bed. He squeezed his eyes shut, but it was no use.

He stumbled to the bathroom and emptied the contents of his gut into the toilet. Bile replaced the whiskey burn in his mouth. "Fuck," he sighed as he hung his head—which he swore weighed three times its normal amount—under the faucet and let the water run directly into his mouth. Then he let the cold water run over his face as well. That helped some. Swirling a shot of mouthwash in his mouth, he tried to study his reflection in the mirror. Yeah, he looked about as good as he felt.

He had to get it together, and he had to do that now. He was going to be late. How poetic. He'd give anything he owned, or would ever own, or would ever even hope to own to not have to go do what he was going to have to go do. But he'd never let her down. Not like that.

Managing to bend over to retrieve his watch, he fought another round of nausea. He had to get to the church. Now. She was marrying that shitlicker in—he willed the dials on his watch to stop spinning oddly in his vision—an hour.

He'd planned to go by the station early that morning and get Kane to give him a saline IV, so he wouldn't have to look like this at the wedding. Charlie would never forgive him for showing up looking like death, no matter how he felt.

This was her day. She'd been planning it for months. He wasn't going to ruin it by opening his big fat mouth and begging her to marry him instead.

Nope. No way. He was not an asshole, and only a guy who wasn't worth the shit on his own boots would do something like that.

He'd had ten dozen chances, and he'd never had the balls to take one, so now he was gonna have to live with the consequences as much as he'd rather walk into a three-alarm without his gear on.

Pulling on his black suit and black tie, he decided it was appropriate that he was dressed for a funeral. He completed his ensemble with a black Stetson. Hell, put his boots backwards in the stirrups of his horse. As far as he was concerned, his life was over anyway.

———

Charlie stared steadfastly at the parking lot from the window of the second-story bridal room at her father's church. Where was he? She could not get married without her best friend there. She mentally tried out that sentence in her mind leaving off the words *without her best friend there*. She could...not get married. She rather liked the peace that settled over her when she allowed the thought to take hold. Oh gravy, that could not be a good sign.

His big brother, Ford, and his extremely pregnant wife, Callie, were already there. So were his parents. But where was he?

Had this dress been this tight when she'd picked it out? She was certain she was going to vomit, but that was just nerves. Wasn't it?

A knock on the door jerked her attention away from searching for Jamie's truck. "Delivery for Charlotte Tilson." A man dressed in a cap and florist's apron held up a bouquet of alabaster white lilies.

"Well, wasn't that thoughtful?" Charlie's stepmother, Louann, commented. Was Charlie the only one who thought she didn't sound very sincere? She'd never known her stepmother to fib. Her father wouldn't have allowed it.

Louann set the lilies down on the antique vanity table and handed Charlie the card. *I can't wait to start our lives together— Ed.* She managed the words, "It was thoughtful," before she had to stop speaking lest she have to race to the bathroom. She hated lilies. They smelled like death. The funeral home had been filled with the dreadful flowers the day of her mother's burial, and she'd hated them ever since.

They were Ed's favorite, however. Charlie had vetoed them across the board for the wedding flowers. Was this some kind of passive-aggressive dig about that? Ed could be whiny when he didn't get his way, so maybe.

She rushed back to her post by the window. As she passed her younger sister, Becca, she formed her hands into a ring like you'd use to choke someone and made the same shaking motion. She'd been doing that with regularity ever since Ed and Charlie had announced their engagement. "You're going to regret this every day for the rest of your life," she whispered yet again.

Charlie had stopped arguing several months ago. Her sister never wanted to get married. Men were entirely too controlling according to Becca. Charlie didn't necessarily agree with that, so she'd assumed she didn't agree with Bec's opinion of Ed. He was a good man. He really was. He took such good care of her patients at the Pecan Crescent Nursing Home where she was the occupational therapist and he was the chaplain. He was kind, and generous, and somewhat patient...and boring.

"It's almost time for us to go down." Louann's reminder shattered the tense moment. "Can I help you with your veil first, sweetheart?"

She held up the lace-adorned tiara.

If she put that thing on Charlie's head, she knew she would somehow suffocate through the lace. "No. It's okay. I can do it. Thank you, though."

Louann nodded and draped the lace across one of the old wingback chairs in the room. She took Charlie's hands. "I remember when I was marrying your daddy and both of you girls." The faraway look in her lovely blue eyes made Charlie smile her first smile of the day. That couldn't be a good sign, either, but it was true. Louann had insisted that Becca and Charlie both have their own wedding dresses because she wanted them to know that they were just as important to her as their father was. As stepmoms went, she was pretty much the greatest. "I couldn't wait to get down that aisle." She chuckled. "I signaled to the organist to speed up the processional so that we could get on with '*Here Comes the Bride*.' It's still that way now too. I can't wait for your daddy to come home from the church. I look for him whenever we're apart." She squeezed Charlie's hands. "He's my very best friend. I think that's the secret to what makes marriage work. Think about that while you're up there today."

"I will," Charlie tried to assure her, but she needed to sit down. All of the blood in her face was making a rapid transit to her feet. Was that some kind of warning? She watched her stepmom and her sister slip out the door, with a final mouthed, "Don't do this," from Becca.

Charlie was sure she just had cold feet. That was it. Everyone did this while they got ready to go down the aisle. Didn't they? Ed probably felt the same way. *Maybe he won't show.* She had no control over her thoughts at this point.

As she stared out the window again willing Jamie's truck to appear, her eyes landed on the nearby cemetery. Her mother's grave was back in Oklahoma City, but the headstones in her vision weighted her with their cold, heavy silence just the same.

It had been more than two decades since the fire, and she still wished for her mother at least once a week. She loved Louann, of course, but Charlie suspected that her mom would've been able to tell that she was completely freaking out.

Her eyes trailed down the lattice trellis right outside the window.

Where was he? Jamie was the only person still on the planet who could calm her down, who always said exactly what she needed to hear, who knew she was coming unglued. She was officially unglued. Why wasn't he here yet? She refused to walk down the aisle without him there.

Again, her mind centered in on the first part of the sentence—refused to walk down the aisle. Why did that sound so utterly appealing, like a lifeline to her when she was drowning in lace and invitations and silk and…lilies? Ugh. But Charlie was the ever-reliable sister. Unless it involved Jamie, she did what her father expected. Becca was the wild child. Not Charlie. Never her.

Her eyes flitted from the parking lot for a moment to take in the dated room surrounding her. Deep teal-and-maroon-striped wallpaper looked frighteningly like prison bars. The bookshelves that lined one wall held small single-bud flower vases. Since Charlie's father had gotten Ed a job at a church in Odell so he could leave the nursing home, which he didn't love the way Charlie always had, Ed had been helping her father out around the church.

One of his current jobs was to handle all the flowers for the church. He'd hand selected the ones in those vases as well. He must've been distracted with all of his jobs lately, because every single flower was withered and dried. They still held color, but their stems were brittle. One touch and they would fall apart. Charlie hated that she recognized herself in them.

That's what he wants. He wants to stick me in a vase at his new church and let me wither as long as I keep up appearances. She shook that disturbing thought from her head.

From her vantage point, she watched two of her favorite residents from Pecan Crescent Nursing Home being helped up the church steps by Trisha, her fellow OT. Mrs. Garcia was so excited about the wedding. If Charlie didn't go down the aisle, would it disappoint her?

Wait. Was she really considering not going down the aisle?! Being an OT was the single most satisfying thing in Charlie's life. She loved her patients, even if they occasionally didn't like her because of what she encouraged them to do in order to retain skills. Pride overlaid her nerves for a brief moment. Should she love her job more than she loves her fiancé? Was that normal? Dear God, she had no idea. She'd never even thought of it before that moment. It wasn't normal to rank things in your life. She was being insane.

Ed had wanted her to quit and start a family. Charlie's last day had been the day before and she was still sick over giving up her job. Trinity Church, where he'd just gotten a new job, expected her to be the subdued, submissive pastor's wife, just like her mother—only her mother had never been submissive.

Deep breaths. She tried to breathe, remembering to draw air into her belly and not just her lungs to help ease the anxiety. Big, huge mistake. She flew to the vanity, grabbed the vase of flowers, and dropped them into the trash can in the restroom. Then she slammed the door shut, trying to shut away the fragrance, the sorrow, every single thing she was feeling.

She had to get out of there. In moving the bouquet she'd released the toxic stench. She couldn't stand the smell. Death and weddings had always been diametrically opposed in her book, until they weren't. She had to get away from both.

Her instincts took over. She had to survive. And survival came with clean air to breathe, and that was anywhere outside of the tiny church where she'd been a leader in the youth group, a Sunday School teacher, and the role that had defined her entire life—the preacher's daughter.

If she was going to do this, if she was going to be able to breathe ever again, she had to execute this perfectly. Grabbing her purse, she checked to make certain it contained her inhaler. Then she took her toiletry bag. She wasn't certain when she was going to stop once she got to her car, but it was going to be a long, long time. Deodorant and a hair brush were necessities.

Timing her exit, she watched from the window as the last few guests made their arrivals. The church doors were sealed. She eased the window open, stuck her head out, and inhaled deeply. Thankfulness and possibility rushed into her lungs.

She set the two bags on the roof and shoved. They rolled and bumped along to the gutter. Gathering the skirt of her dress in her hands, she wiggled her butt up onto the sill and managed to get one leg out and then the other.

CHAPTER TWO

Charlie scooted to the gutter. She was supposed to walk down the aisle in six minutes. The first chords of Nocturne No. 2 were playing. They'd be seating Ed's grandparents now. That's what they'd practiced the night before over and over and over again until she'd wanted to scream.

With her will to survive still running the show, she shimmied to the lattice work on the side of the church away from the stained-glass windows. Wedging the toe of her high heel in the lattice, she began her descent. She'd explain to Ed later. Perhaps when she understood herself. She still half prayed that he'd had a change of heart as well. That would be so much less awkward.

Holder County gossip hens would have a field day with it still, but at least that way no one would really be hurt. She didn't want to hurt Ed. She just also didn't want to marry him. Her father would be so disappointed in her. That was the only thing that gave her pause, but it wasn't enough to make her stop.

She took another step down, lowering herself to freedom, and god it smelled so good. Moving faster now, she made it another few feet, and then accidentally stepped on the dress and wedged it inside the lattice. The sound of tearing fabric alerted her to the misstep.

Crap. Using the water downspout to secure herself with her hand, she tried to lift her foot and ease the dress out from the lattice and away from her heel that was now anchored in the torn lace.

She tugged with one hand and held tight with the other. And then...the downspout pulled away from the brick building and the lattice work snapped under her weight. She slipped down the next few feet and swung there suspended in midair against brick, held up only by her heel, which was still serving as a tack for her dress. The skirt portion was now up over her face. Everything god had given her was now on display for everyone, and she couldn't see to figure out how to get down. She fought but was afraid of falling the last fifteen feet to the concrete walkway below.

Oh my god. Oh my god. Oh my god. Everyone's going to see me like this, not only fleeing my own wedding but wearing entirely see-through white lace panties as well. She'd told herself maybe the panties would inspire Ed to some kind of dominant passion. The ever-present Oklahoma wind teased her butt cheeks as if to make a point. She tried to be thankful that she'd opted not to get a sleeveless wedding gown she'd admired so much, since it would've turned completely inside out, and she'd now be naked and sprawled out on the pavement. She never thought she'd actually be thankful for the scarring along her ribcage and breast, but currently she was glad they'd kept her from the other gown. As it was, the long sleeves were saving her life.

Although at that moment, death coming early for her so she would not have to endure this didn't sound too terrible. *Stop being so dramatic.*

She could just make out the chug of truck motors, but she was fairly certain that the grim reaper did not drive work trucks. Wagering that it would be better for however many people were in those trucks to see her than it would for the entire freaking town to be witness to this, she decided to burn any pride she'd ever have to the ground and squeaked out a, "Please get me down! Please! Help," she added hopefully.

———

The wedding started in ten fucking minutes, and Jamie was just passing the old schoolyard. How the hell had he had more game when he was twelve than he did now? More balls too. At least he'd asked her out back then.

But god she was just so good, so...perfect. And he wasn't. He wouldn't ever be. Too much hot-blooded cowboy, too much adrenaline-addicted firefighter, to ever be what Charlie Tilson would need. He was going to endure this stupid ceremony with the flask in his back pocket, and then he was getting out of town for however long his family would let him be without interrupting.

He turned into the church parking lot. Jamie didn't trust his own vision nearly enough to believe what he could've sworn he was seeing with his own eyes. No way. The same adrenaline that made him a kickass firefighter launched him into action. He threw the truck into park in the middle of the gravel lot. No fucking way.

But the pleas for help were undeniably his Charlie. He swallowed hard, but his mouth was once again so dry there was nothing for him to press down his esophagus. Tender red, lace-covered curls, that he'd fantasized about for decades, were on ripe display right along with her perfect ass—almost as pale white as the dress that was only half covering her. She was tangled in a ball of lace.

"Charlie?" He finally managed the single word.

"Oh my god. Jamie!" Thankfulness washed through her tone. "I have to get out of here," she begged.

His brother, Wes, who'd never made it to church on time once in his life had pulled in behind Jamie. He was surveying the situation and trying not to laugh.

It took Jamie a half beat to remember that he had a ladder in his truck. "Hang on. I'll get you down." As he turned to sprint back to his truck, he growled out a warning to his brother, "Do not look at her."

Wes held up his hands. "Man, get a grip. You need my help. If we don't get her down, everybody's gonna see this," he spoke between his teeth.

Jamie had the ladder leaned up against the church in the next minute. "You hold the ladder, but you fucking look the other way," he demanded of Wes.

That earned him a complimentary eye roll.

Taking it three rungs at a time, Jamie wrapped his right arm around the most perfect woman in the whole fucking world and cradled her to his body. "I've got you," he soothed. She sat that perfect little ass right in the crook of his arm and he swore he almost came in his suit pants, a problem he hadn't had since that night when they were sixteen at the Renegade Rodeo and he'd almost kissed her.

He managed to get most of the dress back down to cover what it was supposed to cover, revealing the mass of red curls on top of her head instead of showing off the tender ones that covered what he wished every goddamn day belonged to him.

Her face glowed redder than her hair. She buried her face in his shoulder as he carried them down. "Thank you," she managed in a horrified gasp.

"Charlie, honey, are you running?" He had to ask, although the answer seemed fairly obvious.

She stared at him like he'd lost any good sense he ever had. "No, I just decided to walk around on the roof and tripped." She rolled her eyes. Then terror filled those beautiful eyes. "Sorry. I didn't mean that. I'm a horrible person," she confessed like he was some kind of priest who could absolve her. He was about as far from a priest as you could get.

"No, you're not. Don't ever say that. If you don't want to do this, don't do it."

"I just can't face everyone right now. Please, will you just run away with me for a little while like we did when we were kids? Anywhere. I'll go anywhere you want that isn't here."

Wes and Jamie carried on an entire conversation using only their eyes, as siblings could so often do.

Wes eventually gestured to Jamie's truck. "Get her out of here. I'll buy you as much time as I can before they start looking for her."

"Thank you," Charlie gushed. "And will you tell Ed I'm sorry if you get a chance?"

"I'll do my best."

Jamie still hadn't fully set her on her feet. He was incapable of removing her body from his arms. It would be like pulling skin from bone.

He scooped her legs back up into his arms and carried her to the truck. As he secured her, Wes saluted him. "Honestly, man, it's about damned time. Don't fuck it up, okay?"

CHAPTER THREE

Jamie started to flip his brother off but thought better of it in the church parking lot. What the hell did *not fucking this up* look like exactly? Just because she was running away from Ed didn't mean she was running to him. Did it?

No, it definitely didn't. Every single complication that had ever existed between them was still right there. She didn't want to have anything to do with anyone who was a firefighter. Her daddy hated him. He didn't deserve her. And most importantly, they were best friends. What happened to that if anything between them romantically fizzled out? Jamie had seen enough relationships end to know that it occurred with frightening regularity. That was one of the reasons he avoided them.

"Are you sure I'm not evil?" she whispered as he pulled onto the main drag through town.

She was an angel. Charlie and evil didn't even exist in the same universe in his book. "Would it have been better for you to have gone through with it, hated every minute of today, been miserable the next couple of years until you finally admitted to yourself that you should've called it off before it ever got started, and then to have gone through a divorce? No, it wouldn't. It'll sting today, but he'll get over it. He's a big boy."

"Maybe there will be someone at his new church he could ask out. They'd make him way happier than I would anyway."

Seeing her almost butt nekkid hanging from the church had completely sobered him up. Adrenaline coursed through him constantly, and he had no good place to put it to use. As he eyed her seated beside him staring up at him like he was her own personal hero, his cock heartily disagreed with his assessment. "See that. It's good you left when you did. You're already trying to fix him up with someone else. That ain't how love works."

She nodded. "You're right. I know you're right. It's just...I never really saw myself as the runaway bride type. Dad will be furious."

"Your daddy'll get over it too."

"Where should we go?" She switched topics fast.

"If we're getting out of town for a few days, I need to let the chief know. Wes can tell everyone else."

"Jamie," she laid her hand on top of his on the steering wheel. It took everything he had not to immediately wish he could hear her groan out his name as he forced climax after climax from her. "Thank you for always running away with me."

He turned to stare into the endless green fields of her eyes. "That's my job, carrot top."

She rolled her eyes. He was the only person she'd let get away with calling her that. He used it sparingly, relishing that he owned that single small part of her when no one else did. The thing was that her hair didn't look like carrots. It looked like flames. So, the part of her she allowed him wasn't real. He hated that.

Fishing his phone from his pocket, he pressed the station number from his favorites list. "Holder County Fire Station. You're talking to Yeager." Jared Yeager, a relatively new guy on the team, answered.

"Hey, man, is Chief Riggins around?"

"Yeah, hang on. Wait, aren't you supposed to be at that wedding?"

"Had a change of plans."

"Oh..kay, here's Chief. It's Holder," Jamie heard Jared inform him.

"Holder? Aren't you at Charlotte Tilson's wedding?"

"Not exactly. Listen, about all that vacation I've got saved up—I need to take some of it now."

The chief chuckled. Jamie wondered what that was about, but he knew better than to ask. "Tell me something, son, is Charlie with you right now instead of standing down at that altar?"

"Uh, yeah. She is."

"I see. Well, you take your vacation. We'll try to get by without you. If I can take a liberty here, can I just say don't fuck this up. For chrissakes it's about damn time. Better late than never I s'pose."

Okay, was everyone in Holder County reading from the same script or something? This was ridiculous. Jamie rolled his eyes. "I'll let you know when I get back."

"I'd appreciate that. Does your daddy know you left with her?"

"I figure he will in another few minutes."

"Can't wait to hear Barrett's take on this. If you're looking to get out of town, you might want to take 75 instead of 412. There's a pile-up on 412. It's a mess, so I hear."

Jamie cringed at that. "Anybody hurt?"

"Nothing major. They'll all recover."

"We'll head north then. Talk to you later."

"I'm sorry for making you use your vacation days," Charlie lamented when he ended the call.

"Stop it. I've just been letting them build up forever. I need a break. Spending time with you is all I ever want to do anyway. Chief says 412 is a no-go for a while. Where do you want to go? I could take you back to the ranch."

"No," she was suddenly adamant. "I want to get out of Holder County. Out of Oklahoma. Out of...everywhere. I don't want anyone to know where I am except for you. I need to...breathe."

Jamie considered that. So, she thought Ed was smothering her too. Good, they agreed on that already. "How 'bout our chalet in Telluride? Mountain air's good for breathing."

"No. As soon as everyone knows I left with you, that's the first place they'll look. But I do wish I knew somewhere to go that wouldn't require me using a credit card for hotel rooms. Ed set it up so he gets alerts on all of my purchases." She rolled her eyes.

Jamie gripped the steering wheel until his knuckles were white. "Don't you make a shit ton more money than preacher man?" leapt from his mouth without his permission.

She grinned. "I didn't know you didn't like Ed," she commented.

"I guess you do now." He'd never seen any point in not fessing up when she had him dead to rights.

But then she did something that she'd never done before. She leaned over the console of his Ford and brushed a kiss on his cheek. "I'm not sure I ever liked him either. He just seemed like the next thing I was supposed to do." Jamie swallowed down raw hunger. It burned down his chest and threatened to ignite in his gut. He had to get a grip. This was him and Charlie. There was too much at stake to do something stupid, especially when she was in a bad place.

Rescuing people, when they were having what would likely be the worst day of their whole life, was who he was. Running out on her wedding sure as hell wouldn't even make the top five of the worst days of Charlie's life, but saving her was his drug. Making her smile, listening to her dreams, just being in the same room with her—those were the driving forces in his life. Nothing else even mattered. If he got to just hang out with her for the next week or so it'd still qualify as the greatest week of his whole life, even if they were in separate beds. Which they would be. Because that's how they worked.

But thoughts of Ed being on her list of things to *do* made Jamie want to kill him again. "I doubt you're wanting to camp out down on the low creek on the ranch like we did whenever we ran away when we were kids, so where are we heading for this impromptu vacation?"

"I have no idea."

"How 'bout I pay for the hotel room," he amended her plural version of the word though he wasn't certain why he'd done that.

"No. I cannot let you bail me out of this. That's too much. I'll take care of everything."

Jamie considered. As sweet as she was most of the time, when she was of a mind to do something, she'd dig her heels in. He suspected she was going to hold fast to not letting him pay for stuff on this trip. He'd have to deal with that later. "How far away are you wanting to get?" That would at least give him a direction.

"I don't know. Is out of the country an option? Australia maybe? I saw this documentary on people living off the grid down there. No internet. Not even a telephone. That sounds perfect."

"My truck'll go over a lot of things, but the ocean ain't one of 'em. Plus, if you're wanting to hang in the outback, I'm going to need to go back for some gear. 'Bout the time you lock eyes on some of the critters they have down there, you'll be demanding that I get after them with my ax."

She grinned at that. "I wish either one of us had family away from Holder County. Somewhere we could just hide out for a little while and not think. The farther away the better."

"I do have family not in Holder County," Jamie offered.

"You have family that doesn't live in the county named after them?" Skepticism rode hard in her tone, but then her eyes lit like sparklers. "Colt! Oh my gravy, I wasn't even thinking."

Grinning at her cute phrase to avoid using the Lord's name, he nodded. "Yeah, Colt. I bet he and Avery would be okay with us staying up at their place for a while. Nebraska ain't Australia, but Camden Ranch is pretty damn remote. Nothing up there but cows and corn. If you toss your phone out the window, you'd be off the grid."

"Don't tempt me."

"I'll help him out on the ranch in exchange for room and board. Does that work for you?"

"I'll help too. That way we aren't putting anyone out."

CHAPTER FOUR

Jamie touched his cousin's name from his contact list.

Colt answered on the first ring. "And here I was thinking I was gonna have to drive my ass down to Oklahoma and remind you that I still exist. How the hell are you?"

"Sorry I haven't called in a while. Been a little busy. I'm good. How're you?" Instead of Colt answering, there was a heartbreaking wail of what sounded like a newborn baby.

Colt sighed. "'Bout like that. He's got his days and nights confused. Avery and I are beat. She keeps trying to wake him up to feed him more during the day, but he ain't real fond of that idea."

"He sounds like his daddy. You were the one who preferred to go out and party all night and then show up hungover trying to saddle a horse the next morning," Jamie reminded him of the good old days. Not that he was one to talk since his head was still throbbing and the sunlight pouring through the windshield was excruciating.

"Yeah, well, that was a long time ago. I'd rather be tired 'cause of one of my youngins than 'cause I was being a dumbass. How are you?"

"I'm all right. I was gonna ask a favor, but it sounds like you've got your hands full."

"Nah, you kidding me? Ask. I don't plan on stopping making babies for as long as Avery's on board, so that ain't a good excuse not to do something for you."

Chuckling at that, Jamie considered. "I don't know, man. Charlie and I need a place to stay for a few days. Need to get out of Holder County, but..."

"Charlie Tilson?" Colt's tone took on that same knowing timbre that Wes's had.

"Yeah, you remember her, right?"

"Jamie, you were practically her shadow for years. I remember her. For a while I figured it'd make more sense for Aunt Sara to just adopt her. That way she wouldn't have to keep running away to the ranch when her daddy tried to lay down the law. But why are you needing to get out of town?"

Jamie glanced at his passenger who was studying him intently. "Uh, well..." he lifted his eyebrows to Charlie in question. "Can I tell him?"

"Of course." She squeezed her eyes shut like that might also close off her ears.

"Well what?" Colt had never been known for his patience. Jamie was glad some things hadn't changed.

"She was kinda supposed to get married this morning and she decided that wasn't what she wanted after all. We were thinking we'd get out of town 'til the..."

"Parishioners with pitchforks find something else to talk about?"

"Pretty much."

"So, let me get this straight. Charlie Tilson was to marry someone who wasn't you, but she up and ran away *with* you."

"Yeah."

"What'd her daddy say?"

"Haven't heard from him yet."

"What'd Uncle Barrett say?"

"You're the only person I've talked to."

"All right then, come on up. You don't want to stay here with me, though. You won't get any sleep. I'll talk to Brock. We got a little cottage kind of thing down by the entrance gates. We've been fixing it up. Y'all can stay there as long as you want. Only got one bedroom though." That was a test if Jamie had ever heard one.

"I'll sleep on the couch," he supplied.

Charlie shook her head. "No, I will," she corrected him. He rolled his eyes at her.

But Colt was laughing. "Uh huh, I'll let you two work that out. Can I just give you some unsolicited advice before you head this way?"

Jamie spoke before he thought. "Let me guess, don't fuck this up and it's about damn time?"

"Exactly. Now try actually letting that advice get through your stubborn head. It's the first house after you drive under the Camden Ranch sign. You can't miss it. It's off to the left. I'll meet you down there. Will you be here by supper, you think?"

"Not sure we'll make it much before dark. Got a lot of drive ahead of us."

"We have to stop for clothes," Charlie reminded him.

"And apparently we're stopping to shop."

"Women," Colt teased. "But if she's still wearing a white gown, I guess we have to give her that."

"She is. Thanks for letting us stay up there. We'll see you tonight." Jamie ended the call and sincerely wished his family and his chief would stay the hell out of his head. He'd spent the second half of his life trying, and obviously failing, at keeping anyone from knowing that he wanted Charlie to be his. He was fairly certain Charlie didn't know, though, and that was all that mattered.

"I still cannot believe you and Wes saw me like that," she whimpered. "I'm so embarrassed."

He had absolutely no idea how to respond to that. God, the image of her in deliciously innocent white lace panties. He was still sporting a semi and that was with a headache. But the desperation to save her was always his only goal. "Don't worry about it. I made Wes look the other way while I got you down, and your ass is gorgeous so nothing to be embarrassed about." Okay, well, that was several dozen steps too far. She always took down his guards. She was the only person he'd ever really been real with.

She laughed and shook her head. "Thank you for making Wes look away, and my ass is even more pale than the rest of me and hasn't seen the inside of a gym since we took it together in ninth grade, so I know you're lying."

Sexiest ass I've ever seen. Made me think how fucking good it would look with my cock buried deep in that tight little rosebud between those lush cheeks. He sank his teeth into his tongue to keep from informing her of that. "I ain't lying. Are you hungry? There's a little diner just inside the Kansas line." Changing topics was the only safe way out of this.

"I am kinda starving. I couldn't eat anything yesterday, and I only got down a few crackers this morning. Every time I thought about the wedding, I got sick to my stomach."

"You still thinking you shouldn't have run?"

"I thought it was just nerves."

"It was your good sense trying to get you where you needed to be."

———

"You're right." Charlie knew he was. Only, if that were true, did that mean that where she was supposed to be was with him? Of course it did. He was her favorite person in the whole world. But...there was something different about him or maybe it was something she'd ignored before.

There was a hunger in his tone, maybe. Or maybe she was just imagining that or wanting it to be so. She reminded herself of all the many reasons why a relationship with Jamie Holder would never be for her. She couldn't stand it when he was at work, and it would only be a million times worse for her every single time he left the house if they were anything more than best friends. There was a difference in loving someone and being *in* love with someone. And she had to remember where that line was and respect it.

Louann's advice wasn't for her. She could never marry her best friend. Not happening. Jamie wouldn't be interested in her anyway. She couldn't even stand the thought of being undressed with anyone and, well, he was Jamie-freaking-Holder. The Holder boys all had a well-earned reputation. Every woman in Holder County, save her, had uttered or at least thought the phrase—save a horse, ride a Holder. According to town legend, they always exceeded their reputation.

Besides, she was probably just making all of it up in her head anyway. That husky, lusty tone she swore she heard in his voice wasn't really there. She was starving and obviously having a completely insane day. She was off-kilter. That was it. Food would help. "A diner anywhere sounds great, but I don't want to traipse around in this stupid gown any longer than I have to, so after food we need clothes." Instinctively she turned around to check out the back window again. For some reason she couldn't shake the feeling that someone would be chasing her, trying to tie her down again.

She hated to stop at all but Jamie didn't look like he felt all that great, and she didn't want him getting sick, especially since he was being so great about her completely disrupting his life.

Jamie was always great. No matter what crazy idea she came up with next, he just always made it happen, no questions asked.

"Thanks again for doing this. You're the best," she vowed.

That earned her a full-fledged Jamie Holder cocky grin. It was her favorite and he didn't show them off very often. "I know I am," he assured her with a wink. "This gets me out of at least the next dozen times you want me to watch one of those girlie movies you love. *How to Run Off a Loser in Ten Easy Steps* or *Hootie and the Smallmouth Bass's Long-Ass Record* or whatever it is.

Laughter erupted from deep in Charlie's belly. "It's ten days, and I think you're talking about *Nick and Norah's Infinite Playlist*, goofball."

"Infinite being the operative word in that title. Woulda been better if there'd been fishing."

"All right, fine, you get to pick the movies for the next dozen times, and now that Ed is no longer my problem I can totally watch movies with you again." She hadn't exactly meant to admit that out loud because she hadn't exactly told Jamie that Ed had repeatedly requested that she not hang out with him anymore. Her plan had been to ignore his request the same way she'd completely ignored her father's order to stay away from Jamie when she was younger.

Every single time her father had out-and-out demanded that she never go to the ranch again, she'd sneak out, ride her bike all the way to Jamie's parents' house, and talk him into running away with her.

They almost always camped down near the low creek on Holder Ranch.

They'd leave word with Mrs. Holder to please tell her daddy that she'd think about coming home if he promised she could go to Jamie's house whenever she wanted. She always suspected that Jamie's parents knew where they'd gone, but they hadn't told her father, not that he could've navigated the ranch even with directions. His parents had let them stay out there several times. Eventually, Barrett Holder would come out and negotiate a peace treaty between Charlie and her daddy. For the next month, her father would preach on children respecting and obeying their parents and the wisdom of the elders. She didn't care. Just then, she had to admit that running away wasn't completely new for her.

"Ed had something to say about you watching movies with me?" Jamie spat the words like they were laced with venom.

"Kind of."

Jamie shook his head and visibly locked his jaw. Charlie wondered what he was keeping behind those perfect teeth of his.

"I would never have listened to him. You know that. People have been warning me off about hanging out with you since we moved to Holder County. In case you're just now figuring this out, twenty-some-odd years later, I don't really take kindly to people telling me who I can be friends with."

That got her a grunt. She barely managed to keep her eye roll at bay. Jamie grunted when he refused to say what he really wanted to say. "Just spill it," she ordered.

"I wasn't aware I was someone people needed to warn you off about."

Oh good grief. "You're not."

Another grunt. Why did cowboys have to be so frustrating? That was yet another reason she shouldn't even try to imagine what it would be like to be in a romantic relationship with Jamie—to wake up in those impossibly strong arms every day, safe and warm, to trace the trail of dark brown hair that she knew ran from his abs down into his shorts with her fingers, to feel the slight friction burn from his short beard on her chin and...points below, to finally find out exactly what Jamie's lips tasted like. She imagined straight whiskey and pure sin.

She knew he'd be the kind of kisser who could get girls drunk off his mouth. She knew because she'd heard it all through high school, and then every time he was home from Oklahoma State, and for the rest of adulthood. Other women were in and out of his life constantly. They never stayed around long. She'd asked him once why that was. He'd shrugged and gotten a weird look in his eyes. They'd never discussed it again.

CHAPTER FIVE

Jamie finally got the call he'd been waiting on. "What happened?" he demanded of Wes.

"I tried to buy her as much time as I could. Told everybody not to go up and get her out of the bride dressing room thing 'cause you were up there and needed some time to talk before she walked down the aisle."

"How'd that go over?"

"They sat for a good little while, but then her sister tore down the aisle and went running up there. Her daddy followed after. Tell you the truth, I didn't know her preacher guy had any fire in him, but he was pissed the fuck off. Got to threatening you. Saying you'd turned her against him. Poisoned her mind or whatever. Her daddy assured Ed that you'd been a bad influence on her since middle school. You know he don't much like cattle ranchers in general which is funny since that's who makes up half of his congregation. He thinks we're all un-American. Says the whole town puts Holder land and family above the good Lord, and that makes our ranch an idol. Dad reminded him that Holder Land and Cattle paid a good portion of his salary, so he might want to think on that. Ed got the bright idea that he'd fight you for her. Maddog and I reminded him that there were a lot more Holders than he wanted to take on, and that we didn't mind whipping his pansy-ass if he even thought about going after the two of you. He told us we'd go to hell for it. Maddox told him Satan was scared of us too."

Jamie laughed at that, but Wes continued. "That might not'a been the thing to do though. Last thing I heard before he went into Reverend Tilson's office with her daddy was that something was going to have to be done about the Holders. Things went from bad to worse real quick like as you can see."

"They can all suck my star-spangled firecracker for all the shits I give what they think of me. I just wanted to make sure no one was heading our way before I stopped to get her something to eat."

"For right now, no, they're not looking for you. I wouldn't come back home 'til this all blows over though. It can't possibly be good for anyone involved, Charlie most of all. And if people start talking shit to her, we all know you're gonna throw down every chance you get. Just let everybody get used to the idea that this whole wedding ain't happening."

"That was my plan."

"Right now the church ladies are trying to decide if it'd be okay to cut the cake for everyone."

Jamie turned to Charlie. "You care if everybody at the church eats the cake?"

"Nope. Tell them to enjoy it. It cost me a fortune, but me not having to eat it is worth every penny."

"Tell 'em to go ahead. Give Ed some. Maybe he'll simmer down."

"I doubt that'd help. Where are you two heading? You're not going on their honeymoon with her are you, 'cause I'm telling you that might drive Ed right over the edge. Guy's got a mean side, that's for sure."

"Nah. I figured we'd go up and see Colt for a while."

"That's a good idea. I won't let anybody know that I know where you are. Tell Colt I said hey."

"Will do. Let me know if anything happens there that I need to know about, and would you mind..."

"Checking your cattle and your hay every damn day you're gone?"

"Yeah. Sorry about that."

"Dad and I decided we'd divide the work between the three of us brothers. Hallie says she'll help out too. But, listen, it's gonna up our workload, which means we aren't gonna be able to keep an eye on Ed and Pastor Tilson, so keep your head up. Speaking of your head, if you can finally get it out of your ass and figure out what everybody but her daddy, and Ed, and maybe the two of you have known for years, it'll be worth it."

"It ain't gonna go like that, Wes."

Jamie couldn't quite make out what his brother grumbled, but he was pretty sure it was *dumbass*.

As soon as he ended the call, Charlie leapt. "Who exactly is going to be sucking your firecracker?" She couldn't even say it without laughing.

Jamie smirked. "Ed and your daddy."

"I was afraid of that. What's Daddy saying? I'm sure he's being awful." She understood what had driven her father to be so overprotective of her and her sister, but why did that have to include being unkind to her favorite person in the whole world?

"Same shit he's been saying for years, plus that I poisoned you against Ed or something along those lines."

Charlie ground her teeth. "Ed poisoned me against himself. I should've known better than to get involved with him when Dad was the one that kept inviting him over. I think I felt sorry for him honestly. And I worry about Dad after his heart attack."

"Your daddy is doing fine, and Ed's ego's bruised. He'll get over it," Jamie insisted.

"I don't think he really cares too much except that the new church that hired him wanted him to be married, but surely that's not like a requirement. That wouldn't even be legal, I don't think. They can't make you be married to preach."

"Even if they tried to, him having a job ain't your problem. He'll get over it like I said."

Every time Charlie caught a glimpse of herself in the reflection in the window she winced. "I really, really want to get out of this dress."

Jamie coughed oddly over what sounded like another grunt. "Where do you want to go get clothes?"

"Preferably somewhere inexpensive. I have a little over a hundred dollars cash in my wallet. I'll use that."

"Just let me buy you whatever you need. You can pay me back after we get you unleashed from Ed."

"Maybe." She considered that, but she was sure that was asking too much. Being unleashed from Ed was precisely how she felt. How had she ever found herself tied up with him in the first place? Had she been slowly giving away her freedoms without even realizing it? Fear that she'd done just that slithered up her spine.

Apparently, it also stirred the hunger in her belly, which chose that exact moment of quiet to make itself known.

Jamie chuckled at her. "Just a few more miles."

"Guess I'm hungrier than I realized."

Her shoulders eased a little when they flew past the "Welcome to Kansas: The Sunflower State" sign. Putting some distance between herself and Ed, and her father, and everything else in Holder County felt far better than it should. She leaned a little closer to Jamie and got another smile.

True to his word, ten minutes later he was pulling into the gravel parking lot of a diner that looked like it had stepped right out of the fifties. Appropriately named The Three Squares, there was even a gas station across the street that was almost equally nostalgic. It was perfect, sitting there in an open field like it had been planted years ago just for them to arrive at this moment in time.

Jamie helped her lift the small train of the dress so it didn't drag in the gravel dust, not that she needed it pristine. What she needed was to get rid of the thing.

But it wasn't until they stepped inside The Three Squares that Charlie began to understand that letting other people inside this runaway trip of hers was going to be awkward...very, very awkward.

"Oh my soul, Les, would you look at this!" A woman, whose name tag read Lena, clasped the dishrag in her hands and rushed toward them. Jamie stepped slightly ahead of Charlie as if to build her a blockade out of his body. He really was the best. "Newlyweds! I just love young love. Here, now let me get a picture for the wall." She gestured to hundreds of Polaroid shots of diner guests over the years that were tacked to the yellowing wallpaper. Before Jamie or Charlie could stop her, she retrieved a camera that was almost as old as the diner and snapped a shot of the two of them. Apparently, posing and smiling weren't necessary for diner pictures, which would explain the multiple images on the wall of people with food in their mouths.

"Um," Charlie tried to give weak protest, but Lena looked so thrilled she hated to correct her. She was waving the photo back and forth trying to get it to develop.

"Sit in the round booth. That way you can cuddle."

They both stood frozen until Jamie relented and guided Charlie toward the table. "Are we going along with this?" he spoke through his teeth.

"She looks so happy. I hate to ruin it."

"Got it." With that, Jamie wrapped his arm around Charlie's shoulders and pulled her closer rather intimately. She absolutely should not have done it, but she couldn't help herself. She laid her head on his substantial shoulder and for just one minute let herself enjoy the warmth of his body and the scent of his cologne mixed with saddle leather that clung to Jamie always.

But as she turned to let him help her into the seat, she caught the faint scent of smoke that had her moving away quickly. Just like the saddle leather, it was a part of him, and that was the part she couldn't handle.

CHAPTER SIX

Okay, so pretending to be married to Charlie was both reckless and stupid. It came far too easily to Jamie. He should've hit the brakes, but the day, the night before, the months of absolute dread that he'd held for this day that had turned out to be the greatest day of his life so far —it was all too dizzying for him to make good decisions. Or maybe that was the remnants of the hangover.

All he knew was he needed about four plates of burgers and fries and maybe a milkshake to clear his head. Surely, that would help.

To his shock, Lena set down two waters on the table and then scooted into the round booth beside Charlie, which in turn moved her right up against Jamie. Damn. Charlie smelled good. She always did. Like vanilla and cinnamon and some kind of musk he figured had to be from heaven because he'd never smelled anything like it on earth. She was an aphrodisiac without even trying, and she was pressed up against him like she really could be his.

"What can I get you?" Lena urged.

Jamie glanced down at the still unopened menus. "Maybe give us just a minute." He tugged at his collar and decided to dispense with the tie altogether. He couldn't fucking breathe.

Charlie opened her menu to block her face and then shot him a *help me* glance. Once again, he wrapped his arm over her shoulders and propped it on the back of the booth wall trying to create a little more room for her.

"Well, while y'all decide tell me how you met." Lena wasn't leaving it seemed.

"Uh well," Charlie tried and then came up short. Girl never had been good at lying. She was much better at being openly defiant and telling her daddy to get over it. Yet another thing Jamie adored about her.

He threw all caution to the wind and figured he'd go with the truth. Surely, things couldn't get any more awkward. "She moved into my hometown when we were in middle school. They brought her into my classroom on her first day of school that year, which also happened to be my birthday. I'll tell you the truth, I figured God himself had gotten me a birthday present. I didn't need to blow out the candles. I got my wish."

Charlie turned to stare him down. There was a whole different look in her eyes, one he'd never seen before. "Was it really your birthday?" she whispered.

He nodded.

"How did I not know that?"

"You'd been through hell up to that point," he gently reminded her. "By the time it rolled around again the next year you'd forgotten exactly when you arrived at school. No big deal."

"That is a big deal," she corrected him. "It's a huge deal. Birthdays are so important."

Before she could continue, Lena was visibly swooning. She grasped Charlie's arm. "Oh honey, you have got yourself a good one. You better hang on to him. Men like that are once in a lifetime. And I know. Les's my fourth husband." She gestured to the kitchen.

As if on cue, Les leaned in from behind the cooktop. "Lena, honey, leave 'em be."

"Well, all right, fine." She scooted out of the booth. "Y'all just flag me down when you're ready to order. We have cherry pie today. Cherries are so fresh and ripe, you'll love it." Jamie really needed her to stop talking about cherries. "I top it with some fresh cream. Let it melt just a little all over. Get the cherries nice and creamy." Dear god. "Now, don't let me catch you letting him get his hands under that dress," she urged.

Charlie's mouth hung open, and Jamie choked on the water he'd been drinking. When Lena finally left, Charlie turned her appalled look to Jamie. "Is there some kind of diner fetish in Kansas that we're unaware of?"

"I doubt you want me to Google that." She gave him one of her infectious giggles, and he relished every moment of it. "Does that mean I'm not allowed to finger you at the table? Lena seems like it'd disappoint her if I don't at least try."

Charlie punched him in the arm rather hard. "Would you stop?"

"I thought we were supposed to be married. If we were married, I'd flirt dirty with you constantly. I'm just getting into character." Okay, so he'd never outwardly flirted with Charlie, because that would cross that very firm friend/lover boundary that they'd always kept in place, but it was even more fun than he'd always imagined it would be.

She rolled her eyes. "You're just trying to embarrass me because you think it's hilarious that I still blush."

"It is awfully cute."

"What do you want to eat, Holder?"

He almost said *you*, but thought better of it. "I don't much care what, so long as there's a lot of it."

"Agreed. And I still can't believe you didn't even mention it was your birthday that day. You just let me follow you around like a lost puppy and never said anything about it."

Which was why he never said anything. He'd been given the best gift he ever could've come up with, so why say anything more about it. She'd kept right on looking at him like he was her personal hero, and that had been all he'd ever needed.

"Do you know what you want?" Once again, he changed the topic.

"I know that I'll likely never be able to look at cherry pie the same way ever again."

"Thank god. I thought it was just me. Also, I kinda want to ask if we can get this table wiped down again. Little worried about what Lena and Les do when the diner's empty."

Charlie gagged and lifted her arms off of the laminate. "If I wasn't starved, I'd say we should drive until we find something else."

"There ain't a lot between here and Lincoln so we need to get while the getting's good. There's a Target about three hours north of here and there might be some fast food up there, too, but I'm too hungry to wait that long."

"Me too."

While they were splitting a piece of peach pie, because cherry was absolutely out of the question, Lena pushed two of the wax-coated menus toward Charlie. "You should take these with you so you remember all of the things you did on your honeymoon."

Charlie officially melted. Jamie bit back a grin. The girl kept everything. Every movie stub, every concert ticket, every everything they did together. She'd print them all out and keep them safe in all of her scrapbooks. She kept root beer bottles and pressed flowers into books to keep those too. Everything that ever meant anything to her or represented anytime they'd had fun together, she still had. But Jamie knew she'd also lost everything, including her mama, when she was little so he never questioned her being sentimental. He liked it. She was like his own personal diary. He told her everything. Everything except that he'd always wanted more of her.

"Thank you," Charlie gushed. She gave Jamie a soft grin. "I will definitely keep them." And just like everything else she saved, she pressed the paper smooth, ran her fingers gently along the red tie binding, and carefully tucked them near her.

"Are you just passing through here? Where are you headed?" Lena asked with entirely too much exuberance for someone not traveling with them.

"Um...Nebraska." Charlie seemed to realize how odd that likely sounded.

"Oh," Lena's face fell. "Well, that's...nice."

Okay, so Nebraska wasn't exactly on any top ten honeymoon destination lists, but they weren't really going on a honeymoon.

They endured an awkward lunch with Lena constantly joining them at their table to ask uncomfortable questions. Jamie's ears perked up while he was paying when Lena asked Charlie, "What would you say was the first thing that attracted you to him?"

Charlie smothered a giggle and considered for a minute. Jamie stared her down. "Come on, honey. What was the first thing that attracted you to me?"

Heat stained her alabaster cheeks and turned her lips the most beautiful shade of pink he'd ever seen. Somehow he knew she'd be just as pink and ripe between her legs, and god, he wanted to confirm his suspicion.

"Honestly," Charlie grinned, "he's the greatest guy I know. He'd do anything in the world for me, and he was there for me during the worst time in my whole life. He was little back then, and he'd sit and hold my hand while I cried. What twelve-year-old boy does that? Plus, he's got the best lips. Don't you think?"

"Oh, I agree," Lena assured her. "So masculine. Nice strong jaw too."

Personally, Jamie thought his pecs were more impressive than his lips, but he wasn't going to be picky. Mildly concerned that Lena was going to try to kiss him, Jamie yanked his "wife" out of the diner. She put a whole lot of space between them as soon as they were out of view of the diner windows. Disappointment sank slowly through him. It turned the two loaded cheeseburgers he'd eaten into a brick in his stomach.

A few hours later, they pulled into a Target in Junction City, Kansas. Charlie swore she'd never been so thrilled to see a store. Once again, Jamie helped her keep the train off the pavement. "All right, how long are we staying at Colt's so I know how many pairs of underwear to buy?"

Charlie considered. "I don't know. How long do you think we'd be allowed to stay?"

He shook his head. "We're allowed to do anything we want. You're not breaking any rules. How long did you take off work for the honeymoon?"

"A week. Kind of. I turned in my notice before I left because Ed didn't really want me working, so I guess I don't have to go back other than to clean out my office." She shuddered involuntarily and wondered if part of her desperation to run wasn't the thought of spending an entire week alone with Ed. *Really should've considered that before today.* She felt like the walking embodiment of the head slap emoji.

"What the actual fuck? You love your job. And why the hell didn't you tell me you were doing that because I would've stopped it."

"I know. I was...really, really stupid. Okay, there I said it. I was a complete idiot. After Dad's heart attack last year, I've been so worried I thought it would be better if I did what he wanted me to do. I'll call them Monday and beg them to give me my job back because not having it makes me want to cry." She'd lost so much in her life. She'd told herself that bowing to her father's wishes would be better for his health. She wasn't certain she could survive burying another parent. Reverend Tilson was doing very well health-wise lately. She hoped her stunt didn't set him back. But losing her job felt like a death to her. She cherished it. Loved it way too much to have ever let Ed discourage her from it. Not to mention, she'd worked awfully hard to get where she was.

Once again, Jamie seemed to be damming back a flood of words with the might of his teeth. It took him a full minute before he unhinged his jaw. "All right, we'll start with a week. Do you need my help or are we grabbing what we need and meeting back up at the registers?"

"I've got it. I'll meet you back up here, but I want to change out of this gown before we get back on the road."

"Then we'll make that happen."

Charlie got a cart and headed toward the women's section. She'd picked out one shirt and was looking at the jeans when Jamie returned with a full handbasket. "I've been up front five minutes. Are you okay?" He sounded genuinely concerned.

Completely unable to believe that he was ready to go on a week-long trip in less than ten minutes, she inventoried his basket. Large pack of boxer briefs, two pairs of Wranglers, a stack of T-shirts and a package of socks. Toothbrush, toothpaste, some of that dude combo body and hair wash, and deodorant. She rolled her eyes. "Women's clothes don't come in packs. It takes us longer."

"Women are objectively the smarter sex so that sounds like something y'all need to get to fixing."

"You didn't get pajamas, so see, you're not finished either." Victory rang in her tone, but she tried not to sound too smug.

"I don't wear pajamas." He chuckled at her expression.

"Well, whatever you sleep in, you didn't get it."

"I don't sleep in anything, unless I'm at the firehouse and then I sleep in skivvies, so I've got everything I need except you."

It took Charlie entirely too long to get her mind to focus on anything but what Jamie would look like completely nude tangled up in bedsheets. She blinked several times trying to clear the erotic imagery from her mind. Nothing worked. "Um, well, okay then. I'll hurry."

"Here, let me help. What size jeans do you need?"

"I'm not telling you that."

"Oh for fuck's sake. All right, how 'bout what do you sleep in? I'll go over there and get that." He pointed to the adjacent section in the store.

Charlie had no idea what possessed her to say it, but she smirked. "Maybe I don't sleep in anything either."

"Good to know. Looks like we're gonna get to know each other real, real well on this trip."

But thoughts of actually having to sleep in the nude in the same house with Jamie had her backing down quickly. "I don't actually sleep naked," she whispered. "Just grab me some sleep shorts and a shirt, please. I'll get everything over here."

CHAPTER SEVEN

Jamie wandered into the women's lingerie section and realized he'd made a grave mistake. First of all, what the hell were sleep shorts and how were they different from not-sleep shorts? Far more importantly, how the hell was he supposed to pick out what Charlie was going to sleep in?

It was going to be like walking a minefield. If he picked something too sexy, she'd either be pissed or figure out that he couldn't seem to get his thoughts out of her crotch. If he picked some kind of granny nightgown thing, she'd really be pissed. Then there were sizes. Jesus. Why had he volunteered for this?

He passed a display of panties, and his mouth went dry all over again. Did she ever wear thongs? That seemed so un-Charlie like. For as long as he'd known her, she'd been a one-piece swimsuit, high-collared shirts, keep-all-the-best-stuff-covered kind of girl. Apparently Ed got to see her in lace panties, however. His fists clenched tight around the basket in his hands.

He wandered around and found some short flannel shorts that had to be sleep shorts. All right, well, she had asked him to pick them so he located the shortest style he could find and gambled on a medium. If he could get a few glimpses of those lush cheeks of hers again, it'd fuel his fantasies for the next twenty years.

Now for a top. They had a hundred different T-shirt things that said stuff like *Tiaras and Coffee*. None of them seemed to fit Charlie though. As far as he knew tiaras were not something she had any interest in. She liked coffee, but he saw no purpose in advertising that on clothes only the two of them were gonna see her in. They already knew she liked coffee.

He located full-on, zip-up, adult-sized footie pajamas on the clearance rack. What the actual fuck? Must be what nuns wore. He moved on to shirts that had those tiny little straps on them. Now they were getting somewhere. The shorts he'd gotten were blue and green plaid, so he grabbed a white top and congratulated himself on a job well done.

But as he headed back to Charlie, praying that she'd made some headway or they were going to be there all damn day, he got a text from Wes. *Went by the preacher's house after I checked your cattle. No car in the carport. Drove around town and I don't see evidence of him anywhere. If he left town, I have no way of knowing where he's heading.*

Fuck. They were far enough away from Oklahoma now that Jamie wasn't too worried, but it pissed him off nonetheless. Guy just didn't know when he was beaten, did he? The fact that he might've had the audacity to come after Charlie when she didn't want to be found pissed him off even more. Of course, preacher man could be anywhere. Maybe he went on his honeymoon alone. Were preachers allowed to have revenge fucks when they got left? Probably not. Not that he deserved one anyway.

He responded to Wes, let him know how far they had to go until they were on Camden Ranch, and rushed back to Charlie. "Hey, so Ed apparently left the building, and no one knows where he is. You ready to get back on the road?"

"Do you seriously think he's going to come looking for me? That's just...so unlike him." She grabbed a bunch of T-shirts off a display and tossed them in the cart.

"He didn't want you working, didn't want you hanging out with me, didn't want you doing anything you like to do. Sounds to me like he's a controlling prick, so yeah, I do think he'd come looking for you. He better pray I don't find him first, or I'll beat my opinion of him ordering you around into his self-righteous face."

"You seem to have a lot of pent-up anger. I wish you'd told me you hated him a long time ago."

"You wouldn't have listened. You were too worried about your daddy. What else do you need? I got these." He offered her the pajamas hopefully, the way a kid gives his mama a dandelion from the front yard that he stuck in a mason jar for her.

"Um," a harsh swallow contracted her delicate neck. "These are fine." She tossed the shorts in the cart. "Just not this." She held the shirt like it might've been some kind of wasp nest. "I'll hurry."

"Okay," he shrugged, "I'm gonna grab a hairbrush. I did forget that."

———

Refusing to meet Jamie's eyes, Charlie laid the tank top on the cart and loathed its existence. She watched her best friend trail off toward the groceries, while she grabbed another pair of jeans and threw in a pair of shorts just in case.

She shoved the offending top on a random rack in the pajama section and picked out a full coverage T-shirt instead. Everyone had chapters of their own books that they didn't want anyone to read. She just didn't want to think about the scars right then. She didn't want Jamie to see them. He was the only person in her whole life who'd never treated her any differently after he found out what had happened to her mother, to her whole life. She never wanted him to feel sorry for her.

The scars told the part of her story she didn't want anyone to read, not even him.

She grabbed a week's worth of panties and another bra. Then she headed Jamie's way. *Next time I run away, I need to remember my suitcase.*

That thought made her cringe. Did she always run from her problems? Maybe. Ugh. She so did not want to be that kind of woman. She just needed everyone else to quit telling her who to be and what to do.

She didn't run from anything she'd ever personally chosen. That soothed her somewhat.

Twenty minutes later, they were both standing outside the Target restrooms looking much more themselves. Charlie had her stupid wedding gown wadded up in her arms. She didn't know what to do with it but felt bad dumping it somewhere. Maybe she could donate it to one of those places that made them into other things. It struck her that as much as she loved to keep things, she'd never once kept a menu from any of the restaurants Ed had ever taken her to, and she had no desire to keep the gown at all. Once again, she lambasted herself for not realizing all of this earlier.

She tossed the dress in the back of Jamie's truck, thrilled to be done with it.

Jamie chuckled at that. "Want me to cram it in the toolbox?"

"I don't care what you do with it as long as I never have to wear it again."

He stopped at a gas station and filled up. When he returned from the store, he had two Dr. Peppers, a bag of Jalapeño Cheetos, and Red Hots. "If we're gonna road trip, we gotta do it right."

She suspected he didn't want her to worry about Ed's whereabouts so he was acting like it didn't matter. But she wasn't worried about Ed or anything else, except maybe her father. She almost never worried when she was with Jamie. He was like a sanctuary away from everything in the world that might hurt her. "You are the best!" she gushed.

"I told you, I know." He winked at her, opened his Dr. Pepper, and they were back on the interstate.

CHAPTER EIGHT

They made good time and got to Lincoln just a few hours later. With every state line Jamie put between Charlie and Ed, his breaths came a little easier. Just another couple of hours and they'd be at his cousin's ranch. No one would come looking for them there. Hell, he doubted Pleasant Glen even showed up on most maps.

"Oh look, they have gas stations here named after most of your relationships." Charlie pointed to the Kum and Go Gas Station and giggled.

"Ouch," Jamie pretend to be wounded.

"Aww, I'm sorry. But you cannot deny it."

"I didn't say I could, but still ouch. You only get vicious when you're hungry. Do I need to stop for supper 'cause there ain't nothing between here and Camden Ranch. And when I say nothing, I mean literally nothing but cornfields."

She studied him for a minute. "Why don't you ever go out with anyone for more than a few dates?"

He hated lying to her, but he couldn't give her the actual truth —*because none of them are you.* So, he shrugged out his lie. "Just haven't met the right woman, I guess."

"So, you do think she's out there somewhere then? I'm not so sure

I believe in that anymore. I'm thinking of just becoming a spinster, like in old books. Becca can get married and have kids and I'll just be their favorite aunt or something. I'll keep candy in my purse."

"So, you're just giving up on love and kids and the whole deal? You always wanted to be a mom."

"I know, but it's not worth it. Plus, I'd be terrible at it."

Jamie paused but went on with the question, "What's not worth it exactly?"

"Having to give up a life I love for a guy I don't. I could have a kid without a man, if I wouldn't be a terrible mom, but I would because I didn't have one for a long time so I probably missed some kind of crucial information you're supposed to have or something."

"Stop it," Jamie demanded. "You'd make a great mom, and you shouldn't have to give anything up. That's not how love is supposed to work."

"And you know this how?" she countered.

"I don't know it specifically. I just know that ain't how it's supposed to go. You're supposed to make each other better. It's supposed to be like you don't ever want to not be with the guy you fall head over boots for. You should see Ford and Callie," he reminded her of his older brother and his wife. "She still looks at him like he's some kind of cattle-ranching superhero or something."

Charlie shook her head. "You're the only person I never get tired of being around, so that doesn't work. I just don't want to get some kind of reputation for being a runaway bride, like in that movie."

"If it was the right guy, you wouldn't run away." Jamie mentally corrected— if it was *me*.

"Maybe." Her eyes lit a moment later, set off by the sinking sun behind the Lincoln skyline. It set her hair ablaze, made the bronze flecks in her green eyes dance, and made him ache with need. "We should have one of those deals!"

"What kind of deal?"

"Where if neither of us gets married by the time we're like fifty-five, then we marry each other."

Another sucker punch right to the chest. The pain made his heart trip over the next beat. His mind, however, began coming up with ways to keep her single until they were fifty-five so she could finally be his. But God, he didn't want her to be alone. He didn't want to be alone either. But letting her know what he really thought of that wasn't a gamble he could risk. What if it didn't work?

They'd had one fight in their twenty-plus year friendship, and it had started the day he'd signed on the dotted line at the fire department. She hadn't spoken to him for weeks. She'd never told him that she didn't want him to be a firefighter. She didn't have to. Every time he got near her in an effort to get her to scream at him or hit him or something, tears would pierce those gorgeous eyes and she'd walk away. He couldn't live through something like that again. He'd finally gone and sat in her office at the old folks' home where she worked and had refused to leave until they talked. He'd offered up never talking about his other career. She just kept saying how much it scared her to know he was in danger and that she never wanted him to go through what she'd been through. The thing she didn't get, the thing she refused to see, was that she wouldn't be sitting beside him, they never would've met at all if it hadn't been for the fireman that got her out of that house. "Fifty-five, huh?"

"Yeah. Don't you think so? You'll retire around then."

And there it was. So blatantly obvious and yet she still refused to acknowledge its presence. "If that's what you want, you know I'm in."

"Okay. Good." She paused again and stared out at the main drag through the city. "Would it be bad for us to eat again? I don't want to make your cousin wait up on us, but I am kind of starving. I don't know why I'm so hungry."

"Because you're finally relaxed. There's a place downtown that Maddox goes to with a bunch of his army buddies when he's up here. He says it's great food and it's fast. I'll call him and get directions. We'll eat quick and get right back on the road. I need to stretch my legs anyway."

———

After a quick call to his cousin and a few turns, they were heading to something called The Hi-Way Diner. "Did Maddox say anything about

Ed?" Charlie couldn't help but wonder. She didn't want drama over any of this. She wished the whole town would forget about it. Ed especially. But Holder County wasn't known for forgetting much of anything ever.

"Just that no one knows where he is. I'm surprised he hasn't tried to call you."

"He might've but I turned my phone off. I just don't want any ties to anyone there. I guess that's irresponsible, though."

"There's nothing irresponsible about wanting a break. Keep it off. You wanted an escape so let's take the one we have."

"I should at least check to see who all might've called." Charlie eased the phone from her bag like it might've been some kind of feral cat and turned it on. There were six missed calls, so it could've been much worse. Three from her father, two from Becca, and one from Louann. None from Ed. Somehow the only thing she found surprising about that was that she'd expected it. Nothing about Ed not attempting to phone her was shocking at all, and shouldn't it have been surprising? Communication had been something she'd told herself they'd develop after the wedding. Again, so stupid on her part.

Before she could debate listening to the voicemails, the phone rang in her hand. She jolted and tossed it back in her purse. Jamie glanced her way like she'd truly lost what was left of her mind. She retrieved the phone again and relief washed over her, restoring a little of her good sense. "It's Becca." She answered before voicemail could pick it up again.

"Hey, listen, I'm so..."

"Do not apologize! This is the coolest thing you've ever done. I've waited my whole life for my big sister to grow a pair and you finally did. Where are you? No. Wait. Don't tell me. I suck at lying. How long are you staying out of town? No. Don't tell me that either. You should've seen everyone's faces. It was priceless. Also, I may have told Ed to suck it, which I know wasn't nice, but then I also called him a twat-waffle. Because he is. And I decided I don't feel bad about it. If a guy's a twat-waffle someone ought to tell him."

Having no idea how to respond to any of that, Charlie's mouth continued to gape but she produced no sound. Finally, she came up with, "You called Ed a twat-waffle?"

Jamie choked on the sip of Dr. Pepper he'd just taken as he burst out laughing.

"Yes, I did. Because he pisses me off with the way he treats you. He acts like you're lucky to be with him when it should be the other way around. Plus, he's so controlling. Gross. He's lucky you even gave him the time of day. It's about time you realized your worth." Charlie wasn't entirely certain that was why she left, but she knew better than trying to reason with her sister. It would be more productive to beat her head against a brick wall. "But now you're finally with Jamie, and this is exactly what was always supposed to happen. I am so fucking excited for you. Plus, as your little sister you owe it to me to tell me everything about you and Jamie in bed. The boy has a reputation as I'm sure you know. Save a horse, ride a Holder and all."

"Bec," Charlie huffed, "that is not going to happen. Ever. Why would you even think that?" The sucker punch of disappointment in her own belly brought her up short. Where had that come from? That wasn't allowed.

"Why?" Becca whined.

Why? Charlie rolled her eyes. "You know why."

"No, I know the shit you tell yourself and anyone else who asks—it would ruin our friendship, you could never be in a relationship with a firefighter after what happened to Mom, he wouldn't be interested. But those are lies, and you know it. Bottom line is that you won't let it happen because you're scared."

"I am not scared," Charlie gave the reflexive answer primed on her tongue.

"Bullshit."

"Becca, I'm hanging up now. You're being ridiculous."

"Am I?"

"Yes, you are."

"Tell me this then—you spent all freaking morning in your dress staring out the window into the parking lot. Who was it you were looking for? On your freaking wedding day, Charlotte, who were you searching for?" Her family only called her Charlotte when they wanted to make a point. And her sister had one, damn her. "That's what I thought," Becca stated triumphantly. "You've done the hard part. He's right there beside you. He is *always* right there beside you. He always will be. I don't give a bull's hindquarters what Dad says about him. Stop being afraid to live. Stop doing what you think everyone else wants you to do. For once in your life, take a chance on something. He'd never let you down. But even if it doesn't work out, you'll be okay. I won't let you not be okay. Plus, you're stronger than you give yourself credit for. You and I got out of that fire. Mom wouldn't have wanted us to just survive. She'd want us to be happy. Now, I love you. I miss you, but do not come back home until you've got your shit figured out. God, if you won't do it for yourself, do it for Mom. She was a badass, and you are too, when you let yourself be."

CHAPTER NINE

Charlie sat in the Hi-Way Diner not really tasting the food, though she was sure it was delicious. She'd lost her voracious appetite.

There was a loud group of guys in the back-corner booth. They had to be ex-military. They all had the look. They seemed to be having a good time, cutting up and joking around. One of her favorite pastimes was occasionally eavesdropping on strangers. She liked to make up backstories for the people she encountered. In her made-up stories, everyone got to have a happy life. They got to fall in love and have babies and marriages never ended and there were never fires. There were never scars.

She couldn't get Becca's words or her question out of her mind. Why did she make up happy stories for everyone else but never imagined one for herself? That seemed...sad. Her mother would be disappointed to know that's how Charlie thought.

"Hey, what did Becca say to you?" Jamie finally asked. "You haven't said a word since you got off the phone. You look like you just walked out of a morgue."

How apropos. Jamie had always been able to read her like an open book. She used to love that about him. Currently, she wished she could shut herself up tight with a lock like those diaries she used to keep when she was little. The ones that had been turned to ash.

She shrugged. "Becca said that I needed to stop being afraid to do what I want to do."

"Girl runs wild, but she's got a point. All right, so what is it you want to do?"

Kiss you. She shook her head back and forth telling herself no. "I... have no idea," she lied, and she suspected he knew it.

"You don't know, or you don't want to tell me?"

"I tell you everything." Another lie.

"Except whatever's going on in your head right now. And you didn't tell me Captain Twat-Waffle didn't want you hanging out with me, so you don't tell me everything."

Charlie half smiled over Ed's new rank and name. "I should probably have asked Becca if she knew where he was."

"It don't matter where he is. I've got you. If he somehow figured out where we were and wants to come looking for you, he can come through me."

Rolling her eyes at that, she shook her head. "I don't need you to protect me from the Captain. He's completely harmless." Her smirk at least got him to grin. His harmlessness was one of the things that had first attracted her to the idea of Ed. He was safe. Nothing to fear because there was nothing to feel at all.

"Yeah, well, I like protecting you. Always have. Always will. Gets me hard thinking you need me."

Charlie was quite certain her own shock was reflected back in Jamie's eyes. Did he know what he just said? Did he mean to say that? "Uh," he promptly panicked. "I didn't mean that. I mean it...uh... makes me feel...good to know that I can be a good friend. Good?"

Holy baby Moses in a basket. Her eyes were the only part of her body not frozen. She managed a few blinks. Slowly, her head seemed to thaw, and she remembered how to nod.

"You gonna eat that?" Jamie pointed to her mostly uneaten meatloaf. Charlie slid it across the table to him and watched him devour it all in a few bites. She suspected he was shoveling food in his face so he didn't have to look at her and wouldn't have to talk.

It was just a slip. He hadn't meant it, like he said. She should tease him about it to prove that she knew it meant nothing, but her mouth was still incapable of producing words.

She sat in awkward silence listening to the guys in the back corner. It sounded like one of them had just told the others that his wife was pregnant again. "I thought you two were just friends," one of the others harassed.

Finally, it was all too much. She had to rescue Jamie. He'd rescued her a dozen times over. That particular day being the biggest rescue of them all. She owed him. "Hey, I know you were just kidding," she offered the lie that would save them both.

Relief softened his hazel eyes. "Yeah, I don't even know why I said that. That's not what I meant."

She wondered if any table in that old diner had ever held as many lies between the patrons as the one they were sitting at. She nodded out the next. "You were mad about Ed."

"Yeah." Jamie leapt on that. "Guy just pisses me off."

"Becca says I deserve better."

"You do."

"She says I deserve someone who won't ever let me down."

"Agreed."

"Yeah, my kid sister went and got smart on me."

"Then there's hope for Wes and Dalton yet, I guess."

There. Now, they were talking like two old friends. She forced a smile. "They have a great big brother so they'll be just fine."

"Does that mean you're taking total credit for Becca?"

"Of course."

He laughed and looked even more relieved than she felt. They were such good friends they could even overcome the mother of all awkwardness. She needed to remember that.

Jamie tossed his napkin down on the table. "Are you ready to get back on the road? We've got about two more hours give or take."

"Definitely. I don't want to keep Colt up. It sounds like he's not getting much sleep as it is." At least that was the truth.

———

Jamie mentally beat the crap out of himself as they drove on in silence. What the hell? No, better question—*where* the hell had that even come from? The fact that it was the truth did not matter. He'd been keeping that truth from her for decades. He had to keep on doing that.

Jesus, he needed to get to Camden Ranch and get his head together. He hoped Colt had something about a hundred proof that he could down before he crashed on the couch. It occurred to him that alcoholism wasn't attractive on anyone, and he'd had way too much to drink over Charlie in the last few days.

Moving on to another plan--he'd skip the booze and just hit the sack. Maybe getting a decent night's sleep would restore his common sense.

"I've never seen so much corn," Charlie commented as the fields flew past their windows.

"Really? I just drove you through Kansas."

"Yeah, but this is the Cornhusker state."

"True. It'll be good to see Colt. He hasn't been home in a long time."

"Do you think he still thinks of Holder County as home or does he think of Nebraska as his home now?"

Jamie considered that for a beat. "Honestly?"

"Of course," she urged.

"I think he considers Avery home. Doesn't much matter where he is as long as she's there."

Charlie gave him one of those smiles that seemed to somehow align the light of her soul with her emerald eyes like a prism. "That's so sweet."

Jamie shrugged. "Just calling it like I see it."

"Do you think I should call Daddy?" she asked all of a sudden.

"To tell him what?"

"I don't know. That I'm okay and I'm sorry."

"Are you sorry?"

"That I left? No. That he spent money on the ceremony that never happened? A little."

"Do you want to talk to him?"

"No."

"I thought we were working on you doing what you wanted to do."

"That's true." Charlie seemed relieved at that answer.

They'd talked all the way to Lincoln, and Jamie had forgotten all about music. Managing the steering wheel with one hand, he fished his phone out of his pocket, used his teeth to hook it into the sound system in his truck, and turned on the playlist he'd made of all of Charlie's favorite songs. He needed more of those grins of hers. They were a drug. He required another hit to keep himself sane.

When Garth started singing, she beamed. Yeah, that was the good stuff. That was the stuff he'd tried to find in a bottle the night before. That's why he'd kept drinking. Nothing was as intoxicating as her. "You're the best," she vowed.

"I keep telling you, I know." He winked at her.

There was one road that led through Pleasant Glen, and it ran parallel to the train tracks. They drove past Saddleback's Bar and Grill and both of their brows furrowed.

"Is that a church sign they're using to advertise the bar?" Charlie asked.

"Looks to be." The fact that the church sign informed everyone that a band called The Original Sinners would be performing Friday night made it all the more odd and hilarious.

Jamie was yawning when they pulled under the gates of Camden Ranch. Exhaustion weighted both of them. He wondered how much sleep Charlie had gotten the night before.

It wasn't that late, but he suspected the sheer relief she must feel had let her relax.

He followed Colt's directions and parked the truck outside of the small cottage near the gates. There were several trucks nearby. Jamie hoped the entire Camden family didn't feel like they needed to be there to welcome them or anything.

He secured their luggage, which was really just her makeup bag, five Target bags, and a sack of snacks from a gas station. She tucked close to him as they made their way to the porch. It was a chilly night without a single cloud in the sky. There was a full moon, but she hadn't seemed to notice, and he wasn't going to bring it up. He knew she hated them.

Charlie was doing that thing she did when she was nervous where she gnawed on her thumb nail. "You okay?" he whispered before he knocked on the door.

"Yeah, but I feel like we're imposing."

"I don't think they mind. We'll help out while we're here." He hoped her nerves were really about being polite and not about staying with him. They hadn't spent the night together since the last time they'd run away to the creek when they were sixteen.

Colt pulled open the door. "'Bout damn time." He laughed and yanked Jamie into a full-force hug. There were several other Camdens standing in the living room. "How the hell are you?" He slapped Jamie on the back and then tipped his hat to Charlie. "I haven't seen you in years. How are you, Charlie?"

But Charlie didn't answer. Jamie turned to stare at her. He followed her line of sight to the fire roaring in the fireplace. *Fuck.* She was whiter than a sheet and trying and failing to clutch his hand. Her arm wouldn't seem to lift. That's okay, if she couldn't move, he always would. He wrapped his arm around her tight and forcibly turned her head and laid it on his shoulder, trying to get her away from the sight of the flames. "Colt," he growled quietly through his teeth.

Obviously confused, Colt glanced from Jamie to Charlie and then to the fire. His eyes widened in horror. "Shit. I'm sorry. I forgot." He cringed and quick-stepped to the fireplace where he made the flames disappear with the flip of a switch. "It's a gas fireplace. No chimney. Goes out completely when you turn off the gas."

Jamie appreciated his cousin trying, but he doubted those reassurances were going to be enough.

Colt cleared his throat and went on with introductions. "This is my Uncle Ev and Aunt Jessie. And you probably remember my brother Brock from the wedding."

Jamie shook everyone's hands and made his offer to Mr. Camden. "We appreciate you letting us crash here. If I can be of any help, sir, don't hesitate. I know a thing or two about running cattle."

Ev chuckled but he was eyeing Charlie with a great deal of fatherly concern. "You're family, son. You're welcome up here anytime. 'Sides, we seem to be running a refuge ranch for runaway brides. The thing I noticed the last time this happened was that what everyone really needed was a break."

Mrs. Camden beamed at them. She gently rubbed Charlie's back when she hugged her. "We're so glad you two are here. Now, what can we do to get you settled in? There's some coffeecake for the morning and there's hamburger meat and a few steaks in the fridge, too, along with a few other things for making meals. Katy said she'd drop off a few casseroles tomorrow, but you all are more than welcome to come up to the big house to eat."

"Who's Katy?" Charlie whispered to Jamie. At least she'd found her voice again, but she was clearly on high alert.

He searched the recesses of his mind, but he'd only ever been around the Camdens for Colt's wedding and he hadn't quite memorized the names. "One of the brother's wives, right?"

Jessie smiled. "Yes, and don't worry about keeping up with them. Just about the time I think I got a handle on the number of grandkids we have, one of them up and has another one. I've lost all count, and they're my kids."

Everyone except Charlie laughed. Jamie had seen her like this twice before. Once when she'd come out to the ranch unexpectedly when they'd been doing some spring burning. The other when they'd attended a wedding for some friends of theirs in Tulsa. The reception had been held at some historical house, and they'd had every fireplace roaring. The fire that had killed her mother had started in the chimney one cold winter night. Her father had built a fire early in the evening and then had put it out later on. They'd thought they were safe.

"Your ranch is beautiful," Charlie commented robotically.

Colt, Brock, and Ev all gave her a concerned smile. Ev nodded. "Thank you, sweetheart. We do what we can with what we have. Can't really do more than that. It's not quite Holder Ranch, but we get by all right."

Jamie wasn't certain what to say to that, so he tried, "Yeah, well, there's a few more of us to run all that land. Besides, my daddy and his brothers have had a competition going for years to see how much of

Oklahoma they can slap the Holder brand on. I'm not sure they even know where to put the fences anymore. 'Bout the time we get 'em up we're having to move 'em to expand. It's too much."

"Cattle rancher can't ever have too much land, now can he?" Ev countered.

"Hear, hear," Colt agreed.

"Where are the babies?" Jamie asked his cousin. Charlie loved kids. That might be the thing to get her to come back to the present with him.

"We're getting ready to send Chase back to UN in the fall. Jaxon is starting middle school if you can believe that. Brock's wife, Hope, has Annabelle up at the house with her cousins, and Avery's at home trying to get the newest one to sleep. She'll be down here tomorrow so you can meet them all."

"Good. I need to fill them all in on a few of your wilder stunts just so they have something to hold over your head."

Colt laughed at that. "I wish you wouldn't. They already have me wrapped so tight around their fingers I hurt."

Jamie was thrilled to see his cousin so happy. He was also jealous, but he'd deal with that later. "All right, I'll keep my mouth shut, but I do want to meet them. We're beat tonight anyway." He didn't want to be rude, but he needed them to leave. He was the only person who'd ever been able to coax Charlie out of the flashbacks when she had them.

"Of course."

Jessie took Charlie's hand. The touch seemed to ground her somewhat. "The bedroom is this way. There's a few more blankets in the closet if you need them. If you can't find something, just give me a call."

"We really do appreciate this so much, Mrs. Camden. I know you weren't expecting guests. We won't get in the way." Charlie almost sounded like herself with that. She appreciated everything. Jamie suspected it was because she knew what things like hospitality were worth and what they cost.

"Honey, you are never in the way. We're thrilled you're here. Relax.

It sounds like life owes you a breath of fresh air. We've got that in spades."

Jamie doubted Colt had elaborated too much on Charlie's asthma from the smoke inhalation, so it was interesting to him that Mrs. Camden seemed to know right away what she needed. Must be a mom thing.

CHAPTER TEN

Still trying to regulate her heartbeats, Charlie made a third pass through the small house. Checking and checking again. Not that she knew what exactly she was checking for, but she was certain if she'd just checked her house when she was little, she would've noticed something that would've saved them all.

She felt terrible for reacting the way she had when they'd walked in. She knew the Camdens wanted the cottage to feel cozy, but fires never felt cozy to her. Their heat never felt soothing to her, either. They smelled like melting synthetic carpet and plastic appliances and disintegrating siding turning to liquid before her eyes. And those smells would never leave her lungs. They smelled like life being turned to ash. She couldn't let them go. She refused.

She blinked away the memories as best as she was able. Jamie was staring at her, gauging her, she knew. Charlie joined him at the window. She just needed to be close to him. He'd make her forget for a little while. He always did.

"Do you want a beer or something? I saw some in the fridge," she offered hopefully. She was trying to convince him that she was fine, even though she wasn't. She hated feeling weak and scared. She prayed he wouldn't want to go to bed already. She just needed him up and talking and being her Jamie for a little while longer.

"Nah," he eased closer to her, almost instinctively it seemed. "I had way too much to drink last night. I need to lay off. But I'll get you one if you want."

That explained why his eyes had been bloodshot that morning. She didn't allow herself to think of why he might've gotten drunk the night before. Focusing instead on the back deck, she immediately wished she hadn't. Everything around them glowed pale blue from the full moon. She'd refused to acknowledge it on their drive.

That's the thing about the moon—it's the same in Oklahoma City, and in Holder County, and even in Pleasant Glen, Nebraska. It changed cyclically. Always showing different faces to the world below, but when it was full, like it was that night, and the air was just right, it always looked like a frozen sun to Charlie, eerily hanging too close to the ground. It showed entirely too much. Things no one would ever want to see. "Will you check the smoke detectors, please?" she begged suddenly and immediately wished she could just get a grip.

"Hey," Jamie wrapped her up in his arms, and she was able to breathe in his scent. It replaced the acrid smoky death. Saddle-oil-infused life rushed into weak lungs. "Of course I will. It's been a long day. But I am right here, and you are safe. I've got you. It's a gas fireplace, baby. No chimney. Safest you can have."

She knew that. She knew that he had her, too, but as soon as she lifted her head from his chest the memories yanked her under their riptide again. Something about the stupid moon or maybe it was what Becca had said, talking about their mom, plus the fire or something. "You know they don't really work," she insisted. "If your house is on fire, you can't even hear them. Not really. You can't hear anything. They melt. I saw them." She'd seen them by the light of the moon. She clamped her mouth shut so hard her molars ached, but she didn't care.

The gentle grip of Jamie's hand on her chin centered her just a little. "Look at me," he demanded in a somehow soothing, yet forceful, order. "Right here in my eyes." She obeyed as best as she could. "That's it. Deep breath for me." She could no longer draw deep breaths. She wasn't in his arms. "I know you hate full moons. If I could, I'd climb up there and turn the thing off for you. I'd do it in a minute, but I can't do that mostly because I refuse to leave you here. But I will never let anything hurt you. Never. I've got you." He tucked a wayward strand of her hair behind her right ear and smiled. "Hey, you know what I was thinking about earlier?"

Charlie shook her head in his hand. She focused only on the soothing tone of his voice.

"Remember that time we skipped Sunday School and went to the gas station and got candy instead? But then we got back too late. Church had already started, and we had to sneak you up to the balcony before your daddy realized you weren't there?"

He replaced the terrifying memories with one that always made her laugh. "Yes," she nodded, "you caught a bullfrog and dropped him in the back window of the church and then when it started hopping down the aisle and people started laughing, we ran up the back stairs. I can't believe we didn't get caught."

"The window wasn't open but a little bit and they're stained glass so no one saw me. Plus, I am pretty much the best at what I do."

"Louann found a Butterfinger wrapper in the pocket of my dress, but she never told my dad."

"Guess we owe her a nice bottle of Crown or something then."

Charlie laughed at the very idea of her stepmother drinking. Her father strictly forbade it in his house. The Holders' penchant for whiskey was yet another thing he disliked about them.

"Maybe I will have a beer," Jamie changed his mind. "You want one?" He casually kept her hand in his and guided them into the kitchen. Everything in the cottage was so new and fresh. The hardwoods still smelled like the faint odor of wood stain. Charlie focused on that scent and kept her hand tucked tightly inside Jamie's.

"Sure." She gratefully accepted the beer. She definitely needed a drink. It had been one hell of a day.

An hour later, the TV was running constant reruns of some sitcom, and Charlie was leaned up against Jamie. God, it would be so easy. So fucking easy to let his hands drift gently over her breasts. So easy to coax her sweet body fully into his lap and make her forget everything that had her tense. So easy to sink his lips to hers and get her drunk on him.

The fire that had killed her mother was a constant back draft in her life, threatening to erupt again and consume as only a fire can, and he hated that. He could make her forget it all for a nice long time if she'd let him. She was so soft and warm against him. He ached with the comfort.

She yawned again, and he forced himself to talk, though he swore he would've sat on that couch half-holding her for the rest of his life just to know she was right there beside him always. "We should probably go on to bed. You're worn out. I'll grab some blankets for the couch, and brush my teeth, then the bedroom is yours."

Another slight complication with the cottage guest house was that it only had one bathroom to go with the one bedroom.

"I'm sleeping on the couch," she corrected through another deep yawn.

Jamie might not know much, but he knew she didn't really want to sleep in the room with the fireplace in it. "Don't get stubborn on me now. You are not."

"I am too." God, he loved how she defied him with a naughty smirk. Her disobedience wrapped a tight fist around his cock and squeezed. He'd love nothing more than to turn her over his knee, but that wasn't who they were.

"Charlotte Grace Tilson, no you are not."

"Oh, full name," she giggled. "Am I supposed to be scared?" At least she seemed to have come back to the land of the living.

"Yes." He joined her laughter.

"Okay, I'm terrified, but I'm still not taking the bed after you left your whole life and both of your jobs to run away with me just because I didn't have backbone enough to tell Ed no when he asked. This is my fault, so I get the couch."

"It's not your fault. If you ask me, Ed stepped in and took advantage when your daddy had that heart attack. It's his fault."

"Even if that's true, I'm still sleeping here."

Jamie grunted his annoyance. "Fine, sleep here, and then once you're out I'll move you to the bed."

"You will not. I'm a very light sleeper, and I know where you're ticklish."

"Is that a threat?"

"Obviously." She waggled her eyebrows.

"Women are so damn stubborn."

"It's part of our genetic makeup," she informed him.

"You're not wrong."

"Wait, I have an idea that will make this fair." Charlie looked far too pleased with whatever she'd just thought of. "I'll thumb-wrestle you for it. If I win, I get the couch."

Jamie ground his teeth. She knew he'd let her win because he was afraid of hurting her hands.

"How about if we take turns?" he negotiated. "I'll sleep in the bed tonight since you're being a brat and then tomorrow night we'll switch."

Her mouth hung open in mock surprise. "I am not a brat." But then another fit of giggles overtook her, and he had to get out of that room lest he pin her down to that sofa and drink the laughter from her mouth.

"I just call 'em like I see 'em."

"Okay, maybe sometimes I am, but I'm not right now. You look exhausted. You drove all day long and had to witness me hanging outside of the church with a dress over my head."

"It wasn't a bad view at all," he informed her.

She shook her head at him, crawled out from beside him, took two of the Target bags, and disappeared to the bathroom. Charlie wasn't one of those girls that spent a long time getting ready. That was yet another thing Jamie liked about her. She was naturally gorgeous and rarely even wore makeup. But that night, she stayed in there a long while.

He threw away the beer bottles and made the couch up for her, complete with two of the pillows from the bed and three blankets. Nebraska got cold at night even in spring. The thought of her being out in the living room shivering made him hate the idea of her sleeping on the couch even more. The next day he was determined to get her to trade places.

But when she stepped out of the bathroom wearing the pajama shorts Jamie had stupidly picked for her and some kind of oversized T-shirt, all thoughts left his head completely. Hell, he couldn't even remember his own name. He swore everything he'd ever known flew out of his mind, everything but her.

Her face was scrubbed clean, and her hair was up in a loose bun in one of the cloth bands she'd gotten when they stopped.

Innocence personified. That wedding dress had been one thing but this, this was something else entirely. This was perfection. His traitorous feet took two steps toward her before he could order them to stop. God, he wanted to hold her, to devour her.

She couldn't be walking around looking like *this*. As many times as he'd imagined what it would be like if there were more to them, he'd never fathomed this. His imagination wasn't that good.

Yet, he couldn't have this. He didn't deserve anything that looked so utterly untouched. So clean when he was who he was—either covered in cow shit or grease from the ladder truck that held the other half of him.

To his shock, she moved closer as well, like they were magnetically linked, impossible to keep apart. And they were. They always had been.

She brought her thumb back to her mouth and nibbled.

"What's wrong?" he managed in a harsh choke.

"Nothing."

"It's something. Just tell me. I know you don't want to sleep in—"

"Maybe I'm sick and tired of being scared," spilled from her beautiful lips. His mouth clamped shut.

He nodded and pried his jaw apart. "You lived through hell. It's okay to be—"

She cut him off again. "Not of the fire." She shook her head which seemed to erase whatever she wanted to say next. She took another step closer until she was near enough that he could feel her breath on his chin.

Refusing to lose sight of her eyes, he lowered his head. And suddenly, mercifully, confusingly, she brought her lush lips to his.

Half certain he was dreaming, he was too weak to deny himself the flavors of her.

CHAPTER ELEVEN

She'd done it. She was kissing Jamie. Disbelief stunned the hunger that had driven her to do this very thing. Jamie kissed precisely the way she'd always imagined he would. She may've started it, but oh, he was now running the show. He moved her lips rhythmically with his own.

His hands gripped her hips as he dragged her closer. He guided her hips as well. They moved apart from her thoughts at the insistence of his hands. Everything she'd ever wanted was on the very tip of her tongue.

She encountered the evidence of his potent, steel-stiff need at his zipper line. And that drove her harder. Being desired was like a drug. Being desired by Jamie Holder was some kind of liquid nirvana she swore she'd sell her soul to have. For a girl who'd spent years certain that she would never be beautiful, this soothed every scar that marred her skin and the vicious ones that crippled her heart—the ones even she couldn't see.

She could hide the others. She always had. There had never been a medicine that took away the searing ache, until that moment.

He lifted his head before he dove back in for more, allowing her a quick breath, enough for his scent to banish the fear to the past where it belonged. But when his hands slid instinctively up from her hips to her waist and then higher, the fear brought reinforcements. They rushed back in with a vengeance.

She pulled back and gasped for the breath her lungs had willingly given away. She needed that back along with all the reasons why this wasn't a good idea.

His mouth was swollen, and a low flame of need flickered in his darkened eyes. He licked his lips like her taste lingered there. "What was that?" His lust-soaked, husky tone almost drove her back into his arms. She wanted more. She wanted to drag him into that bed and beg him to satisfy the heavy ache between her legs. She needed friction and pressure and to be full of him. She needed to be safe under him, against him. She needed to feel.

She forced herself to remember that he had to have felt the bottom of the scars at her rib cage and his hands were headed to where they were much worse. She couldn't let him. She just...couldn't.

Her nostrils flared as she fought the disappointment that stung her throat. "We should go to bed." She pointed to the couch with her injured arm. Her occupational therapist had made certain she had full range of motion, but on occasion she swore her arm was still heavy with the weight of it all.

"What if I don't want to go to bed? Not without you." The last three words were ashen like his throat couldn't quite produce them fully.

She closed her eyes and called herself several horrible names. How could she have used him like that? He was her best friend.

She shook her head. "I'm so sorry." She rushed to the couch and laid down facing away from him. A coward once again. But that was okay. Cowards were safe.

His footsteps were heavy as he paced to the bedroom. She prayed that he didn't hate her and ordered herself never to act on impulse again. What was she thinking? She'd all but thrown herself into the fire and dragged him with her. So stupid. Safe was better than satisfied anyway.

Five minutes later, she heard the click of the lamp and the rustle of bed sheets. Her breaths came a little easier. She lay awake for hours listening to his light, rhythmic snores. She couldn't sleep. Her eyes couldn't look anywhere but at the cold metal glow of that fireplace in the bands of light from the moon outside the sliding glass doors.

Squeezing her eyes shut, she willed sleep to come. She was exhausted, but the kiss had awoken some part of her that she didn't recognize. It was like some other person also existed in her mind. Some kind of untarnished twin, or maybe the girl she would've been if everything had been different.

The girl wanted to be held and tended. She wanted to be desired. To know what all the fuss was about the Holders, maybe. And if Charlie closed her eyes hard enough, she was brave enough to admit that she wanted Jamie's aggression, his hunger, his filthy words in her ears. She wanted to be one of the women he picked up with such ease at honkytonks, one that he took home and used.

Tossing the covers off, Charlie glanced around the room. When her eyes had popped back open, the hazy moonlight looked precisely like smoke. Sitting bolt upright, she got to her feet and rushed to the bedroom to check on Jamie. If he was all right, that was all that mattered.

He was still snoring lightly. She smiled. The moon outside wasn't the only one out that night, it appeared. He'd kicked the covers off and his ass—and lord what an ass it was—was on full display. She couldn't imagine what it might feel like to be that free. To have a body that would allow you to not care if someone saw all of it.

With a harsh swallow she eased closer, unable to help herself. He was a work of art. For the first time since the fire, she actually appreciated all that the moon revealed. The lithe muscles of his back bunched and eased with his breaths. Even relaxed, the rolling muscles that comprised his arms looked mighty enough to keep anyone safe. The good lord had obviously chiseled Jamie Holder with a blade dipped in sex appeal. She found herself wishing he would turn over. There was so much more she wanted to see.

In the muted silence of that thought, she remembered that Jamie wasn't hers to appreciate this way. Girls like her didn't get guys like him as anything more than a friend. She needed to walk out of that room, but her feet refused to move. Every cell in her body wanted to climb in beside him and see what happened. The fear be damned to hell.

When Jamie shifted in his sleep, she panicked. What kind of weirdo would just be standing there staring at someone while they slept? With hasty tip-toed steps, she slipped back out of the room and returned to the couch, and the fireplace, and the frozen moon.

The explosion of heat woke her. "Becca!" Charlie couldn't see her little sister's bed. It was right beside hers. Where was Becca? Scrambling out of her own bed, she screamed for her mother. She couldn't see anything. Something pressed in around her, filling her lungs, blinding her. A veil of smoke.

Frantically feeling along in the blackened cloud of darkness, her hands landed on the other bed. "Becca," she pled. "Please, please wake up." She lifted her little sister out of her bed and stumbled to the bedroom door.

"Put me down," Becca finally whimpered.

"No. We have to go get Mommy."

Charlie jerked her hand away from the doorknob as it scalded her palm. Gritting her teeth, she endured the pain and flung open the door anyway. Another explosion of heat knocked the girls backwards all the way to the wall. Flames blistered Charlie's legs as she screamed into the roar of the fire. But the fire was louder. It drowned out everything.

She had to find her parents. Becca scrambled out of her arms. "Come on," she urged. She helped Charlie stand and they both ran, not for the windows, but for their parents' bedroom. Their mother would know what to do. She always knew what to do. She would keep them safe and make everything okay again.

The putrid odor of melting plastic and the sounds of Becca asking Jesus to protect them were the last things Charlie fully understood. She hit the ground. The pain wrapped its vicious fists around her throat and smothered her.

———

"Charlie." Panic speared through Jamie as he lifted her off the floor in front of the couch. He hated himself for not insisting she sleep in the bed. "Hey, shhh, it's okay. I've got you." He seated her in his lap on the couch. Her eyes were soaked with tears, and she was gasping for breath that didn't seem to be coming.

It took him entirely too long to feel around on the floor for her purse. He shook her inhaler. In his best soothing firefighter tone, he urged, "Deep breath for me, okay? Ready?" He placed it to her lips, and she did as he instructed.

But she coughed the albuterol back out with her sobs. He tucked her head to his shoulder and rocked back and forth. "It's gotta get in your lungs. Okay. Shh. It's all right. I've got you."

Her chest rattled her body, making her tremble with each cough. "One more time for me. Look at me," he soothed. She set her tear-stained eyes on his. "Ready?"

This time she gave him a nod. Once again, he got the inhaler to her lips and managed to get the medicine into her lungs this time.

When she was maintaining steady breaths, she tucked herself against him once again. She trembled in his arms, either from the meds or the terror. He cradled her tenderly and wished for the thousandth time that day alone that she'd be in bed beside him every fucking night. He'd starve those nightmares until they held no power over her. Hell, he'd slay dragons to have her. All of those demons that wouldn't give her rest—he'd vanquish them to hell. They could burn there. He just had to figure out some way to make her understand that he'd trade his last breath for her. "Want to talk about it?" he whispered, but she shook her head and clung to him tighter.

"You're not sleeping on this couch," he ordered, and he no longer cared if she wanted to argue with him. Standing with her in his arms, he whisked her to the bedroom and laid her gently on the bed. He crawled in beside her and guided her head to his chest. Friends who sometimes kiss with enough need to make him hard-up for weeks also share a bed on occasion, apparently. Fuck it. Rules had never been his forte anyway.

"I'm sorry I woke you up," she croaked. She sounded a great deal like a terrified frog.

"Nothing to apologize for. Nightmares suck. I'm glad I'm here with you. It'd kill me to think that you have them like that when you're alone."

She cleared her throat. "I'm always alone when I have them."

"Not anymore." He gave all sense of caution and discretion a big middle finger. He was done with it all.

She tucked her face tight to his chest and mumbled out, "I dreamed about the fire."

He'd figured that. Turning on his side, he tipped her face back up. "Does it happen in the dream the way it really happened?"

"Sometimes. Sometimes I can't get Becca to wake up, and...." Another violent shiver coursed through her.

"Okay," he cradled the back of her head with his hand and kissed the top of her head. "It's all over now."

"When they got me out of the house, I woke up for a few minutes," she choked out. She rarely said anything about the fire. What little Jamie knew he'd found out by searching the records from the OKC fire department. She didn't know that he knew anything at all. He assumed she wouldn't want to know that. He nodded, afraid to say anything at all that might not let her talk this out. "I hurt so badly I kept passing out, but I woke up when the fireman was carrying me out to the ambulance."

He knew both girls had been rescued by a man named Clint Masterson. That night had been his first structure fire. Guy had to have been scared out of his mind. Jamie had called Clint one day a decade ago to thank him and tell him that both Becca and Charlie were doing well. They'd spoken on the phone numerous times since then, just talking firefighter shit. Jamie didn't have anyone he could talk business with. Charlie was terrified of his job and his family just didn't get it. Clint always asked how the Tilson girls were doing. Jamie always filled him in. As a firefighter, he knew what it meant to get those calls, to know you'd made a difference. "That's our job, sweetheart."

"I know, but I never thanked him." Panic seemed to bolt through her again. She sat up off of his chest. The absence stung. "I should thank him."

Taking another reckless chance, he sat up with her and brushed more soothing kisses on her cheek then he guided her back down beside him. "I thanked him for you."

"You did?" He could see the questions painted in her eyes as she lifted her head.

"Yeah. I did. He's a lieutenant on a ladder truck now, but he was a newbie the night he saved you. He remembered pulling you and Bec out of the house that night. He's a good guy. Got a few kids of his own now."

"That's the same as you are now. A lieutenant on a ladder truck, I mean." Even her sniffles were adorable.

Jamie smiled at that. "Yeah, but it's harder to get up to that rank in OKC, since they have a hundred times more people than we do out in Holder County."

His mind was a little sluggish. It took him a beat too long to understand what she'd been saying. If she'd passed out from pain, that meant…she'd been burned. But that made no sense. She'd never said anything about actually having been burned in the fire.

Scared? Of course. Lung damage? He knew all about that. But pain to the point of losing consciousness? How had she never spoken of that? He was her best friend.

CHAPTER TWELVE

Charlie was so touched that Jamie had thanked the man who'd saved her life, but of course he had. That was such a Jamie thing to have done. "I can't believe he remembers us. He must do that kind of thing all the time."

She wished she could talk to his wife. She wanted to understand how the woman was ever able to exist even moderately peacefully when her husband was at work.

"That was his first fully-involved house fire. You never forget that. Plus, I think Becca tried to bite him when he was getting her in the ambulance."

Charlie cringed. "That sounds like Bec."

"She was scared," Jamie gently reminded her.

"I know." She tucked herself closer to him once again. It felt so right to be where she was. So warm and safe in his arms. He didn't seem to mind that she was there or that she'd woken him with one of those stupid dreams. Until her engagement made it to the papers, she hadn't had the nightmares in years. Lately, they came once a week, minimum. "I really appreciate you calling and thanking him. That was so sweet of you. But I need to thank him too."

Jamie brushed a kiss on her forehead, and she told herself not to think too much about it no matter how good it felt. "I enjoy talking to Clint. We're the same rank on the same kind of truck, like you said, so he knows what goes on with that."

Charlie had always been distinctly good at reading between the lines. Jamie liked talking about firefighting with Clint, someone he'd likely never met in person, probably because he couldn't talk about it with anyone else, especially her.

Guilt swiped through her belly. She swallowed down bile-soaked fear. "I know...well...that it scares me when you...you know...talk about fires and training and stuff. But I can learn. I can be okay if you just give me some time. I'm your best friend. I want you to tell me things." There. She'd gotten the words out. Now, she just had to work on actually believing them.

"I don't want you to have to learn. Things work for us the way they are."

His voice had fractured on his lie, like the words themselves were icy shards. She stared up at him and watched that still eerie moon shimmer in his gorgeous eyes. In the reflection, she found that she didn't mind its presence so much. She kind of liked it even. It was then that she was suddenly awake enough to realize that she was in bed with Jamie Holder, and he was naked. Deliciously, perfectly, gorgeously naked.

Her mind scrambled. Her breasts were heavy. The right one pulled on the damaged muscles and scar tissue on her side. It made her all the more aware that nothing in this world was as real as he was in that moment. Right there beside her. Heat emanating from him. Life itself in the breaths she could feel cascading through her hair.

The desperate desire to share a small piece of heaven with this man who would walk through hell for her won out over every potential complication this would inevitably bring.

She let her hand drift down his chest. His evident strength tensed under her touch. His breath grew ragged. It stirred the need she swore was coiled tightly beneath all of the fear she let rule her life far too often. "If you could do anything in the whole world you wanted to do right now, what would you do?" she whispered. His eyes drifted closed and a hungry grunt filled her ears, but he said no words. The grunt spoke a compendium of lust, however. It drove her onward. "Please tell me."

"I can't." He shuddered against her and caught her hand in its track down his abs. "Can't," he managed the word again. It was laced with raw defeat.

"Why not?"

He shook his head against the pillow and refused her an answer. Her bottom lip slipped through her teeth as she considered. The movement triggered a choked curse from him, like he was being tortured. Charlie couldn't stand the sound of him in pain. She had to rescue him, to rescue them both.

The words quaked as she spoke them, but she refused to shut them away again. "I'll tell you what I would do." He gave her a single nod, like he was afraid to make more movement than that. "We'd make some kind of plan where whatever happens tonight in this bed doesn't change us. And then, I'd do this."

She cradled his cheek in her hand and let the friction of the whiskers of his slight beard enliven her. Her mind instantly wished she could feel that friction between her legs. She tried to guide his lips to hers, but he held himself away from her for entirely too many seconds. He was so much stronger than she felt.

"Mean what you say," finally rumbled from him, low and pierced with hunger. "Don't start something you don't want to finish. I've fucking dreamed...fucking needed you...too damn many times to stop once I start." The ragged warning pumped some kind of dangerous form of yearning through her veins. Strong and urgent. More desperate than anything she'd ever felt before. It should've frightened her, but instead it tore away a little of her practiced caution. She could feel the tantalizing evidence of his arousal, fevered and thick, against her thigh. Slick need leaked from him, marking her.

A frantic, desperate noise she'd never heard from her own lips before filled the air between them. "I don't want you to stop, unless you want to." She felt she should offer that. This wasn't only about what she wanted. She needed this to be for him.

"I'll never want to stop," was the last warning she received before he expertly rolled her underneath his impressive body. The weight of him, pressing her into the mattress, centered her. She was right where she was supposed to be. The doubts distanced themselves until she could no longer make out their bothersome reminders of why this was going to blow up in their faces.

"Please, Jamie."

———

He had to be dreaming. This, her, the delicious words she'd just uttered, her begging him—it had to all be a dream. He'd never deserve this. What if she regretted it? He told himself to stop. It'd kill him if she regretted anything that had to do with them, but he knew he couldn't.

She'd just had a nightmare. She was supposed to have married another man that morning. There were a thousand reasons why he should refuse, and not a single one of them was enough to get him to do what was right. Yet another reason he didn't deserve the angel in his arms begging him to own her.

But damn him to hell if he'd ever turn her down. He just wasn't that strong. He'd fantasized about this too many times to deny himself the forbidden fruit that lay before him, begging to be tasted.

He had to get some control. Jesus Christ, what if he was too rough with her? What if he hurt her? His dick was hard enough to drive fence posts into concrete.

"Whatever you're thinking right now, stop," she ordered. "You don't have to be gentle with me. I'm not a china doll."

"You can't say shit like that to me." His warning was too rough, too urgent. She had to stop, or he wasn't going to be able to. His cock was already fucking weeping for her. Weak bastard that he was.

"Why not?" she whispered. "It's true."

He kissed that nonsense off of her lips. The kiss became a warning itself. He wasn't gentle, had no finesse. He sought her surrender like that would make him somehow less insane with need. Every time his lips touched hers, he swore he tasted his future. She tasted like his.

He just took and, my god she gave in return. He was certain she was out to prove that she wasn't delicate, didn't mind him getting rough. He knew better. He'd spent the past twenty years certain that she'd come equipped with a halo that must've been burned up in that fire. But that didn't mean the shadow of it didn't still exist in its rightful place.

Maybe she didn't even know she was lying to him, but he knew. She was too sweet, too good, too perfect for him to fuck her the way he'd always wanted to. Holding her down. Making her drip. Slamming into her over and over again until the only name she knew was his. Her long auburn hair tied up in his fist while he came hot and fast down her throat. Punishing that alabaster skin until he'd left his marks of ownership. Things he was ashamed of. Things he'd never wanted with any other girl. Never with anyone else had he ever wanted to imprint himself on her. Not with anyone but Charlie. The urges to dominate her were rooted in raw possession. His. He had to make her all his.

Her hips were already restlessly bucking against his cock. His precum marked the deliciously innocent cotton. How the hell was he naked and she fully clothed? That was not how he did things. Seeking to rectify that situation, he slid his hands to the warm smoothness of her belly. She quivered under his touch. Oh fuck yeah.

But as he slid the T-shirt upwards, seeking the lush mounds of her breasts, she pinned her arms tight to her side. "Please. Don't." Her eyes begged him as well.

"Why the hell not? I want all of you. You're so goddamn gorgeous. Let me see you. Don't be shy with me."

She winced, but he wasn't certain if that was from his filthy language or if she was afraid he was going to force her out of her shirt. He was sure as hell not into making women do anything they didn't want to do, but her begging to be taken, rubbing her heat up and down the stiff ridge of his erection, and then not wanting to be undressed made no sense.

To further his confusion, she wiggled until he leaned up off of her, and she proceeded to shimmy out of those sinful little sleep shorts, or whatever the hell it was she called them, and panties exposing her ripe little pussy all for him.

And as he stared down at the moonlit glistening heaven she was offering, he decided he'd deal with the shirt issue later. He dragged rough fingertips over her creamy little peach already swollen up nice and tight. "You're soaked, baby."

She shuddered and a half-starved moan echoed from her lungs. "Please. Jamie, I need…" She sank her teeth into her bottom lip, afraid of the end of that sentence, he assumed.

"I know what you need, angel. I'm gonna take good care of you. Tender little pussy already showing me just how sweet it's gonna be for me, isn't it? So creamy and tight." She bucked against his exploring fingers and clawed at the white sheets beneath her. So fucking responsive to him he damn near came across that fucking T-shirt she was still clinging to. He knew her better than anyone, and somehow that translated to knowing exactly what she wanted to hear from him.

He brushed kisses at the tender spots where her pussy met her legs as he pressed two fingers gently through her folds. With no more warning than that, he found the tiny, hidden away opening that she was begging to be filled.

He tried with two fingers, but she was too tight. Holy shit. He managed with one and asked a question he needed an answer to. She was a preacher's daughter after all. He supposed it was possible. "Have you ever done this…with anyone else?"

She nodded. "Yeah, just not in a long time." Pain flashed in her eyes making him want to hunt down and beat whoever had caused her to look that way when she thought about sex. He doubled down on his determination to be gentle with her.

"Not with Ed, then?" He loathed the thought.

"No. We were waiting. Preacher and all."

"You're so damn tight," he coaxed her G-spot with his index finger, "try to relax for me. I don't want to hurt you."

"The only way you'll hurt me is if you stop. That feels so good." Her eyes drifted closed again, and she bore down on his hand. Her sweet little pussy nursed at his fingers. My god, she was going to feel incredible on his cock.

"I know it feels good, baby. I'm about to make it feel even better."

Keeping his strokes deep and even, he sank his mouth to her pussy lips and coaxed her clit with his tongue.

A choked groan sobbed from her as she locked her thighs against his head. Her pussy fucking wept for more. And he indulged her with gentle flickers of his tongue until her clit peaked enough for him to draw it in his mouth and suck.

"Oh god. Oh fuck that's...good," she gasped. It took all of his lacking concentration to keep from laughing. He'd never heard her so much as use the word damn before that moment, and she'd gone right for the ten-dollar word. Maybe that halo of hers could be set aside for a little while, if he did everything right. "I'm..." she whimpered and writhed. Her body seized.

He locked her hips down with his available hand, keeping her right where he needed her. "Let it come, angel," he urged. "Let that sweet honey drip down my throat. You taste so fucking good." She tasted like his.

But she fought the release like she somehow couldn't allow herself the pleasure. Now, she was keeping herself from him both physically and sexually. He couldn't stand that.

Determination throbbed through his muscles. He craved her climax more than his next breath. "I want it, Charlie. I want to own it. Give it to me," he commanded and then set to work.

CHAPTER THIRTEEN

She tried. She tried so hard to do as he ordered. Wanting nothing more than to please him, her mind scrambled. A tidal wave of fear tore her in two. She couldn't relinquish control, not even to Jamie. Orgasms made her unable to breathe.

But holy mother, that felt so good. It was all-encompassing, absorbing her entirely. She longed to be able to throw herself completely into it.

"That's it," he continued to coax. Her tenacious grip on her own sanity slipped another degree in the sexy smoke of his voice. "Let yourself have it, baby. Let it feel good for me."

He didn't sound frustrated, but surely he was. Both of the other guys she'd slept with, all of once, had gotten extremely frustrated with her. She tried not to think of that, and only to focus on how insanely good Jamie's masterful hands felt on her body.

Her body.

Oh god. Panic walloped through her midsection forcing the amazing sensations aside to make room for more doubt. A whimper sprang free from her lips, but she wasn't certain which side of her mind had created it—the side that swore she'd never recover from the awe-inspiring work of Jamie's hands and his tongue—good lord, that wicked tongue—or the side that was frantically trying to make certain her shirt stayed down and didn't reveal the scars.

She wanted to let Jamie know how much she was enjoying being with him like this. And oh Great Jehoshaphat, what had they done? This was her and Jamie.

The panic and the awe went to war. They held a draft, each claiming soldiers for their sides. She couldn't think through the drowning doubts that cinched tightly around her throat. They became a blockade to the pleasure that threatened to pull her under. Some part of Charlie was thankful for them. For the control they allowed her to regain. Control was how she remained safe. It helped her to remember the thing she wanted most—for Jamie to enjoy this.

But the other side, the one that aligned her pulse with the deep, forbidden strokes of his fingers, the one that rushed her own essence to his feasting tongue, wanted more. Her inner vixen, one she hadn't known she possessed until she'd laid down beside Jamie naked, wanted his dominance, his force, his fervor. She wanted to be the object of his obsessions.

Perhaps that was the neutral ground where the peace accord could be drawn. She wanted to be with him. She'd never been able to climax with a guy before, so she'd do what she always did. She'd fake it.

"Tell me what you need, baby," Jamie urged. She knew he'd likely do anything she asked.

If she was going to have to fake it, then she wanted the full experience. The tug of emptiness she existed with daily longed to be full of him. She wanted to ache with his occupation, though she was certain she shouldn't want things like that. At that moment, she didn't care. She'd go back to being the preacher's daughter, and hell, a different preacher's almost-wife later. The seclusion of Camden Ranch bolstered her.

"That feels so good," she assured him, "but I want all of you. Please."

When he lifted his head from between her thighs, his lips were slick with her cream. That did nothing to give her courage. Embarrassment stalled the rush of blood in her veins.

"Are you sure, angel? I was loving the sounds you were making when I was between those fuck-me thighs, but then you stopped. I want to make this good for you. Just tell me what you need."

"I'm sure." She tried to grip his substantial shoulders so she could pull him back on top of her. His weight on her was the only thing that made any sense at all.

He complied, crawling up her body like a lithe predator intent on his prey. She moaned instinctively. Her heart sped, and her breath tangled in her lungs. "Just breathe for me, baby. I'm gonna take good care of you."

Jamie always knew the right things to say to her. She drew a deep breath soaked with his raw masculine scent and forced herself to ignore the hint of smoke that clung to him. Her body bucked against his and she relished the thick heat that brushed against her overly sensitized pussy. Shuddering with each pass, she continued to tempt herself with the tantalizing promise of his erection.

And again, he indulged her. Gripping his cock, he pressed it against her folds, so slick with need she was still embarrassed, and he slid it back and forth. Every thickened vein and ridge of him made her tremble. Nothing had ever felt so good.

She almost forgot to worry about the shirt and about needing to breathe and about every reason she was going to struggle with this. Almost.

———

"That tight little pussy is needing to be fucked, isn't it?" Jamie growled. He was too far gone to guard his words. Besides, the filthier he talked, the more ravenous she seemed to get. He never would've guessed Charlie would like dirty talk, but he should've. She was the most perfect woman alive.

"Yes," she was clawing his back now, completely unaware. Sexiest damn thing he'd ever felt, but he knew as soon as he sank himself balls deep inside of her nothing else would ever compare. "Please," she whimpered out again.

Girl was driving him wild. His precum leaked all over those tender auburn curls that reminded him to be gentle with her despite every ragged desire tearing through him that longed to make her ache with force.

There hadn't been a woman yet that he couldn't get off with his tongue. It was a skill he'd honed. He knew when to suck and when to tease, when to let her feel the scratch of his beard and when to ease off and press her until she was clinging to the edge. But if that wasn't what Charlie wanted, he was fine with it. Hell, it didn't matter what she needed for him to own her pleasure, he'd do it. He was nothing if not adaptable.

She jolted and moaned out his name with his next pass of his cock against her. He swore he could get off just listening to her say his name like that. Fuck. He had to get it together, or he was going to become the only Holder to ever wear the two-pump-chump crown.

"Condom." He bought himself a moment to think as he leaned up off of her, trying to get his head straight.

But she linked her arms around his back preventing his movement. Girl was strong. She had to be in the field she'd chosen. Taking on the weight of full-grown men when they needed her help was a part of her job. "Pill," she pled. "I'm on the pill. Just please." She closed those gorgeous eyes. Her head shook back and forth against the pillow.

"Please what, angel. Say it. Tell me you want my cum soaking down those tight walls, dripping down your thighs when I finish. Tell me you need me to defile that pussy, so sweet and innocent."

"Yes. God...yes. Please." Her entire body was strung so tight, Jamie swore under his breath. With no more provocation than that, he sank himself a few inches into her warm, wet heaven. She was too tight for him to even move. The welcoming heat of her body licked at his cock. He wasn't going to survive.

"Jesus Christ, you feel incredible, honey. So damn good," he grunted, "too fucking good." He was in some kind of divine agony. He knew in that moment he'd never be able to go back to just being her friend. He'd always want this. He'd always want more.

"Jamie," she gasped. "I need..." her eyes flashed open begging him of their own accord.

"Tell me, sugar. Say it, whatever it is." Concentrating on what it was she was needing gave him a moment to gather his staying power, what little of it there was left anyway.

She spread her legs further and coaxed him deeper inside. "Move," she urged.

He allowed himself another inch, maybe two. Her tender little pussy nursed at him now, tempting him. So fucking perfect. He met her on her next urgent buck, slamming inside of her. He hadn't meant to use that much force, but he longed to tear away every ridiculous reason why this couldn't be their forever.

He knew she was a gift from the Good Lord. He'd always known that. But burying himself so deep in the atonement of his best friend was somehow more than holy. Like he was heaving every mistake he'd ever made onto some kind of sacred fount set for him alone, so she could wash him clean.

Her body quaked with her need. She stared up at him. A thousand questions glimmered in her eyes like the stars in the endless Oklahoma sky. He vowed to himself to find the answer to every single one.

There was nothing between them. It made this all the more holy. "Charlie, baby, this is incredible," he tried to explain but there weren't words. Words hadn't yet been invented for the way he felt.

"I know," she choked. "Please don't stop."

"Never fucking going to stop. Never," he vowed as he sank himself in deeper with each pass. His cock was so sensitive he felt her clit swell against him. Holding himself up on one forearm he reached between them to stroke that swollen little nub so anxious for his attention.

A choked scream from Charlie rattled in his ears. His roar of ownership met it in the darkness. She tightened like a bolt of ecstasy as he rutted on her like a wild beast. With every deep, hungry thrust, the bolt tightened until the agony in his balls was unbearable.

"Come for me, angel," he begged. "Fuck." He shook with the desperate need to unload inside of her. Not yet. Leaving women unsatisfied was not something he did. Ever. He refused to count his teenage years, or to even acknowledge them.

But his release surged through his veins hot and insistent. "Let it go for me," he urged again. "Give it to me." Nothing was working. She writhed and the word yes hung on her lips, but she also fought her own release. He wasn't certain she was even aware she was doing it. Her pussy spasmed around him.

And it was too late. He couldn't stop it. Hot cum shot through him as he gripped her hips, slammed her against him so deep neither of them knew where he stopped and she began, and he filled her full.

He rode her through every spurt as he unloaded, praying that maybe the motion would send her over. It didn't work. Fuck.

He collapsed back beside her and set to right his wrong. But when he reached for her, she stopped him. "That was amazing," she insisted.

"For me, yeah. But not for you. I'm so fucking sorry."

"Why are you sorry?"

That seemed painfully obvious to Jamie, but apparently she was going to make him say it out loud. He squeezed his eyes shut and flipped through several curse words in his head. "You didn't come," he forced out between his teeth. "Here, let me..." he tried to reach between her legs again but she stopped him.

"I know, but it was still amazing. I can't ever do that with someone else. You were everything. It was so good I forgot to fake it. Thank you. But please promise this won't change us. I can never lose you."

The terror that galloped through her voice brought him up short. "Back up just a minute. What do you mean you can't ever do that?"

Now, she was the one looking at him like he'd lost his mind. "I meant exactly what I said."

"You've never had an orgasm?"

She shook her head. "I have them...you know...when I'm alone, just not when I'm with another person. It's totally normal."

He weighed and tasted each word before he freed them from his lips. "It may be but that ain't how it's going to be between us. Tell me what's different about when you're alone. What do you think about then?"

She turned the approximate shade of her hair. "No," she defied. "And you can't fix this. It's fine. Seriously, being with you like that...it was everything. I'm sorry you didn't like it." Now, she was refusing to even look at him.

He gripped her chin and forced her gaze back to his own. "Hear me, Charlie. I loved that. I loved every moment of it right up until I realized you hadn't gotten off. That ain't how it's supposed to work. I want to figure this out. I want to fix it. Sorry if that's not what you want to hear, but..." he trailed off, not certain what else to say.

She brushed a kiss on his shoulder and then his neck. "If you're determined to fix it, can we argue about it in the morning? I already know it can't be fixed, but we're both exhausted."

"How do you know? Did a doctor tell you that?" Jamie refused to let this go, if for no other reason than his certainty that he'd just blown the one chance he had to prove to her that they were meant to be.

She brushed the hard angles of this cheeks and chin, trying to soften his scowl he assumed. "No, a doctor didn't tell me that. But it's my body, so I should know. I'm sorry you're upset. It's not your fault at all. I'm not fixable."

"Stop apologizing to me. I'm the one that's supposed to be apologizing to you," he huffed.

"But you didn't do anything wrong. It was amazing, like I said. I wish I could explain what that meant to me. I'm so afraid that it's going to change us, though."

She laid her head on his chest and nuzzled her face against him. He wrapped his arms around her and tried to sort through the barrage of emotions now swamping his mind. It was going to change them. He wasn't going to let her excuses or their families come between them anymore. He'd failed her in the past, and he was going to fix it.

CHAPTER FOURTEEN

In the early morning hours, long before the sun ever made an appearance, Jamie's phone buzzed on the bedside table. He'd spent most of the night in debate over what to do next to convince Charlie that he was the man she'd needed all along. Even if he wasn't that man right now, he would become anything she wanted. She just had to give him a chance.

Keeping her cradled gently in his arms, he cleared his throat, answered the phone, and whispered a half greeting to Colt.

"Sorry to wake you," Colt sounded like he wasn't any happier to be awake two hours before sunrise than Jamie felt. "There's a small ranch about five miles west of ours. They were shipping early this morning. Trucks had just made it back to the main road when a couple of our bulls got through the fence. They ran out in front of the first truck. He slammed on the brakes and ended up jack-knifed. Truck behind that one hit the first. It's a mess, and Mr. Clayton says he smells fuel. We could use some help. None of us know what to do. Those trucks are gonna go up in flames, and that's all of their cattle for spring shipping. We've got to get the cattle off of those trucks."

Jamie eased himself away from Charlie without waking her. He made it to the living room before he spoke. "I'm on my way, but as long as the engine block doesn't spark, the fuel isn't going to ignite. We'll get it taken care of. Any of the cattle hurt or just spooked?"

"I don't know yet, and it's gonna be a bitch getting them off of there because they're likely to run as soon as they're free. I've got some fire extinguishers just in case."

"Good. Bring those, but unless you've got an FSI extinguisher that ain't gonna do you a bit of good on a fuel burn."

"What is that?"

"A foamer. Grab as many sandbags as you can get your hands on to go with those extinguishers. I'm betting moving the herds is gonna be more of a bitch than the fuel, though."

"I'll get the sandbags we've got in the barn for flooding and pick you up in just a few."

"I'll be outside."

Jamie snuck back into the bedroom. The sight of Charlie peacefully sleeping with her long auburn hair painted out across his pillow took his breath away. The sheets had shifted when he'd gotten up, and as his eyes traveled over her lush lips slightly opened and her delicate neck, he couldn't help but stare. She was so beautiful it almost hurt. Hurt that he'd failed her. Hurt that she didn't think she was worth trying to work through whatever held her back from fully being with him. Hurt that he doubted his own ability to convince her that they could have a future together.

His hands tingled to touch the soft skin of her face, but he didn't want to wake her. He also didn't want to leave her, but he'd told the Camdens if they needed anything he was their man, and he never went back on his word. Grabbing a new pair of Wranglers and one of the T-shirts he'd gotten the day before, he turned to dress in the living room. Something caught his eye as he edged away from the bed. The T-shirt she'd slept in had ridden up just a little creating a gap of fabric. The sheets covered her lower half, but a band of moonlight from the blinds illuminated her side, a part of her she hadn't allowed him to see the night before.

The skin was puckered and disfigured at the bottom of her ribcage. It curved in oddly from obvious muscle damage. The scarring climbed underneath the cover of the shirt. He had no idea where it ended. His heart fractured. Did she really think that he would judge her because she'd obviously been burned? My god, he was a firefighter. But the pain she had to have lived through swelled in his throat until he could barely breathe. She'd never told him.

A few pieces of the puzzle he'd been obsessing over most of the night locked into place. Maybe if he could convince her that there was no amount of scarring on her body that would change how he felt about her, he could prove to her that the orgasm issue could be fixed. He needed her to trust him with everything. Just like always, Jamie's head leapt ten steps ahead of what was going on. It was part of what made him a good firefighter. He could assess every potential outcome and create solutions to problems that might occur. And if he could prove himself to her, prove that they could work through this together, well then that was a big step toward getting her to give them a chance. Potential pulsed through his veins. He just had to figure out exactly how to go about this. And that left him drawing a blank.

He dug through the kitchen drawers until he found a stack of notepads under some candles and a lighter. He debated exactly what to tell her. He made a quick note that there had been a cattle truck accident and that Colt needed his help. He promised to be back as quickly as he could but told her that moving the cows could take all morning. He didn't want her to worry, so he made absolutely no mention of the potential fire. "When I get back, we need to talk," was his parting line. Calling himself a pussy for good measure, he scrawled a lopsided heart at the bottom and scribbled his initials, not that she'd doubt who'd written the note. It was more out of habit than anything else.

He heard the chug of Colt's truck motor outside and slipped out of the house. He grabbed his equipment bag from his own truck before climbing in his cousins.

"I'm sorry about this," was Colt's greeting.

"Day in the life," Jamie assured him.

"Yeah, I know, but you're supposed to be getting down and dirty with Charlie finally, and I got you out of bed. If you tell any of your brothers I didn't leave you be, they'll skin me. Aunt Sara, too, for that matter. I feel bad it was our bulls that caused this is all."

Jamie grunted instead of commenting, since he didn't have anything to say to that.

"Avery made coffee," Colt gestured to a travel mug in the cupholder nearest Jamie.

He helped himself. "Tell her I'm much obliged. You got yourself a good one."

Colt grinned at that as he pressed the accelerator harder. "I do, but you do too. Just gotta convince her of that, right?"

"Something like that. Not gonna be easy."

"You think? Seemed to me that you never struggled to talk women into your bed."

Hiding his eye roll, Jamie shrugged. "Don't just want her in my bed. There's a lot more to this than that."

"Oh yeah? Like what?"

"How many head were on those trucks?" Changing topics really was the only way out. The uncertainty and the determination were coiled much too close to the surface, and he refused to discuss what had happened last night with anyone. Partly because that seemed like it would be disrespectful to Charlie, but also because he didn't really want to admit to anyone that he'd failed.

"I got no idea and I need to stop thinking about it, so indulge me. I might could help."

"How you figure?"

"I talked Avery into giving me a shot. Two babies and a bunch of years later it seems like I might know a thing or two about women that could help. Plus, I owe you."

"How you figure that?" Jamie genuinely wanted an answer to that question. Colt didn't owe him anything. He'd always been a Holder through and through. He'd never let them down as far as Jamie was concerned.

"You bailed me outta jail twice for fighting, talked the cops out of arresting me a third time, and that's just the beginning," Colt reminded him.

"Yeah, but it was Avery who got you sorted, not me. Besides, you gave me a place to bring Charlie, so we're even."

"We're not even by a mile. Come on. What's your game plan for this? I know you have one."

The truck bounced over the flat lands surrounding them as Colt veered off the gravel road and took to the grass, trying to save time, Jamie assumed.

If there was one thing he knew about his cousin, it was that once the boy had hold of something he never let go. Maybe it was that knowledge or the fact that he still didn't really have a plan that made him consider talking. That coupled with the exhaustion made him uneasy, so he decided to test the waters with Colt. Maybe he really could help.

"Things didn't go that great last night. I may've fucked everything up."

"What'd you do? It can't be that bad. She looks at you like you hung the fucking moon for her."

"Never say that to her, okay? She's not like other girls. She hates the moon."

That brought Colt up short, and Jamie was thankful for the reprieve in talking. But the silence didn't last long. "That still don't tell me what you did. I can't get you out of what I don't know you're in."

Jamie shifted uncomfortably and pretended to stare out the window. The smell of diesel permeated the air blowing through the AC in the truck. That wasn't good.

Colt huffed, "Fine, you don't want my help, I won't help. I could give Uncle Barrett a call and tell him you're struggling. Maybe Uncle Gentry, God knows the man's got advice for every situation."

Thoughts of either his father or one of his uncles knowing that he was struggling drew the confession from Jamie's lungs. "I left her wanting last night."

Colt nodded and sported a half smirk. "Give yourself a break, man. You've been dreaming about getting with her for decades. You just got a little ahead of yourself. She'll let you make it up to her I'm sure. That ain't so much a problem as an apology."

"Yeah, I did that already. There's more to it than that." He clamped his mouth shut, not certain what Charlie would think of him saying much more.

"Hey, I know how you feel. Avery struggled a lot after our first was born. I felt like a failure. She was frustrated and scared. It was bad for a few weeks. I had to—"

Jumping on that before Colt even finished his sentence, Jamie was suddenly grateful his cousin had been outright nosy. "What'd you do? How'd you fix it?"

"I was getting to that," he chuckled. "I talked to Dec."

"Who the hell is Dec?"

"Holly's husband."

Jamie rolled his eyes again, this time letting his cousin see. "Which makes my next question fairly obvious."

"Holly is one of the Camden kids. The youngest as a matter of fact. Her husband used to be a sex therapist. Now, she is as well. They do that and handle addiction counseling and any other kind of thing that comes up around here. Guy's a genius. Not a great cowboy, but he's decent. Never tell him I said that. We can't be all things to all people. But if you ask me, he's better behind a desk than on a horse."

"What'd he tell you to do?"

"It was kinda specific to Avery, and I'm not going into that. But you can talk to him."

"I don't know how Charlie would feel about me doing that. I don't want to piss her off."

Another smirk formed on Colt's features. "Seems to me you doing a little talking might make her feel real, real good, wouldn't it?"

He had to give his cousin that, but this situation felt like it was spinning rapidly out of his control.

They pulled up on a gruesome scene. Jamie expected and then accepted the sucker punch that always came when he assessed a scene. Two good bulls lay on the ground that he already knew were likely going to have to be put out of their misery. One of the Camden brothers was down on his knees making an effort to save them it seemed.

The trucks were a mangled disaster of metal, and fuel drenched the road and ran off to the prairie land nearby. It was going to be a long ass day.

He flung himself out of the truck and into action. All of the

Camden brothers looked to him for direction, and he was going to get the job done. "Get sand on the fuel as fast as you can. Once it soaks it up we can shovel it away. One of you keep an extinguisher ready for that engine. If it hisses, hit it. Two of you get back in your trucks, go a mile down the road each way, and block traffic until the state police get here. I've got bolt cutters. Let me get the doors off, but as soon as they're open we're likely to get run down by cattle. So the rest of you get ready to rope and ride. Decide where there's a field big enough to drive 'em to and keep 'em there."

A man stepped up. Jamie recognized the burns on his neck that came from seatbelts. He had to be one of the drivers. "I called and they're sending out more trucks but they won't be here 'fore nightfall." Guy had a cigarette hanging out of his mouth but had been smoking long enough that when he spoke with it perched between his lips he was still able to be understood.

Colt leapt. "You maybe wanna get rid of that? We're not looking to set the whole damn town on fire."

Jamie shook his head. "You could put a butt out in diesel and it still won't ignite. Too wet. Just keep it the hell away from that engine."

There was a guy in a Styx T-shirt and black jeans. The tattoos covering one arm set him apart from the crowd of cattle ranchers. Jamie wondered if that was Dec.

CHAPTER FIFTEEN

A grin spread the width of Charlie's cheeks when she awoke. Leaving her eyes closed, she relished the rubbed sensation between her legs. If she just never opened her eyes or never got out of bed, maybe she could go on existing in that moment of bliss. She wouldn't have to deal with whatever was going to come of their escapades the night before.

It took her mind a few minutes to remember the conversation after the sex. Ugh. Jamie would never let the orgasm thing go. She knew. She'd just have to assure him that it wasn't a big deal, that being close to him, seeing him enjoy her was more than enough. No one had ever made her feel the way she felt last night. And that's exactly what she would open with this morning.

Sliding her hands across the cool sheets, she continued to keep her eyes closed. She wanted to indulge her senses in him. But when she found his side of the bed empty, her eyes flashed open and disappointment tamped down a little of her outstanding mood.

It was still pretty early. Where was he? Easing from the bed, she noted the twinge between her legs as she whisked to the bathroom. Yep, definitely needed to make certain that he knew she'd enjoyed every single thing he'd given her last night. As long as nothing had changed between them, this was all going to be fine.

She ignored the twist in her stomach that seemed to argue otherwise.

After she'd slipped into a new pair of jeans, she went through the process of breaking them in. Several deep knee bends and a few butt wiggles and then she finally got them buttoned.

Heading into the living room to locate coffee and, more importantly, Jamie, she came up empty on both. On her way to the coffee maker, she located a note he'd left behind. Her face fell. What if the driver was hurt? And surely the cows would be. He should've woken her up so she could help. She didn't know much about the muscle and skeletal structures or injury recovery for cattle, but she'd figure it out. Adapting for patients was a part of her job.

She had no idea how to find Jamie so she texted him. "If you need some help, let me know." Certain he was busy, she switched her sound on and started finding everything she'd need for coffee. If she could figure out where he was exactly, she could take Jamie some and something to eat. He was probably starving.

To pass the time, she Googled muscular and skeletal information on bovine. A knock on the door had her rushing to see who it was. Maybe they did need help and had sent one of the Camdens to fetch her.

When she opened the doors, she found Jessie Camden and another woman she'd never met.

"This is my daughter-in-law, Katy. We thought we'd come see if we could keep you company while Jamie's helping out down at the wreck," Jessie explained.

"Oh, thank you. That's so kind, but I might be able to help if you can tell me how to get to wherever he is. I was just studying the myology of cows and it's not much different than humans really. If any of them got hurt, I might could work with them if they'll let me. I think I've come up with a way we could splint their legs if any of them are broken that would keep them standing but not continuing to damage the bone."

Both of the women beamed at her. Charlie noted that Katy's belly was adorably round with a baby. A twinge of jealousy tugged at the corners of her mouth.

Jessie shook her head. "Ev says they've got it down to a system now following Jamie's instructions. Luke's a vet and I think he's dealing with the injured ones, but he says we're gonna lose one of the bulls. I don't think anything can be done to help. Would you mind if we came in?"

"Of course not." Charlie felt odd welcoming the women into a home that was technically theirs, but she was certain Katy probably wanted to sit down.

"I brought you a loaf of banana bread and a casserole," Katy commented as she set the food on the counter.

"Thank you so much. You don't have to do that."

Katy gave her another kind grin. "I don't mind. I love to cook, and," she blushed as a sheepish look glimmered in her eyes.

"And what?"

"Well, I've never met anyone else who ran out on their wedding, so I feel like we might be kindred spirits or something." She wrinkled her nose. "Please don't think I'm weird. Grant said you were gonna think I was crazy."

Charlie chuckled at that. "I don't think you're weird or crazy, and I read Anne of Green Gables like a dozen times when I was in the burn unit. I always wished I had a kindred spirit." She cringed. She never talked about those long months and didn't understand how it had come out all of a sudden. "I, uh, used to think I was more Diana than Anne, though. I don't think I have quite that much spunk. Um... I take it you left your wedding too? I'm assuming the one before Grant." She gestured to Katy's belly and prayed that they wouldn't ask questions about the burn unit. "Can I make you both some coffee?"

Katy had a kind laugh. She settled in one of the living room chairs. Charlie was thankful to have something to focus on besides the fireplace. "It was the one before Grant, and I'd love some, but I've already had my allotment for the day."

Jessie located a mug in one of the kitchen cabinets. "I'll drink Katy's for her." She winked at Charlie.

"I'll help," Charlie beamed. "What made you run?" She was being nosy but she couldn't help herself.

"I found out he was cheating on me with one of my closest friends about five minutes before I walked down the aisle."

Charlie's mouth gaped open. "That's terrible. You had every right to run."

Katy wrinkled her nose. "I also keyed his car on my way out so that might not have been my finest moment, but it all got me here so I'm not complaining."

Charlie liked Katy. Definitely kindred spirit material. "Yeah, well, I got tangled in my dress climbing down the church, so it wasn't my finest hour either."

Jessie shook her head at both of them. "You're both on my ranch now and that's right where you're supposed to be. You didn't run into Jamie's truck with your getaway car, too, now did you?"

Charlie cringed at Katy. Poor girl really had been having a rough day. "No. Jamie's been my best friend since we were kids. He's always been the one to run away with me whenever I wanted to. He's the best."

Katy and her mother-in-law shared a conspiratorial glance. Katy managed to scoot a little closer to Charlie. "If he's the best, then why weren't you marrying him?"

Shocked at that question, Charlie shook her head. "I could never...I mean...he wouldn't want to...I'm not the kind of girl he likes...plus he's a firefighter and I...well, I mean I couldn't...I would be too..." she sealed her lips shut and clenched her teeth tight around them to keep any more words from escaping.

Jessie raised one eyebrow. "Honey, I saw the way he was looking at you last night. You aren't the kind of girl he likes, you are *the* girl he likes."

"No. I'm really not. It's just that we've been friends for so long. We love each other in a friendly kind of way. Nothing more." Except the night before had been a whole lot more. She wasn't going to tell Jessie Camden that, however.

"There's definitely more," Jessie corrected her. "Now, go back to the firefighter part. There's enough meat in that statement that we could have ourselves a barbecue."

Jessie asked questions the way all moms asked them. The kind where you didn't really feel like you had the option not to answer. Charlie cleared her throat. "Uh, well, the parsonage where my family lived when I was little burned. My mom...." She glanced out the window praying that Jamie would make a sudden return. She wanted to run away from this particular line of questioning. "She didn't survive the fire." That statement performed like some kind of twist valve on a pressurized tank. Everything else spilled from her mouth like she was vomiting out the words. "So, you get how I could never be in love with a firefighter. It's too dangerous. I'd never sleep. I'd have panic attacks again. All the time. Even now every single time I know he's at work and I hear sirens I have to count to ten and take deep breaths. I just couldn't. I...couldn't." If she said it enough, surely it would stick.

Katy looked crestfallen. "I'm so sorry about your mom. That's terrible."

Charlie managed a robotic nod. It had been terrible and unacceptable and so unfair. Her mom had been such a good Christian woman and Jesus was supposed to protect them and.... She shut down that line of thought for the thousandth time since the night of the fire.

Jessie gave her an understanding nod. She reached and gave Charlie's arm a maternal pat. "Can I ask you something, sweetheart?"

"I guess." Charlie really wished she wouldn't, but manners had been bred into her since birth.

"Do you really believe that it would hurt less if something awful happened to Jamie and you hadn't told him how much you care about him and then seen if maybe the Good Lord's got a future in mind for the two of you together? Heartbreak and pain, they don't exist in measurable degrees, honey. You can't set a dial to make sure if worse comes to worst that you can handle the pain. That just ain't how life works."

Charlie made another nod. "I guess I never really thought of it like that."

"So, maybe think about it. When your time comes, regret the things you've done if you have to, but you don't want to regret the things you were afraid to try. It sounds to me like you think you're negotiating a small amount of pain every single day to avoid the potential of the ultimate pain later on. You're trading a whole lot of happiness for a bag of magic beans that aren't the pills that keep bad things from happening."

CHAPTER SIXTEEN

Jamie mopped the sweat from his brow with a handkerchief he borrowed from Aaron Weber. He'd met Aaron once when he was down on Holder Ranch with Jamie's cousin, Maddox. They'd worked together in the army. Quiet guy but he got shit done, that was for sure.

The heavy-duty wreckers had finally shown up and were trying to figure out how to get the trucks off of the road. Most of the cows were scared but were able to walk without a problem. Two of them, inside the truck, had been fatally wounded. Jamie hated it for the owner and hated the loss of a good bull for the Camdens.

Just like every time he left the scene of an accident or a fire, another round of adrenaline surged through him. Life was precious. He wanted to live it while he had the chance, and dammit, he wanted to do that with Charlie.

That brought him back to the issues at hand. It was getting late in the day. Luke and Austin's wives had brought food up to them twice now. He needed to get back to the guest cottage and try to get Charlie to talk to him, not that he had any good ideas on what to say.

"Hey Dec," Colt called from beside Jamie. "Could you do me a favor and give Jamie a ride back to the cottage? Maybe go the long way," he urged. "I gotta get back and help Avery with the kids. They've probably staged a mutiny by now."

Jamie shot his cousin a glance that let him know he didn't appreciate being forced into this.

The doc gave Colt a weary smile. He was just as exhausted as the rest of them, and Jamie doubted he was in the mood to work on his other profession. "Certainly." He gestured to his SUV.

Feeling every eye surrounding them burn into his skin, Jamie stumbled forward when Colt shoved him. Fucker. "Thanks, asswipe," he muttered under his breath.

"Anytime." Colt laughed.

He was too tired to argue much, so he took the passenger seat in the Suburban. Dec climbed in the driver's seat and offered Jamie a kind smile. "You're not the first, nor will you be the last, unsuspecting guy that one of the Camdens has shoved onto my couch so to speak. I might be able to help, and if I follow my instructions to take you the long way we've got a while to talk."

"I appreciate Colt trying to help and your offer, Doc, but I kinda prefer to figure shit out on my own. No offense."

"None taken. The way Colt explained it to us at supper last night, you've been in love with the woman you're currently sharing our cottage with for twenty years, but she was planning to marry someone else yesterday. So, figuring things out on your own must be working for you." His British accent didn't soften the blow at all. Jamie ground his teeth but still refused to take the bait.

Dec continued talking. "Not knowing much about either you or...Charlotte, was it?"

"Charlie," Jamie corrected but then immediately wondered if Dec had just been trying to get him to speak and he'd just lost that battle of wills.

"Charlie," Dec corrected. "I will say that, for the most part, it matters a great deal more who you're running to and much less who you're running from if that helps at all."

"It's more complicated than that."

"I assumed it was. Advice one could find on Facebook isn't typically why people come into my office."

Rolling his eyes, Jamie conceded a little. "What's going on is between me and Charlie. I don't kiss and tell, even with a sex doctor. Not without her okaying it. I'd never go behind her back on something like this."

Dec's entire expression morphed to one of genuine understanding. "I respect that a great deal, and I apologize if I pushed too hard. To be perfectly honest with you, Colt mentioned the issue to me on one of our trips out to guide the cattle to the field."

"Yeah, well, my cousin needs to keep his jaw shut."

"I might have an idea of how I could help without doing anything that would be disrespectful to Charlie or what she's going through. Female orgasm is something I'm highly skilled at."

"Bet you put that on your business card," Jamie huffed.

Dec chuckled. "I didn't quite mean that the way it sounded. I only meant that I've treated a number of patients who struggle to climax. My wife wrote her thesis on society's implications on female pleasure. I helped her do a fair amount of research on the subject to go along with my multiple degrees."

"What was your idea about how to help without helping?"

"On top of the counseling clinic I run here in town, I am also the head of the online psychology department at UN. Several times a month, I go to Lincoln to give lectures. One of the things I often teach in the Sexual Psychology classes is about female orgasm. What if I simply gave you the lesson I'd give at university. You can take from it what you need. If it helps, brilliant. If it doesn't, maybe you could talk Charlie into coming to see me with you, and together we can work on the root cause of the distress."

Jamie considered that from every possible angle. He couldn't find a flaw, and truthfully he could use some guidance. He cleared his throat, "Uh, so in this class that you teach, do you cover how to help if she can come on her own but not with another person?"

Dec did not acknowledge that Jamie had given anything away. "As that is quite common, it is one of the first things we cover."

"Okay, then let's hear this lecture."

"Glad I can help." Dec launched into the lecture, and Jamie wondered if he should be taking notes. He tried to really focus. He'd always sucked at school, but he sensed this was a critical key to him and Charlie. "Female sexuality is vastly different from that of males. Her views on sex tend to be made up of three major components—what her religion has taught her about sex and her body, what her parents have to say about it, and then what society has imprinted on her as what is and is not acceptable and what is and is not sexy."

"Damn," Jamie sighed. That was a whole lot of fucked up is what it was. "Her Daddy's a preacher. He wouldn't even let her date until she was out of college. That's why I never asked her out in high school. I swear he's wound tighter than a nun's nasty."

"Perhaps don't refer to her genitalia as such," Dec urged.

"I'm not a dumbass, Doc."

"Understood. But if her father is a religious leader, then her parents' views and her religious views are likely intertwined, and they were probably reinforced early and often. That can be a lot to overcome."

"No shit. He was always on her about representing the church wherever she went. I know he's in her head still. She ended up engaged to that shitlicker because of her old man. She still feels like she has to keep him happy."

Dec nodded and slowed the Suburban to a crawl as they drove through a herd of cattle standing along the dirt-packed path. "Holly says just to keep the car moving slowly to get them to move out of the way. I'm always afraid I'm going to hit one."

"Holly's right," Jamie assured him. "They'll get out of the way if you stay in motion, but if you stop completely, they'll set up housekeeping here, change their mailing address, the whole deal."

Dec chuckled at that. "See, we all need advice on occasion."

It sounded to Jamie like Dec's wife could teach him anything he needed to know about ranching, but he appreciated the effort to keep him from feeling like an idiot. "Keep going on the women's sexuality thing. Her daddy hates me, so I'm betting that plays into this." That wouldn't necessarily explain why Charlie had never had an orgasm with anyone else, though.

"It might, but it's far more likely that it doesn't matter who her partner is, allowing herself to climax in their presence isn't something she feels she's allowed."

"So, how do I change her opinion on that?"

"I'm getting there. Remember there are three parts and you're going to need to approach it from all three sides. I'm going to also remind you that her orgasm is not for your ego, and you'll make better decisions if you try to step away from the idea that the only way she enjoys being with you is if she climaxes."

Okay, the ego comment stung a little, but Jamie brushed it off. "She said something like that last night. It's not the destination it's the trip kind of thing, right?"

"Precisely. Intimacy is not actually about sexual encounters, particularly for women. The double-edged sword of this issue is that the majority of women need to feel intimacy in order to fully embrace a satisfying physical relationship."

Jamie hated feeling like he was completely inept, but he had to admit that he kind of was. Swallowing down that momentary irritation, he let Dec's last statement roll through his mind. "Sounds like you're saying I need to get her to trust me outside of my bed before I try to get her to come in it. But she does trust me. We've been best friends forever. I've never let her down. I *would* never let her down. She knows that."

"Perhaps, she trusts you with her present. The key to intimacy is getting someone to trust you with their past and their future. The present is by far the easiest part of the puzzle."

Defeat sank through Jamie. It physically pressed him deeper into the seat. He was already in for a penny, and Charlie was likely already going to be furious with him for talking to Dec, but he'd never wanted anything as much as he'd wanted her as his wife. He'd find a way to apologize for this, but he needed some answers. "From what I could tell, she's got some scars on her side." He gestured to his own ribcage. "They have to be from the fire she was in when she was a kid, but she's never told me about them. I thought she told me everything."

Dec's eyes lit and concerned revelation seemed to tense in his brow. "What do you mean from what you could tell? Have you not seen her fully naked?"

"She wouldn't let me take her shirt off last night," Jamie choked on the admission. The doc was quiet for several beats too long, as if he didn't want to state the thing that was now sitting between them in the truck. "Which means she doesn't really trust me, right?" The inevitable conclusion was worse than a fist to the throat.

Dec offered him an apologetic look. "You can build that trust, but it isn't going to be easy. Communication is going to be key. She's going to need to help you build a bridge so that you can both cross it. Don't press too hard, but the key to her issues might be hidden under her shirt. The thing about scars is that, ultimately, they're the cover to the book. The events that led to the scar are vastly more important than the marking left behind. Slowly and cautiously, never pushing her faster than she's willing to go, you're going to have to be willing to go back in her mind to things she's frightened of. Show her that you're willing to meet her wherever she is and that you'll lead her out of that fear."

"I can do that." Jamie immediately began trying to come up with ways to get Charlie to tell him about the fire. She'd started to the night before, but it had all gotten tangled up in the sheets when he was taking her.

"I have no doubt, but there's another issue with scars. It gets back to the third part of female sexuality. Women are constantly told that if they don't look like cover models that they are not sexy. That point is hammered home dozens of times every single day. You're going to have to prove to her that no matter what those scars look like, you still find her sexually attractive."

"That won't be a problem. She's the most beautiful woman I've ever seen, and I've thought that since the first time I saw her."

"Have you ever told her that?"

"No." Jamie instantly regretted that. "That wasn't us, you know? We were best friends, and she wasn't ever allowed to date when we were younger. Plus," he loathed what he was about to say but it was the truth, "she's not the kind of girl you mess around with. She's the real deal. I thought it was my right to sow my wild oats, so to speak. Plus, she didn't want me. I guess it kinda got comfortable when we were older, and I didn't want to rock the boat. She's terrified of my job. It just seemed like there was too much against us to chance fucking up the friendship."

Dec finally got through the herd, but he wasn't driving the car that much faster. "What changed?"

Considering that from every angle, Jamie once again told the truth. "Ever since she got engaged to Ed, she hasn't been coming around as much. She was busy and Ed doesn't like me any more than her daddy does, but it scared me, you know? I hated it. I missed her every fucking day. When I saw her hanging off the side of her daddy's church yesterday, it felt like it was now or never." Dec made no response, so Jamie kept talking. It felt good to get some of this off of his chest. "And see, I get it. Other people don't because they don't have to. But I'm the guy who cuts people out of cars on the worst day of their lives. I'm the guy who can make five minutes feel like an entire lifetime when I go in to get your family out of a burning house. I know how precious life is, and how quickly it can all be taken away. I can't do this anymore. I want to live while we're all here, and I want a life with her."

CHAPTER SEVENTEEN

Dec stopped the car in the middle of an open field and threw it in park. "Then let's really talk about how you're going to go get the life you and Charlie deserve. I understand that you don't want to betray her trust. If I feel like you might be crossing that line, I'll tell you to stop. But what's happening in this relationship is happening to both of you. Asking for help might be the bravest thing you could do at this point. It sounds like she carries a great deal of trauma from her past and it continues to scar her future. It might not be fair, but I personally believe that you're the man who can help her be able to look at her past and understand that it doesn't have to own her future."

For a split, spiteful second Jamie hated just how good the doc was, but when someone hands you a lifeline you take it. His ego had been running the show for way too long. Hell, his ego was part of how he survived, but he was tired of just surviving. He wanted to live.

"All right," he swallowed down every ounce of pride he had and urged, "how do I get her to trust me enough to allow herself to feel when she's with me."

"It's not unusual for people who've survive a traumatic childhood event like a fire to carry residual trauma with them well into adulthood. Tell me everything you know about the fire. I'd bet my license that the key to her control issues lie in that."

Talking fire was something Jamie could do with ease. As long as he didn't think too much about whose home had been involved, it became a work discussion. "It was a two-alarm when the call went out. Started in the chimney on the north end of the house away from the bedrooms. Two trucks arrived on scene. Fire wasn't yet venting so they followed protocol and sent in a four-man rescue team with an inch and three-quarter. The other truck went defensive from outside. Man named Clint found Charlie and her little sister, Becca, passed out in the hallway near their parents' bedroom. He got them out. While he was getting them masked in the ambulance, the roof caved, and they had to get the team out. Her father survived, but her mom didn't make it."

Dec studied Jamie while he processed that. "A few pieces of advice that aren't in any psychology textbook, these come from my own life— when you lose a parent, especially the parent you were closest to, which so often happens with daughters and their mothers, you don't ever want to gamble on that piece of your heart again. It's already broken and so thoroughly damaged you're not certain it could withstand any more pain. You being so closely professionally involved with the very thing that took her mother away from her became a legitimate excuse for her keeping you friend-zoned, so to speak. You're going to have to show Charlie that you're okay with her loving you in pieces as long as eventually you both are working toward her understanding that you want to love every piece of her until she's whole again. Try to keep in mind that what you're asking her to risk doesn't seem like much to you, but the cost to her is significant. You need to make her understand that you get that."

"I definitely get that," Jamie nodded. "So, where do I start? I'll never break her heart. But I'm telling you, Doc, somewhere deep inside of her she already knows that."

Dec gave him a broken smile. "When you speak about the fire that tore her life apart, you speak of the technical side of it. Even *you* struggle to attach any emotion to the event because you understand that it hurt her. You're going to have to allow yourself to feel the pain through her and for her so that she doesn't have to face it all alone. She's not necessarily afraid that you'll break her heart. If she lets you help her put herself back together, she's afraid the world will take away the glue she needs the same way it took away her mother."

"I'm the glue?"

"You will be for a while. Eventually she'll gain strength and take over that role herself, which is what we want."

"But her being able to orgasm with me and me being the glue or whatever, I can handle all of that at once. I want to do it all. I just need to know how."

"I appreciate a man who isn't afraid of all of the complications laid out before him. I bet Charlie does as well. From everything I've heard, the key sounds like it lies in getting her out of her own head while also getting her to trust you enough to hand the reins over to you for a given amount of time. She likely only feels safe when she's in total control. That's why she won't allow herself to orgasm. Her body taking over her brain would be terrifying to someone who's lived the trauma she carries. The first thing I would do is to assure her that as long as she feels good and is able to feel how much you care about her while you're together sexually, the goal doesn't have to be orgasm."

Jamie watched a few head of cattle dip themselves into a low creek nearby. "You know that goes against everything dudes are told, right?"

"I am aware," Dec chuckled. "It's the road you're traveling not the destination, right?"

"Yeah, I remember." He didn't like it, but he was determined to fake it until he made it.

"Try to get her to tell you what's going on in her mind when she climaxes alone. That's always a good starting point. Fantasy is almost always the key to healing from trauma. But you're going to have to do a lot of talking and convincing for her to trust you with her fantasies. And you're going to have to handle them responsibly."

"I'm a grown man who helps run a county, a cattle ranch, and a fire department. Responsibility isn't something I struggle with, no matter what her daddy thinks."

Dec didn't even miss a beat. "Discovering exactly how much of her father's opinion of you has affected her perception of you is another task you'll need to work on. But I meant what I said about fantasy. That's the best way to get her out of her own head. Let her pretend to be someone else. If you can give her something else to focus on, she's far more likely to allow that version of herself to have the pleasure she's actively denying."

Jamie ran through a few rather common fantasies. He was pretty sure he could pull off most anything that turned her on. "Okay, so fantasies and anything else?"

"Take it a little at a time. Talk first. Get to the physical later. Don't be surprised if you have to reassure her over and over again, even when you feel like you've told her a thousand times how beautiful you think she is. The world screams in women's ears much louder than you'd believe. Sometimes it's all they can hear. Proving to her how much she turns you on would likely do wonders for her confidence levels."

"I can do that." Another few, rather filthy, images flitted through his mind as Dec set the car in motion again.

"Final piece of advice—it takes an incredibly strong person to face the demons Charlie lives with every single day. Make certain that no matter what she shares with you that you show it a great deal of respect."

"She's the strongest woman I've ever met. I'll handle whatever she wants to share. That won't be a problem. Listen, I really do appreciate the help even if I was a little resistant at first."

Dec grinned at that. "You likely won't believe me when I say this but it's the truth—for me, helping people keeps me sane. I'm an addict by nature. I have no choice but to live that. Helping other couples achieve intimacy reminds me that what I do matters. So, you helped me as much as I helped you."

As they were pulling up to the cottage, Jamie offered Dec his hand. "I understand needing to know that what you're doing makes a difference. Firefighters are the same way. It's an addiction all its own, so I get what you're saying."

"It is an addiction," Dec agreed. "Fortunately it's one that makes the world better when so many of them tear it apart." He gestured his head to Charlie who was on the front porch heading their way. "I wish you luck. If you need any more help, find me."

"Thanks, man. I'm just hoping she doesn't scalp me for talking to you."

"I'd broach that delicately, but you have to be honest with her. That's the only way to achieve the intimacy you're after."

"Kinda feel like I shoulda gotten her flowers or something," Jamie admitted.

"Flowers don't speak loud enough. Try pinning her up against the wall and delivering physical promises she needs to hear and you want to give instead. People who cling tightly to control are often the ones who'd most like to be able to give it away safely."

"Now that, I can do."

CHAPTER EIGHTEEN

Charlie watched Jamie crawl out of someone's SUV. Every motion of his body displayed his innate confidence. Her heart applauded in her chest at his return. "Hey," she drawled out into entirely too many syllables. "You're back." Already blurring the lines of their friendship and whatever it was they'd become the night before, she raced off the porch and into his arms.

He seemed delighted by that and lifted her into his arms and held her tight. "Hey there, angel. You okay?"

When he set her down she wrinkled her nose. "I'm fine. I just missed you. Why do you smell like diesel?" She hadn't meant for that to sound accusatory, but the concern tensed in her tone.

"'Cause I was damn near swimming in it. Both tanks on both trucks busted in the wreck."

The frantic beat of her heart no longer felt like applause. It was borderline panic. The fact that he was still against her, holding her was what allowed her to keep breathing normally. "There wasn't a fire, was there?"

He cradled her chin with his rope-callused hand and stroked his thumb along her cheek. The motion set her at ease. "You're so damn beautiful, did you know that?"

His compliment did nothing to soothe her, mainly because it wasn't true. Was he avoiding the question? "Oh my god. There was a fire, wasn't there?"

"No fire. Everything is fine. Honestly, it coulda been much worse than it was. Camdens lost a bull, and the Claytons lost about ten head in all, but both drivers are fine. Wreckers are cleaning up the road now."

Relieved to hear all of that, Charlie took his hand and tugged him up the porch steps. "You must be exhausted. Come on. Katy dropped off food. I'll heat it up for you."

"You don't have to do that for me." He sounded like she'd handed him gold bricks or something. She shook her head at him.

"You've been rescuing people and animals all day long. It's the least I could do. I wish you'd woken me up. I could've helped."

"I didn't really know what I was getting into when Colt called me, and you were sleeping so well. I hated to wake you."

Before Charlie could respond to that, her phone buzzed in her pocket. "Crap. I forgot to turn it back off. I had it on in case you called." She showed the screen to Jamie. It was a Tulsa number but not one in her contacts.

"Might be Ed trying you from another number," Jamie cautioned.

"He hasn't tried to call me from his own number." She rolled her eyes and answered the call.

"This is Barbara from the Bank of Oklahoma. I need to speak with Charlotte Tilson."

Charlie was instantly on guard. Her checking and savings accounts were both at Bank of Oklahoma, but they'd never phoned her before. "Um...this is she."

Jamie's brow furrowed. He stepped closer to her as if his proximity could shield her from whatever this was about.

"Miss Tilson, Reverend Edward Weaver stopped into the Odell branch this morning and requested copies of your bank statements for the last six months. He said he was your new husband. You hadn't added him to your accounts, however, so we were unable to give him any information. I was calling to see if you'd like to authorize him."

Rage throbbed in Charlie's head. How dare he? "He is not my husband," she screeched and then reminded herself that Barbara wasn't who she needed to scream at.

"What'd he do?" Jamie asked under his breath.

Modifying her tone slightly, Charlie went on, "I'm sorry. I didn't mean to yell at you, but I did not marry Ed, so he has no right to any information on any of my accounts there."

"I understand. I'm going to add a note to your account files just in case he tries this again."

"Thank you."

"Have a nice day."

Charlie rolled her eyes, ended the call, and then promptly exploded. "Ed tried to get copies of my bank statements!"

"Damn." Jamie looked baffled but not nearly as angry as Charlie felt.

"I cannot believe he did that. First of all, he lied to them. Second, what the heck? I put down the deposits for the wedding. I'll pay for whatever else they want to charge, but he's not getting anything else from me."

"It sounds to me like he's checking up on you unless he's in financial straits or something. Did he say anything like that?"

"No. He squeezes every penny until it squeaks. Plus, if he needed money, why would he insist on me quitting my job? It doesn't make any sense. And how on earth would having my bank statements from six months ago tell him where I am now?"

"Do you want to call him?" Jamie's suggestion sounded like he'd had to dredge it up from the bowels of his gut and force it from his lips.

Charlie studied him, trying to guess his thoughts. "You don't sound like you want me to call him."

"I don't."

"Why?" Her heart picked up pace. She knew the answer she longed to hear, but it was stupid to even wish for it. It was only going to get them both hurt.

He took a step closer, dominating her space. She wanted more. She couldn't seem to get close enough. Maybe ever. "You want me to tell you the truth?" rumbled from him. She managed a quick nod. "Because I'm possessive as hell, and I want you to be mine. I don't ever want you talking to him again. He had a piece of you that's supposed to be mine, and honest to god I hate him for that."

———

Being forthright came far too naturally to Jamie. He'd kept all of this to himself for what felt like a lifetime. She'd asked for the truth, so he'd given it to her. It was all up to her now. A hard swallow contracted her neck as she gnawed on her bottom lip. The time lengthened between them. He swore it put physical distance between them and he couldn't stand it. "Say something," he demanded.

She pursed her lips. "Impatient much?"

He held up his hands. "Yeah, kind of, but I've been patient for a long damn time already."

Concern tensed in her eyes. "Can I ask a question? Or maybe more than one?"

He took her hand and guided her inside the house. This wasn't the kind of conversation you had standing in somebody else's front yard. "You can ask me anything. You know that."

She eased onto the couch, but the tense set of her body did nothing to soothe him. "What does that look like to you? I mean, me being yours. How does that work?"

Approaching that from every angle, he considered. "It means you let me take care of you. Let me protect you. If you're in trouble, I'm the guy you call. Even if you're just pissed for no reason, I'm the one you let try to fix it. You tell me things, even things you think don't matter. If something makes you cry, you let me hold you. If something makes you so fucking happy you want to skywrite it, you call me and tell me first so I can be happy too. Shit like that."

She gave him a broken grin that he swore stabbed through his chest like a frozen ice pick. "I already do all of that. You are already all of those things to me." She dropped his gaze. "You're everything to me."

He scooted closer to her and took both of her hands in his own and wondered if she remembered the first time they'd ever held hands. The spark and fascination were still there in his palms whenever he held them. "I'm not everything to you. Not yet. I want the physical too. I want to hold you naked in my arms. I want to hear all of those sweet, needy little noises you make when I get you wet. I want to roll over in the mornings and prove that I can wake you up better than coffee. Hotter. Stronger. I want to feel you tremble for me, angel. God, I want that more than I even knew. I want you to trust me enough to let me hold every single fantasy that lives in your head, even the ones that scare you a little. I want to be the guy that makes them a reality."

Well, he had just told her he wanted her to tremble for him and she was, but this wasn't exactly what he'd had in mind. Her hand shook in his. He strengthened his hold. "You scare me, maybe more than a little," she finally choked out.

"You're scared of me?" Absolutely nothing about that made sense, and it killed him.

"No. Maybe. Kind of. I'm not scared you would ever hurt me physically or anything. I know you'll always take care of me, but..." she shrugged, "you're a man and you know how..."

"To do things. To give you the things you're afraid to ask for," he concluded for her. Life anew rushed through his veins now. He couldn't quite hide his smirk.

She gave him another hesitant nod. "Yes, and I don't know how to do any...things, and if this doesn't work..." her jaw tensed as she stared him down, "that scares me more than anything in the world, even more than my memories of the fire. I can't live without you. You're the whole world to me. I can't lose you. I've already lost...too much." The words seemed to deflate her body. She curled in on herself.

Jamie shook his head and scooped under her legs so he could place her in his lap. "You will never lose me. If I fuck this up bad enough that you hate being my girlfriend, we'll go back to being best friends. Simple as that."

"It wouldn't be you that messed up." She spoke that into his chest.

He lifted her head again. "I'm gonna do everything in my power not to, that's for damn sure, but why do you think it would be you?" She went silent for several beats. "Say it," he urged. "Whatever you think it is, say it, so I can prove to you that you're wrong."

"I'm not wrong," she fussed.

"Let's hear it then."

She gave him an exasperated eye roll. "You're going to get sick of me being so bad in bed for one thing."

He swore he could hear the audible squeal of brakes screeching in his mind. "What the hell makes you think you're bad in bed?"

Exasperation rang in her tone now. "All of the things that I don't know how to do including...you know."

"Coming when you're with me?"

"Yes. That."

"You not coming doesn't mean you're bad in bed, baby. Nothing you did last night was bad. My god. How could you even think that? But if you want us to work on you trusting me enough to climax, I want to do that. I want to be there for every part of a relationship."

"You've never even had a relationship so how do you know that? And me not being able to do that with you is not because I don't trust you. I trust you completely. I just can't do it. I'm broken."

"Do you have any fucking idea what it does to me when you say shit like that? It kills me."

"Sorry." She cringed.

"Don't apologize. Just let me prove you wrong."

"And how do you think you're going to be able to do that?"

"You just said you trust me, so prove it. Let me see if I can help you learn to come with me."

"How do you plan to go about doing that?"

"Lots of different ways. Just give me a chance. Please. I'm begging here. You said you wanted to learn how to do all of these things you think you don't know how to do. Let me teach you."

"I did not say that exactly."

"Humor me, Miss Tilson."

That got him another eye roll. "I don't know what that means or looks like in your world."

She still wasn't getting it. Too late to turn back now. "You *are* my world, sweetheart. I just need to hear you say that we can try this together."

"What if this doesn't work out like you think it's going to? What if..."

He gently placed his index finger on her lush lips, quieting her. "Last night when you kissed me, you said you were tired of being afraid. Find that again. Just for a minute. Let that version of yourself decide this."

CHAPTER NINETEEN

Charlie tried. She closed her eyes and tried to imagine what Jamie was describing. She would be insane not to take him up on this offer. How long was she going to let the fear rule her? Her mind continued to supply endless reasons why this was a terrible idea, but hope is an adamant, insistent emotion.

Jessie had been right. She was hurting herself a little every single day to avoid pain later on. For heaven's sake, that's why she'd agreed to marry Ed, just so she wouldn't have to chance a relationship with Jamie that might not work. She knew the pain of losing the most important person in your life, and she knew she couldn't live through that again.

But Jamie was so very, very real. Sitting there right with her begging for a chance. His warmth and his protection and every single thing she already adored about him were right there in the palms of her hands and all she had to do was hold on.

Her heart thundered in her ears. She was dizzy with the possibility, and she was so sick and tired of being afraid. Maybe nothing good ever came from fear.

Cautiously, she pressed the words from her mouth. "What if I have questions? What if there's something I want you to teach me? And these things I don't know that everyone else already does know, will you teach me and not tease?"

He looked wounded at her question, but she needed his assurances if she was going to do this. "When have I ever not answered something you asked me? And for the love of god, Charlie, what kind of asshole would I be if I teased you for having questions about things you haven't done?"

"Please just say you won't."

"I would never. Don't you get it? You asking me things, letting me show you things, teaching you how it could be between us, that's my fantasy."

Shock whisked over her skin. "Really?"

"Yeah, really."

"What happens when we go back home? Does this all stop?"

"That is entirely up to you."

"What about your job?"

"Hey," he brushed her hair away from her shoulder. "Let's take it one day and one moment at a time, okay? We'll deal with Holder County when we get back there."

"You promise this won't change our friendship?"

"I swear to you. Go get me a Bible, I'll swear on it too."

"Okay then." She took a tentative breath. "I want to try."

He crushed her to him, hugging her until she wasn't sure how much longer she'd be able to breathe and for the first time in her life she didn't care. She giggled when he peppered kisses on her cheek and jaw. "So, how does this work? Where do we start? I need a plan."

Jamie laughed at her outright. "Guess that's what I get for falling for an OT."

"Plans are important," she insisted, though she was perfectly willing to do whatever he wanted, plan or not.

"Come take a shower with me. That's where we start cause I'm sick of smelling like gasoline."

As badly as Charlie wished she was the kind of girl who'd hop right into Jamie Holder's shower with him, she just wasn't that kind of girl. "I can't do that."

"Why not?"

"Because."

"Not an answer."

Somehow in all of her negotiations about this she'd forgotten that he'd likely want to see her naked. Or at least he thought he did. "I still need to leave my shirt on when we're together."

"No."

He offered no other words to soften that blow. Her brow furrowed. "Yes."

"You said you trusted me. Trust me with whatever it is you're so worried about that's under that shirt. You're fucking beautiful. Inside and out."

She shook her head. "I'm not beautiful there."

"You're beautiful everywhere, but tell me why you think that."

This wasn't the kind of story that she ever wanted to tell. She certainly didn't want to start at the beginning. "Uh," she let her eyes rove the room, desperate for some kind of distraction. Nothing was readily available, however. "I have some scars. Bad scars."

"From the fire?" he urged.

She nodded and continued to study the wood grain on the floor.

"Look at me," he commanded. She immediately complied. "Do you think I'm attractive?"

Incredulity morphed her features. "Is the sky blue? Are fire hydrants red? Do cows moo? That's a ridiculous question. Everyone thinks you're a hunk. You're Jamie Holder."

"But do *you* think I'm a hunk?" he continued to prod.

She cocked her jaw to the side and rolled her eyes. "Yes."

"Good. Now we're getting somewhere. If I had scars anywhere on me, from some horrible moment in my life, would that make me less attractive in your eyes?"

"Of course not."

He lifted his eyebrows. "But what? You think I'm that much of a shallow prick?"

His words cinched her vocal cords. "I don't think you're shallow at all."

"It sounds like you do."

"You don't understand."

"Then make me understand, baby. Stop being afraid, please."

She did owe him an explanation if for no other reason than insinuating that he was shallow. "The other guys that I slept with," she shrugged like that would brush off the pain and resentment she held.

"Keep going," he soothed.

"They both asked me to put my shirt back on before we...did anything." It sounded even worse than she'd remembered.

Jamie's fists clenched. "Yeah, well, they're fuckwads, and that's what I get for not speaking up about wanting you to be mine earlier. I let you get hurt. But, can I please have a chance to prove to you that I'm not a Grade A douche-nugget?"

"You had nothing to do with it, and you don't have to prove anything to me. I know you're a great guy. I just...if I let you see the scars and you want me to cover them up, it's okay. I'll understand. They're hard to look at."

This time he caught her face in both of his hands. "At some point I'm going to prove to you that the only thing that's hard about looking at you is trying to keep my hands off of you." He stood with her in his arms and headed to the bathroom.

Panic flooded through her. Her heart pumped it out with every frantic beat. "Uh...don't you want to eat first?" Delaying getting naked in front of him seemed tantamount to survival. She hadn't quite had a chance to wrap her head around everything he'd just said he wanted to do.

He gave her another one of those entirely too sexy half grins. "Oh angel, trust me, I'm going to devour you like you're my last fucking meal."

Trying to remember everything Dec had told him, Jamie decided it was high time he took the reins. He'd hoped the shower would make her feel a little less exposed than if he stripped her and laid her out on the bed in broad daylight. He planned to do that as well, but he had to take things slowly. He couldn't afford any missteps.

"You know," she started in as he flipped on the bathroom lights, "even if we have sex in the shower and you're not grossed out by the scars, I still won't be able to have an orgasm."

Jamie ground his teeth but tried not to let her see. He set her on her feet and turned on the faucet. The rhythmic drumming of the water on the tile began to create an intimate feel around them. "Make me a deal," he urged.

"You mean more than the one I just made where we decided to throw all caution out the window and date for however long it takes for us to figure out that we shouldn't?"

Letting his annoyance display on his face this time, he debated but went on with what he'd planned to say. "Actually, this deal applies to us having sex and us having a relationship. I won't make you coming my only goal if you won't go into every experience we have determined that you're not going to. Same goes for you not deciding now that this thing between us will never work. Deal?"

"Fine, but I need you to be patient with me. You're asking me to step way, way out of my comfort zone. I'm not good at that."

Heat stained her cheeks and frantic worry scalded her eyes. It killed him. "I'm not trying to be pushy. Can I be completely honest with you? I don't want to wig you out."

"I want us always to be completely honest, even if this," she gestured to the shower, "doesn't work out like we want." She'd said *we* and that was all he needed to hear.

"Good. I want that too. I'm being impatient with you now because I feel like I've spent the last twenty years being way too patient. I've wanted you for a long time, and I never cowboyed up and did anything about it." Her thumb when to her mouth and defeat tugged in his gut. "Don't do that, please." He eased her hand away from her face.

"Sorry. That isn't entirely true, you know. You asked me out the first day we met." Her grin stoked the embers of need kindling in his groin.

"Yeah, but I never did again. I was a fool. There, I said it."

"You weren't a fool. And..." she eyed him cautiously now, "I've thought about us being together like this before too. Kind of a lot actually. But it just wasn't worth risking the friendship for romance. It still isn't."

"I know that. I spend most of my life calculating risks, and this just isn't one. But right now, I want to hear way more about what's on your mind when you think of us together like this."

The blush that had already bloomed across her face reddened again. She was the perfect combination of sexy, beautiful, and cute. And he was about to make her all his, officially this time.

He yanked his diesel-stained T-shirt up over his head, and let himself enjoy the way she licked her lips as she stared at him. He let his ego loose. It had taken quite a hit last night, so he figured it was okay for a moment. "You like what you see, sugar?"

She rolled her eyes at him but couldn't conceal her grin. "Lust is a sin," she giggled.

"Is it?"

"You didn't pay any attention to the preachers that whole week at church camp, did you?" Her grin continued to expand, delighting him.

"I was too busy paying attention to you," he informed her.

"You're coming on a little strong. Aren't you worried I'll get the wrong idea and start picking out new wedding gowns again or something?"

He popped the snap on his Wranglers and reveled in her gaze making a quick trek down his abs to his happy trail. "Making up for lost time, remember? Plus, you hated wedding dress shopping. You texted me from dressing rooms when you were hiding from Louann and Becca, remember?"

She nodded. "I remember. I just wish I'd seen every freaking red flag that Ed and I were a bad idea."

"Lots of people use red flags for blindfolds. Now," he shoved his jeans down to his boots and skillfully stepped out of both, "come here to me." She hadn't taken her gaze off of the rigid bulge in his boxer briefs. She stood there staring at him like she was rooted to the bathroom tile.

He went to her instead. Easing his hands to her hips, he eased her forward one half step. Panic tensed through her. "Come on, now," he soothed. "It's me. This is us. I thought I was your ride or die." He winked at her and slipped his fingers to the clasp on her jeans. She seemed more comfortable with her lower half being exposed so he'd figured he'd start there.

"You are." Her chuckle was haunted. It carried far more pain than tears would've been able to sustain. He hated that she continued to conceal things from him. "You go on and get in. I'll be there in a minute," she negotiated.

"No." He shook his head.

Her stubborn side resurrected, and Jamie was thrilled to see it. Stubborn he could work with. Her fear crushed him. It robbed him of words. "You don't get to tell me no," she huffed.

"Watch me. I'm not leaving you out here with whatever it is that has you somehow convinced that you're not stunningly beautiful. So, no. I'm not getting in without you. Someday, I'll be able to convince you that I have no interest in you showing me the parts of yourself you keep polished and pressed and whatever else. All the ways you think you have to be out in the world, that ain't for me. I want my Charlie, trusting me enough to be real with me. All the people you have to be Charlotte for, they aren't real and their opinions don't matter."

CHAPTER TWENTY

For the tenth time in the last few minutes, Charlie wished she could just believe that the scars weren't that bad, that she could be fully there with Jamie. That he'd like her no matter what she looked like naked.

She took some solace in his determination. He wasn't going to let her out of this. She didn't really want out of it. His hands made quick work of the zipper on her jeans. He shoved them down her thighs then drove his hands down the back of her panties and gripped her ass.

Somehow the hunger evident in his grip prodded the girl she always wished she could be from deep in her chest. She moved closer to him instinctively. But her cynical side was right there trying to take exact measure of the lusty look in his eyes and the need tensed in his jaw so she could obsess over any changes once her shirt was off. Her mind was not going to play fair, and she knew it. She just didn't know how to stop it.

It seemed Jamie had several creative ways to silence the cruel demons who'd been with her since the night of the fire. He sank his lips to hers, taking her breath hostage and suffocating the cruel voices that wouldn't give her peace. Tired of always being the person who stood in her own way, Charlie gave herself over to the persuasion of his lips.

The kiss was steeped in ownership, and she was more than willing to let him have her...as long as he understood that she would always want to hide her broken pieces, even from him.

He dragged her forward until the evidence of his obvious arousal was nestled against the cradle of her thighs. He was astounding—all focused male, intent on satisfaction. To be the object of his need was, and had always been, her most potent fantasy.

Her breaths tripped as they tried to escape her lungs. He gripped her ass with more force and began to grind her mound against his cock. "Do you feel how fucking hard you make me? Feel how bad I want to be inside of you, baby. That's all you."

She certainly couldn't argue with his evidence. He eased back to give her breath and slipped her jeans to the floor. His confidence in quick ways to undress women did nothing to give her peace. He had way more experience than she did, and for the first time in her life she admitted to herself that she hated that. Jealousy was ugly. She knew it was, but dammit, she didn't know how to fix that either. "You're awfully good at that," she huffed although her tone was deep with her own hunger.

He gave her that signature Holder smirk. "I've imagined undressing you hundreds of times. I've got it all worked out in my head how to get you nekkid as fast as I possibly can."

"I thought it was because you've undressed so many other women." The truth was just too close to the surface for her to keep it at bay.

He paused and then locked his eyes on hers. "You remember yesterday when you asked me why I never kept anyone around for more than a date or two?"

Charlie nodded and wondered where he was going with this.

"It's because none of them were you."

Shock shattered over her. He'd been so open about being attracted to her. She'd always been attracted to him as well. She hadn't thought of it as a secret, really. It was just something they mutually chose to ignore. It was a byproduct of their closeness and nothing else. Until he put it in context of every other relationship he'd ever ended, and there were quite a few of them.

His honesty became a soft blanket she could use to keep herself covered and warm. It was a shield that would keep her safe, when her clothes were off. He'd always been that for her—a safe harbor, a fierce protector, her hero. She dammed the fear and admitted that she wanted him under the blanket with her.

She wanted to share the parts of herself with him even if she knew they were hideous. Gathering her courage into a bundle of ripped shards, she pressed on. "I spent three months at the Parkland Pediatric Burn Center in Texas before we moved to Holder County." The words turned to ashes on her tongue. She assumed that was apropos considering what they were discussing, but she still wanted to gag.

Jamie gave her a gentle nod and eased his hands up her sides. This time she didn't stop him. The sensation of having someone else's hands there was one of the oddest things she'd ever felt. She could feel his warmth through her T-shirt, and somehow it didn't frighten her. "Second degree? Third? Did your dad stay with you while you were out there? My god, baby, I wished I known you then, so I could've at least visited you."

"Um..." the memories vibrated in her chest right along with her heart, "third degree. Less than ten percent of my..." she gestured to her chest, "body, so that was good. That's what the doctors kept saying. That's still what they say. I was lucky, I guess."

"Bet you didn't feel too lucky back then. I bet you were scared, and I bet you were pissed the fuck off."

For some inexplicable reason, that made her smile. He really did know her better than anyone. "A little of those things too. When you have an injury like that on your rib cage, you have to have your arm in an axillary splint to prevent contractures. It, uh," she raised her arm up in the air beside her head precisely the way it had been in the splint for so long, "looks like this. It was miserable, and I just kept thinking that I looked like I was raising my hand to answer a question in school, only..." her voice snagged on the memory, "I didn't understand anything. I didn't have any answers, and I was mostly by myself because Dad and Becca were being treated at Mercy in Oklahoma City.

I was just scared and that made me angry at myself. And I was so sad because...my mom," she tried to shrug away a lifetime of devastation but only succeeded in compounding it further. Her shoulders tensed under the invisible weight. She had to be stronger. That was her job.

"Keep going, sweetheart." Jamie folded her into his embrace, like maybe he could help her carry some of the guilt and confusion. "Tell me everything you felt, or wished you felt, or how it all was just so fucking unfair. I want to know."

Memories continued to resurface in bits and pieces that didn't make much sense. She eased off of his chest, though that was the last thing she really wanted to do. But she wanted to share this with him, to maybe have someone who could help her figure out those months of her life that still didn't make any sense. "That's when I learned to braid my hair." She gnawed on her lip, but the words continued to pour from her. "Maya taught me. She was my inpatient occupational therapist. I loved her so much. She's why I wanted to become an OT. The braiding was for range of motion." She continued to supply far too many details, but Jamie listened intently like he didn't want to miss a single word. "She was so great. I felt so hideously ugly, so she always brought things for me to do that sort of helped that, I guess. I remember one day she brought all of these ribbons, and my goal for that morning was to braid all of the ribbons in my hair. It hurt. God, it hurt so bad. It felt like I was stretching my skin so far I was sure it was going to tear apart. I couldn't stand it, but I refused to stop."

He grinned at that. "My stubborn girl. It kills me that you thought for even a moment that you were anything but beautiful."

She'd always been stubborn. She'd never really been beautiful, but until the moment she'd run from the church the day before, she hadn't really been his either. She loved that way too much. When he finally figured out that they'd be better off as friends, it was going to hurt worse than the burns. She shook that off. "Anyway, every day she taught me harder and more intricate braids. I was so determined to learn them. It felt like..." she shook her head at the remembrances.

"Like what, angel?"

"Like if I could figure out just the right way to braid all of the ribbons and all of my hair into something kind of pretty that maybe I could say and do all the right things so...I could put my family back together too," she choked.

Before the last word left her lips, she was right back in the solid sanctuary of his arms. "That wasn't your job, baby," he soothed as he planted kisses on her head. "You've spent your whole life putting everyone else back together. Let me take care of you for a change."

Charlie wasn't certain what that would look like, what exactly Jamie had in mind. But with everything she'd just confessed she felt lighter just then. Strong enough that the tiniest light of possibility began to shimmer under all of the weight. She wanted to give this a chance. She wanted to stop being afraid, so she nodded. "Okay, but I want to take care of you too."

"You've been taking care of me since sixth grade. It's my turn now."

CHAPTER TWENTY-ONE

"Look at me," Jamie coaxed. When she lifted her head, he caught her pensive stare with his own. "Keep your eyes right here on mine. I want you to know I mean every word I'm about to say. As soon as you give me the okay, I'm going to take your shirt off, and there is not one single scar or marking or skin graft damage that is going to make me not want to carry you into that shower and prove to you just how fucking beautiful you are. Do you understand that?" She managed a nod. "Good. You ready?" This time she shook her head, and he let his hands pause in their work.

"I'm never going to be ready, so just do it," she urged.

It fucking killed him that she was so caught up in whatever he was about to uncover. She'd been left in a burn center alone. She'd never dealt with it. If he could've gotten away with it, he would've strung Reverend Tilson up on a pole and taken a switch to his ass. "I'll go slow," he soothed. He reminded himself that her father had just lost his wife and had two injured kids, so he was obviously overwhelmed, but Jamie still wasn't feeling all that forgiving.

"You used to always say patience wasn't your virtue," she reminded him.

"I get what this has to be costing you, so I'm doing my best." He inched the shirt up exposing her belly. He could just make out the rough patches of skin on her right side. Suddenly, she took over for him. Maybe she didn't like his patience, or maybe she was just finally seeing how good they could be together if she'd give them a shot.

With a great deal of determination, she pulled the shirt up over her head and tossed it on the counter. And now, she was refusing to really look at him.

Truthfully, Jamie appreciated the moment to take it all in. It was much worse than he'd ever envisioned. None of it made him think she was any less beautiful or any less sexy, but the pain she had to have endured sucker punched him. He was a firefighter for fuck's sake. He'd seen burns before. But hers were the worst he'd encountered. Puckered knots roped up her side under the thinned, pockmarked skin. The skin graft scars ran the length of the perimeter of the burns that had also mangled the side of her right breast.

"Please say something," she demanded.

Fuck. How long had he been standing there staring at her? *Nice move, asshat.* "First off, there is nothing about scars that makes you not the most beautiful woman in the world to me. Every square inch of your skin is perfect because it's yours. I do have some questions though."

She finally stared him down. Every single thing about her said she didn't believe a word he'd just said. "Ask me."

"Does it hurt if I touch your side?"

"Not really. There was a lot of nerve damage, so I don't feel much over there." She instinctively moved her right arm forward slightly to cover the damage to her breast. Jamie traced his fingertips over the top swell and her nipple. "Just wanted to make sure."

Her eyes goggled and she leapt back.

"You okay?" He had a feeling he knew why she'd reacted that way, but he needed her to say it.

"Uh...kind of."

"Do you not want me to touch you, honey?"

She considered that for two heartbeats too long, but again he tried to be patient. "It's not that. It's just that no one other than doctors ever have. I'm not sure I know how to react. Even I avoid touching the scars."

"I don't want to avoid touching any part of you, as long as it doesn't hurt you."

"How is this not turning you off?" she finally demanded.

"You're standing in front of me shirtless, angel. Why the hell would that turn me off?" He took her hand and brought it back to the bulge in his underwear.

Confusion now rode hard in her eyes. "But this isn't how I'm supposed to look. No one's supposed to look like this."

"You're not supposed to look like you survived?" he challenged.

She was going to test him, and he was determined to pass every single trial. "My boob is dimpled and scarred and awful and the two of them aren't even the same size."

"No one's are."

"What?"

"Okay, I generally make it a policy not to discuss my somewhat sordid past with you or with other women, but I've had my hands up a fair number of blouses, and none of them are exactly the same size unless they're fake. It's part of the fun."

She ground her teeth. "It's part of the fun?" Each word came out like scatter shot from a .22.

He dodged the pellets with ease. "Yeah. Your tits are perfect because they're yours, and they're about to have my hands and my cum all over them. I want to know every single eccentricity you have. I want to learn your body. I want to know your preferences, and I want to feel every sexy-as-sin curve. I wish you knew even half of the times I've dreamed about being naked with you, getting in a shower with you, getting inside of you. Nothing about those scars changes how fucking bad I want to be the guy who gets to see you like this."

"You are seeing me like this."

"I know. I still feel kinda like this is the best damn dream I've ever had, and I'm afraid I'm about to wake up from it."

That at least got a little bit of a smile. "Thanks for being so great about it."

"Honey, I don't know who made you think that it's some kind of sacrifice on their part to be with you like this, but if I ever meet them, I'm going after them with a hose."

———

Some part of Charlie knew that Jamie would never react the way her past boyfriends had, but the relief was heady. It brought fresh air to her lungs. She wanted to really see what it would be like to climb in that shower with him and flirt and feel and do things she'd never given herself the opportunity to experience before.

Riding high on that wave of assurance and praying they didn't crash on the shoreline, she slipped her jeans and panties off all at once. Confidence coursed through her. She barely recognized it.

"Damn, damn, damn," Jamie half grunted and half growled.

She would always regret that she'd never heard him use that tone before until yesterday. It was wholly unfair that he could sound so utterly sexy, and she'd never known.

He shucked off his underwear and then gave her a sinfully cocky chuckle when her eyes zeroed in on his package. She hadn't really gotten to study it the night before the way she wanted. Thick veins protruded from his blood-engorged cock leading her eyes to his crown. He rose proudly out of a thatch of hair at his base, a technicolor display of male pride in the satisfaction he knew he could offer. Every part of her, the scarred and the unscarred, knew he could satisfy the needy ache she had between her legs. Perhaps, it was just a need to be so full of him she no longer worried about not being enough for everyone else.

"Like what you see there, honey?" Jamie teased.

"Shut up." She giggled.

"Oh, I don't think so. I plan on getting a sign made to put up at home all about how much you love my junk just so everyone knows."

She rolled her eyes at that and headed for the shower doors. As she whisked by him, he popped her backside. She spun around with her mouth hanging open. She wasn't certain which surprised her more— that he'd done that or that she'd liked it. It spoke to the cravings she carried deep within her to be with someone who wouldn't worry about being careful with her because of the scars. "What do you think you're doing?"

"I'm just testing out a theory."

"And what theory might that be?"

"I'll tell you later." He opened the door to the shower and followed her inside.

CHAPTER TWENTY-TWO

Her right butt cheek was slightly pink from his hand. That pleased him more than it should. Jamie stepped into the shower behind her. He swore Charlie with clouds of steam billowing around her looked like an angel stepping down from heaven to rescue him from his shitty existence.

He wrapped his arms around her and eased them under the rush of warm water. She melted into his arms, burying her face against his neck. Perfection. "So fucking beautiful," he spoke directly into her ear, hoping the words would make their way to her heart. She tightened her hold. His cock was an iron spike between them pressed to her belly and slick from the warm water and his own hunger.

When her hands began a thorough exploration of his back and then his ass, a low rumbled growl triggered from his gut.

She lifted her head and gave him a mischievous little smirk. "I had no idea you were so growly."

"I get all kinds of animalistic when your hands are on me. You're lucky I haven't thrown you over my shoulder and taken you back to my cave." Intrigue flared in her eyes, and he shuddered from the throb of need it elicited. "Or would you like that, angel? Like me to steal you away and take what I want?"

That only earned him a deeper smirk. If pictures were worth a thousand words, that little motion of her mouth had to be worth a cool million. He dove in and captured it with his lips before she could take it away. It was his.

His tongue dove past the barriers of her lips, tasting her, devouring her. He braced one hand on her ass drawing her even closer and let the other trace gently up her left side. A full body shiver coursed through her as he worshiped the untouched portions of her body. The water rushed over his face as he lowered his head to tease her nipple with his tongue. Fuck air. Fuck every single life-giving thing that wasn't her. He didn't care. He'd drown to have this. Catching her right breast with his palm, he worked her left nipple with easy suckles and then yearning pulls until both were turgid with want.

A choked moan broke from her chest. Her fingers dove through his hair in an effort to hold him to her breast. It was unnecessary but sexy as hell. When she bucked against him trying to bring her hungry pussy to his cock, he roared against her flesh before lifting his head. "That feels good, doesn't it, angel? So sensitive for me. You kept these needy parts of yourself away from me last night. I can't take care of you the way I'm determined to when you do that." He moved to her right breast and let his hand take over on the other. He grazed the puckered skin gently with his fingertips trying to get her accustomed to his touch there, wishing he could physically pour love through the skin that had been broken.

"Jamie, please," finally reached his ears. He swore he could get off on listening to her beg.

Again he lifted his head. "It makes you wet when I suck those sweet titties, doesn't it, angel?" Her head fell back against the tile wall. Her body rolled with the need. "Tell me," he urged. "Tell me how much it turns you on."

"Yes," she finally whimpered. "Now, please."

Sweet baby wasn't going to be too forthcoming with just how good that felt. He wanted her to acknowledge it, but not nearly as badly as he wanted to wrap her legs around his waist and slam himself so deep inside of her she'd feel him coming for the rest of their week.

As he traced and teased his way down her midsection on a direct course to that needy slip of heaven between her legs, she flipped the script on him entirely.

Her hand wrapped around his length. He throbbed against her palm. Her lips parted on a moan.

"Fuck," huffed from him as she took an exploratory pull from his root to his tip. So caught up in her touch, he did nothing but watch her as she traced the thickened veins that ran the length of him.

"I want to know," she whispered so low he almost didn't make it out over the roar of the water.

"What, baby? Tell me." He wanted to be the answer to whatever it was she needed to understand. Her fingers tightened along his shaft and then fanned at his crown, driving him wild. She seemed to have gotten lost in her research of his cock. "Charlie, sweetheart. Tell me what you need to know before I bury that so fucking deep inside your tender pussy you can't walk."

Her bottom lip slipped between her teeth as she studied him. "What do you think about?" she asked with only slightly more volume. He waited. His only thoughts were on how fucking good this hand job felt. What she lacked in experience she was more than making up for in exuberance. She stopped her work, and he fought not to demand that she get back to it. "If I let you steal me away to your cave, I want to know what you'd do with me."

His mind scrambled. The truth would likely scare the hell out of his mostly innocent angel. Plus, he wasn't able to think beyond his desperation to have her. When he didn't respond, she kept going. "You said you'd thought about us like this. I want to know what kinds of things you think about. I need to know." She stroked him with more vigor now, drawing the confession from him with divine torture. His angel transformed into a vixen before his very eyes.

The sexiest fantasy he had was the one of her being his. Of them walking through town and everyone knowing she was Mrs. Jamie Holder. That she would never want for anything and that she was more than satisfied every fucking night. His balls drew up tight and hot thinking about her waltzing into the fire station with a smirk on her face and a rubbed ache in her panties from what he'd given her the night before.

But that wasn't what she wanted to hear so he let his mind turn to a darker, more depraved place. Suddenly, the absolute truth was the only option because he didn't have the brain capacity to lie. "It's dirty." His warning was ragged and rough.

"Good."

Damn. "Your panties are sweet and innocent, but they're so wet I can see through them," he groaned out. Somehow her tremble shook through his balls and made him see stars.

"What else?" Her words came out in pants of breath.

"You hurt with need. You fucking tell me that." Everything in him knew he needed to stop. She wasn't ready for this kind of shit. But she slipped her hand up and down his length faster now. Jesus, if she didn't stop he was gonna unload all over her fingers. His eyes closed as he let the fantasy fully form in his mind. "You need me," he grunted. "Need me to make it feel better. Need me to show you where only I know it hurts."

"Oh god. More." Her breath mixed with the heat of the shower as it encapsulated them.

"Yeah, angel. That's it. You beg for me just like that. You beg for me to take you how I want." He wrapped his hand around hers, pressing her tighter to his cock and showing her how he liked to be jacked. Her eyes goggled at his force. "Oh honey, there's so much you don't know, isn't there? Your pussy's 'bout a million times tighter than my fist. So hot and wet. Nursing at my cock. Feels so fucking good I'll never be able to get myself off to thoughts of you again. I'll have to come get the real deal. Nothing else will ever feel like you do."

"Then fuck me," she urged frantically.

She didn't have to ask him twice. He released her hand and stroked the tender auburn curls soaked from the shower water but slick from her own need. She shuddered between him and the wall. "Spread your legs for me, angel. Let me get you ready. 'Cause I'm ten country miles past the ability to be gentle with you."

"Good." She widened her stance, and he dipped his finger deep in one smooth pass. He loved that little gasp she made when he entered her, loved that she'd add a groan to the gasp when he replaced his fingers with his cock. Loved everything about this. Loved her.

That realization might've frightened lesser men off, but he'd known for two decades that he loved her. Surely, she knew that too.

He circled his thumb gently over her clit until it peeked out, needy for his love. "Feels good when I touch right there, doesn't it, baby?"

"Yes," she whimpered. "So good."

Now they were getting somewhere. Slippery need coated his knuckles and thumb, driving him wild. Her body continued to pull at his fingers, anxious for more. "Gonna feel even better when I keep teasing that naughty little spot while I fill you so full you're overflowing. Tell me you're ready."

"I am. Please stop teasing me."

He hadn't really intended to tease, but she sure as hell responded. He lifted her right leg and hooked her heel against his ass. "I could take you like this. See, how open you are now. How wet and slick. I could slip right in and make it feel so fucking good, but it wouldn't be enough," he growled. "I'd still need more." He'd always need more, but he couldn't wait any longer to explain that. He lifted her slightly, brought her left leg around his torso to meet her right and impaled her.

The torture of her jacking him off while making him tell her things he knew he shouldn't was nothing compared to the moments he forced himself not to move while she adjusted to the invasion of his cock, deeper than anyone had ever been before.

She wiggled in his arms both to seat him further inside of her and to let her body adjust to his girth. He shook with the divine pain of being denied.

"Jamie, please," she finally begged.

"Don't wanna hurt you," he grunted.

"I want you to." Again, she spoke so softly he was certain he'd misunderstood. His eyes flashed open to take in her burying her face against his neck, trying to hide from her own confession.

"That what you need, baby? Need to feel how rough I was with you with every step you take?"

"Yes," she squeaked.

"Done." He gripped her hips, braced her back on the wall, withdrew by mere fractions, slammed himself deeper, and then rode like the cowboy he'd always been. "So fucking beautiful," he assured her. As he slipped himself out and then pressed back in deeper, "Fucking love watching my cock disappear deep in you," growled from him like he was far more beast than man. She angled her head so she could watch as well. A delicious little moan escaped her mouth. "You like watching me take what's mine, angel? Watching me own you?"

"Yes." The confession tore from her, perforated with shame, he suspected. But she went wild in his arms. She was so slick and his muscles were exhausted from physically helping to move cows out of the trucks that morning. He was scared not to hold her up with both arms, so he improvised.

"Bring your fingers to my mouth," he urged.

Her brow furrowed for a split second before she complied. Damn, but he loved that. Once she had her fingertips near his lips, he licked their tips and then sucked two into his mouth. "Now, reach between us and tease that sweet little nub. Show me how you like it."

She made a quick circle of her fingertips between his abs and her clit but didn't really make contact. "Rub yourself, honey. Like a good girl."

Her eyes closed and she gave herself over to his instruction. Perfect little filthy angel. She shook with the impending orgasm, a combo if he had any say over it.

He throbbed constantly now. His balls were so high and tight he swore he was choking on them. "You're right there, sugar," he grunted. "Let yourself go. Take me with you."

He pled with whoever was in charge of orgasms in heaven that she'd push through her fear, but he was denied. She tensed. Her jaw locked. And she actively denied herself all while urging him on, "Come in me. Please. I want it to drip out of me again. Like it did this morning."

Fuck. Fuck. Fuck. It was too much. She squeezed those internal muscles even tighter against him, locking him down inside of her and he tried. God, he tried to hold it back. Tried so fucking hard he was dizzy, but nothing worked. She was too good. Too tight. Too Charlie. Too much his. And he filled her full with pump after pump, soaking down her walls with hot cum.

When his breath finally returned to him, he gently lowered her back to her feet and held her steady. Disappointment crushed him even though he tried to remember that her climaxing wasn't supposed to be his goal. Fuck that. He hadn't gotten her off. And he felt like a failure.

CHAPTER TWENTY-THREE

Charlie was thoroughly, deliciously melted. She let her head loll on Jamie's shoulder and relished every moment of that. She loved that he hadn't been gentle or worried over her even after seeing all of her scars. No one had ever done that before. She felt deliciously sexy.

"That was amazing," she remembered to inform him. He tensed his arms around her tighter but didn't respond. Great. He was still hung up on the orgasm thing. Disappointment tore away a little of the satisfaction she'd experienced. Why did that even have to be a thing? Why couldn't they just let it feel good, not just good even, completely euphoric? This was why everyone was so hung up on sex. She'd never really understood it before crawling into bed with Jamie the night before. This was why the whole entire town wanted to ride a Holder.

He soaped his hands and began to massage her back. Okay, he was clearly some kind of gift to her from God for being a good person all of her life or at least trying to be. Despite how insanely good it felt when he rubbed her shoulders, she lifted her head. "I thought you were going to be okay with the orgasm thing." She wanted him to feel as good as she did.

"Trying. Not necessarily succeeding," he sighed. He added more soap and took advantage of the slight distance she'd put between them to wash away the seed he'd left behind from between her legs.

Shock robbed her of breath when he slipped his hands to the scars and lovingly washed those as well. She still wasn't certain how to react to someone lovingly touching her breasts, but she fought the panic and allowed it. "Do you still put lotion on this?" he asked with a great deal of caution. She managed a nod. "Do you have it with you?" Another nod. "Then I want to do that too. Gonna fucking prove to you that I think you're goddamn gorgeous. Every square inch of you is perfect."

It didn't take a genius to figure out that he thought her inability to orgasm was tied up in those scars. Maybe it was. But there was so much more to it. She had no idea how to explain that though. She couldn't even explain it to herself.

Besides, she was still woozy and satisfied from the best sex she'd ever had, so words were difficult to produce just then. When the water turned cold, Jamie shut it off, guided her out into the steamy bathroom, and wrapped her up in a thick towel. It was such a shame that they couldn't just stay on Camden Ranch forever. Then they'd never have to face everyone back home. She could just go on ignoring Ed and her father and all of her problems. Spending every waking moment with Jamie and then falling asleep in his arms at night sounded like an ideal life to her.

And that thought paralyzed her. She'd never ever thought that about Ed. She'd spent most of her time trying to figure out how *not* to be around him. What she'd just described sounded a whole lot like a marriage and love. But falling in love with Jamie was stupid and dangerous. What if she lost him? She couldn't lose anything else in her life. She'd never survive. She knew.

"Where'd your mind go?" he whispered as he rubbed another towel over his impressive biceps.

"Nowhere," she lied. Nowhere good, anyway.

After their shower and trying to avoid the awkwardness that hung between them like a physical presence, they decided they were hungry. At least that gave them something else to talk about.

———

Jamie despised the barriers that formed between them as soon as she realized he was disappointed in their shower session. He wanted to fix it, but he didn't know how. He sucked at keeping things from her. Pretending that he wasn't confused and frustrated that he couldn't do to her what she did to him sucked.

Somewhere in the recesses of his mind, he remembered Dec telling him that he was gonna have to be patient. That blew. There was a problem, and he wanted to fix it now. Thinking of his conversation with Dec, Jamie cleared his throat and tossed his napkin on his plate. Casserole had been delicious, but he wanted to get down to business. "Can I talk to you about something?"

She lifted her head from her plate. "Of course."

He tried to gather courage. Damage control was going to be necessary. Surely, if he could convince her that Dec's ideas would be helpful, she wouldn't be too pissed. She'd probably even be thankful that he took initiative. Women liked that shit, right?

"One of the Camden daughters is married to a…uh…psychologist or maybe it's a psychiatrist. I don't really know the difference."

"O…kay." She narrowed her eyes, and Jamie considered bailing out now.

He sped up the next words. "And I think Holly, that's the Camden married to the doctor, is one too."

Charlie gave him a single, cautious nod.

"And they sort of specialize in sex therapy. So, Dec, the doctor, was up helping us with the wreck. And Colt got involved and, anyway, I ended up…kinda talking with him. A little bit."

The napkin she'd had braced in her hand dropped to her plate like a rock. Her jaw cocked to the side for a moment before, "Talked to him about *what?*" She emphasized the what with enough force that Jamie swore he felt the blow from the other side of the table.

He faltered. "Uh…well…I mean."

"What, Jamie? What did you talk to him about?" Fury scalded every word. Rage ignited in her all-telling eyes.

A harsh swallow did nothing to bring the right words to his mind. He produced some odd sounds but none of them were actually words.

"Tell me," she shot.

"Okay, okay. Jesus. Calm down."

She leapt up from the table and headed his way. Definitely not the right thing to say. He held up his hands in surrender. "I just thought maybe he could give me some ideas on how to help you."

And with those asinine words, she ignited like a fuse dropped in pure gasoline. "I cannot believe you. What is wrong with you?" She shoved him with enough force that his chair scooted back from the table.

Before he could react and stop her, she stomped toward the door.

"Wait. I'm sorry. I didn't know it'd piss you off so bad. He did it in a way you probably wouldn't mind if you'd just listen."

He continued to dig his own grave. She spun back. "How dare you discuss anything about us with anyone at all? Did it ever occur to you that maybe there's nothing wrong with me? And if there is, that it's mine to deal with. I'm the one who has to live with everything that came out of that fire. The emotional pain and the physical and no one, not even you, can live it for me. So stop trying!" she seethed. "Did it ever even enter your stupid brain that maybe I don't want to give anything else of myself away? Especially to you. Because if this doesn't work, I'm going to need every piece of myself to be mine so I can put myself back together all over again. But no. None of that ever occurred to you. You just want to 'fix' me." She made liberal use of finger quotes. "If I'm broken, then that's my problem! You have done a lot of stupid things in your life, Jamie Holder, but this takes the cake." She flung open the door and he was by her side in the next split second.

"I'm sorry," he tried.

She rolled her eyes from the front step. "No you're not. You're just sorry you pissed me off. You don't feel bad for what you did at all." She rushed out into the front yard. He took off after her, and she broke into a run. "Do not follow me!" were her last shouted words.

He watched her disappear across the flatlands surrounding them. The weight of her words bore down on him until he landed on his ass on the porch steps. Regret and guilt and a thousand other unnamed but destructive emotions took turns pummeling him. God, how could he have been so stupid?

CHAPTER TWENTY-FOUR

Charlie had no idea how far she'd traveled. The adrenaline-fueled rage had kept her moving far and fast. She'd run until she was out of breath and the stitch in her side demanded that she slow. Worried that she'd need her inhaler, which she hadn't grabbed in her escape, she'd walked slowly from there on. Eventually, the fiery anger subsided just enough to leave the smoke of shame in its wake.

How could he have done that without even thinking to ask her first? Did it never even enter his mind that it would be horrifically embarrassing? Every time she thought of what else he might've told a complete stranger about her and then what might've come out of his fat mouth to his cousin, she dumped more fuel on the blaze.

She could count on one hand the number of fights they'd ever had. Jamie was the one person who just always got her. Or he had been, at least. Clearly, he'd been saving up for the past twenty years.

Shaking her head at that, she picked up pace again. Nothing soothed her. Not the low bellows of cattle in the distance. Not the gradually sinking sun. Not the crunch of gravel under her shoes that marked her progress along the path.

Eventually, she stumbled upon a large house nestled against the few trees on the ranch. A small smile tugged at her lips, but she refused it.

The home was perfect—large porches lined the sides and multiple chimneys stood proudly on either side. She was thankful there was no smoke coming from either. It was a warm night, so surely they wouldn't be lighting those. It was the kind of house that looked like nothing bad could ever happen inside of it.

Instinctively, she walked closer until she heard voices coming through the screen door. She wondered which of the Camden houses it was. There seemed to be several people inside.

Before she had a chance to escape, Mr. and Mrs. Camden stepped out on the porch. They exchanged a quick, concerned glance before they both offered her kind smiles. Jessie headed Charlie's direction. "Are you all right, sweetheart? You look madder than a freshly baptized cat."

A warm flush creeped up Charlie's neck. "I'm fine."

"Honey, I've raised a lot of children, a whole lot of grandchildren, and enough animals to have filled the Ark a hundred dozen times. I know mad when I see it. You're a lot of things but you ain't fine."

It was such a maternal thing to say, Charlie felt bad for lying. "I... just got mad at Jamie. He's a..." she tried to think of what he was exactly. Something between a dumb jerk and an infuriating asshole.

"Man," Jessie provided for her.

That, at least, made her chuckle. "Yes. That."

"And they all seem to be our burden to bear. It's not fair but it's the way it is. Come on inside. I just made some of my fresh salsa. Food's good for figuring things out."

"Thank you for inviting me, but I'm not sure I have much to figure out. I'm just not speaking to him."

Jessie nodded her head and continued leading Charlie toward her home. "If you're not speaking to him, then come talk to me. We can make some bread for breakfast tomorrow. Kneading's good for the soul. Frustration always needs somewhere to go. Might as well be there." As she passed her husband who was making his way down the porch steps, she gave him a knowing grin.

"I'm heading down there," he assured her.

Charlie said a quick prayer that he wasn't going to try to get through to Jamie. God only knew what Jamie might tell Ev Camden.

She shuddered at the thought. How could something that felt so natural have turned out so badly? She should never have climbed into bed with him the night before. The thing that hurt so badly she could barely breathe was that it had been the first time in her whole life where she'd felt like she was right where she belonged.

The tense set of her shoulders eased as soon as she stepped into the ranch house kitchen. It hadn't been updated since the early nineties, but as far as she was concerned it was perfect. Warm and inviting and worn in all the right places. Nothing looked like it shouldn't be touched and enjoyed.

Two women who looked strikingly similar were seated at the table. They both offered her grins that were identical to Jessie's. She gestured to them. "These are my girls, Natalie and Holly. Their better halves are hashing something out about one of Natalie and Aaron's foster kids, down at Dec's office, so I'm making them hang out with me until they get back."

Natalie chuckled. "We love hanging out with you, Mama."

"It's nice to meet you," Charlie replied automatically. The name Holly ricocheted through her head and the shame sharpened its claws and took swipes through her belly. Holly was the therapist Jamie had mentioned. Charlie's only prayer was that her husband hadn't had time to fill her in on everything that had come out of Jamie's mouth.

"You're the runaway bride, right?" Holly beamed at her, like they were suddenly the best of friends.

Charlie took a slight step back. How did the day before feel like it had been a month ago? "Yeah. I guess I am."

"Good for you," Holly nodded. "I like a woman who knows what she wants and what she doesn't."

"It would've been better if I'd figured out what I didn't want a little earlier."

The three Camden women all laughed. Holly waved that off. "Nah, you went out in style. Nothing wrong with that. Sometimes we all need to make a statement." She certainly didn't act like her husband had said anything about Charlie, but maybe she was just good at covering.

Despite her adamant resistance, Charlie kind of liked Holly.

Dangit. This staying mad thing wasn't going to get easier if she ended up confessing anything to her new acquaintances.

"Charlie's getaway ride is being a man," Jessie told her daughters.

They both nodded in solidarity. "Idiots. They can't seem to help themselves," Holly said.

"I don't think he meant to be so stupid," spilled from Charlie's lips before she could stop it. Great. Now she was defending him, but Jamie was so much more than a getaway ride to her. He was...everything.

"Most of 'em don't mean to," Jessie assured her, "they just can't stop themselves before they do something dumber than a pile of manure."

Jamie had paced the length of that tiny cottage until the walls were officially closing in. Then he'd gone outside to walk the yard. He had to fix this. He just didn't know how. He'd figured she'd be a little pissed that he talked to Dec, but that she'd at least hear him out. Girl was almost always sensible, but sometimes she showed off all of her red-headed stubborn. When it wasn't directed at him, he thought it was sexy as sin. But when it was, it took him out at the knees.

Bile churned through his gut. What if she was lost? What if she had an asthma attack from running? She didn't have her inhaler with her. He shook his head and called himself a dumbass for good measure. When was he going to learn that she didn't always need him to rescue her? And why did it have to feel so damn good when she did?

Why did he crave her release the way he did? He longed for her to come apart on his hands, on his cock. He needed her to trust him enough to let him have that part of her.

Her words slammed their fists against his skull again. *Did it ever even enter your stupid brain that maybe I don't want to give anything else of myself away? Especially to you.'*

He swore if she'd taken a metal baseball bat to him, it would've hurt less than those shouted words.

When his phone buzzed in his pocket, he answered it without even checking the screen. Part of that was firefighter training, but most of it was the desperate prayer that she'd call and let him apologize a thousand times. "Charlie? Just tell me where you are. I'll come get you."

But it wasn't Charlie. His daddy's sigh was audible through the phone. "Well, I was genuinely amused about all this, thrilled if I'm being honest, but now, I'm worried. Why do you not know where she is, son?"

The universe was certainly taking its swings that night. "Hey, Dad."

"That doesn't answer my question."

His daddy was a lot of things to a lot of people, but patient wasn't one of them. "We got into a fight." He weighed and measured his words, afraid of saying too much and repeating his mistakes.

"What did you do?" There was no accusation in Barrett's tone, just an assuredness that he already knew who'd fucked up.

"So, you just already know it's me?"

"I did raise you."

Jamie couldn't argue that, but it galled him nonetheless. "I don't know. Things were going okay and then they weren't."

"Do you remember the time you wrecked the brand-new truck I'd purchased for you on your sixteenth birthday because you were messing with the radio and spun the truck out in the Mendelsons' ditch?"

Jamie remembered all too well. "Yeah."

"Good. Do you remember what I told you when you said that you had no idea how you'd ended up in the ditch? It had just *happened*."

Rolling his eyes freely since his father couldn't see him, he sighed just like his daddy had. "Yeah, you said trucks don't wreck themselves. But there was a pothole," he reminded his father.

"Glad to know that occasionally my words stick around. If you'd been looking at the road instead of looking at the stereo, you would've seen the pothole long before you were on it. Now, I'm asking you again, what did you do?"

He wasn't going to get out of this line of questioning and truthfully, he needed some help. He'd just be careful exactly what he told his father. "I kinda talked out of school about the two of us, but it isn't nearly as bad as it sounds."

Barrett was silent for a long, drawn moment. "That doesn't sound like you. I was sure it was going to be something along the lines of you deciding to throw yourself into something dangerous and her finally admitting that it scared her."

"I'm not that dumb, Dad. I know she hates my job. You all do."

"I don't hate your job, son." His father sounded genuinely taken aback by his statement. "Whatever gave you that idea?"

The question triggered a blasting cap of resentment, and he didn't have the energy to keep it contained anymore. "You and Mom cringe every single time I get a call at your house. When I go with you to Cattleman's out in Tulsa, you tell everyone I'm a rancher. You never even mention that I'm a firefighter. You hand out chores like my other job doesn't even exist. I get it, okay? If I'd quit, then I wouldn't have to work so hard. You've made your point a thousand times over."

A huff of air from his father made its way from Oklahoma to Nebraska via the telephone. "I apparently made a point I never intended to make. I'm sorry I ever gave you the impression that I gave you as many chores as I give your brothers because I wanted you to quit at the fire department. You seemed happiest when you were working. I'm the same way. I didn't want you to think I believed you weren't capable of doing both."

"I like working but not all the damn time. How am I ever supposed to put anything together with Charlie if all I do is ride a horse or ride a ladder?"

"Point taken. Your brothers and I are happy to redistribute the work. I'm sorry. I made an assumption and you know how the rest of that saying goes."

"Yeah, well. It's fine. Look, I need to go find Charlie."

"Just a minute. I've had a hand in raising that girl since she was eleven, and I'll tell you the same thing I used to tell her father when you two ran away. She only runs when she doesn't think she has any other option. And until she's ready to be found, you're not going to find her. If you spun out in a pothole by running your mouth when you shouldn't have, I'm assuming you had something you needed to talk about. Just how long did you give her after leaving her fiancé yesterday before you had her in your bed?"

Jamie ground his teeth. "You know, I may have hit that pothole when I was sixteen, but I don't make the same mistakes twice."

"Few hours, then, I'm assuming. I know I told you boys a hundred times if I told you once that I wasn't getting involved in your love lives, but you and Charlie have been dancing around this for decades now. I want you to be happy. The whole town knows that isn't going to happen for either of you unless you're together. That's why her father is so up in arms over this. He resents her running to you instead of running to him. That and he was more than a little embarrassed standing up there at his pulpit with no bride."

"What's your point, Dad?"

"I'm getting there, but quite honestly you just made my point. I know you feel like you've waited a lifetime for this chance with her but try to be patient. That isn't your virtue, and I say that because it's not mine either. Charlie has lost more in her life than most of us could even fathom. She cherishes people the way all of us should, because she knows how delicate this whole damn world really is. That's the worst of it all, if you ask me—broken people love bigger and harder than any of the rest of us are capable of doing. They can't help it, and she cherishes you most of all.

"You're going to have to make her feel secure before you try to alter the relationship you're both comfortable with. Give her a safe, warm place to lay her head at night before you're rolling her underneath you. To be blunt, talk to her before you fuck her. You've always been her safety net, but you don't think you need one. You've created a trust dynamic that does nothing but leave her vulnerable. Show her that you can rely on her as well, because that's what cements a relationship. Stand up and prove yourself. Her heart is already broken over her mother. You're asking her to hand it over to you. From what it sounds like, you've already almost dropped it. Stop trying to earn her love by being a hero and start earning it by being her partner and letting her be yours."

"So, tell her I need her? That's what you're saying."

"That and a thousand other things. You're going to have to go to the places she feels vulnerable and instead of leaning on your own bravado to bandage them, show her that you'll be vulnerable with her.

Instead of telling her that everything is going to be fine if you go from friends to lovers, tell her you're worried too."

Jamie let that idea settle on him. "How'd you know I was worried?"

"Because I was scared to death."

"What? When?" That was the first time in his thirty-plus years of life that Jamie had ever heard his father admit to being afraid of anything. He was Barrett Holder, head of Holder Ranch, legendary cattle rancher, the baron of the entire county, respected by most and feared by the rest.

"When I thought your mother was going to marry someone who wasn't me, and when I finally had the balls to ask her to reconsider. Then I had to become the kind of man who deserved someone like her, which I hadn't always been before. If you want to be the guy that Charlie does meet at the end of an aisle someday, then go to her, be where she's the most afraid, and exist there with her. Show her you're not any more afraid of emotions than you are of fires."

"That's...really good advice, Dad." Jamie hadn't intended to sound shocked but he kind of was.

Barrett chuckled. "You know, your Uncle Gentry isn't the only cowboy on this ranch with life experience."

"Yeah, I know. Hey, listen, somebody's knocking on the door. I'm hoping it's Charlie."

"Good luck, son. You can do this. I know you can."

CHAPTER TWENTY-FIVE

"Well, what do you *want* to happen with Jamie?" Natalie asked.

Charlie considered the question. "I'm not entirely sure."

Instead of helping Mrs. Camden bake bread, Charlie was seated at the kitchen table chatting with Natalie, Holly, and Mrs. Camden, enjoying girl talk with the added bonus of tortilla chips and the best salsa she'd ever tasted.

Holly studied her. "You're not sure or you're afraid to admit to yourself?"

"Probably that," Charlie confessed.

Natalie shook her head. "I know it's hard, but try to do things before the fear gets a word in. It took me so long to finally ask Aaron out, and it ended up being nothing but wasted time that we could've been together."

"You asked him out?" Charlie grinned at that. She loved Natalie's cowgirl spunk, and that she'd gone after what she wanted.

Holly rolled her eyes. "She asked him to teach her the finer points of riding, dirty cowgirl style."

Jessie cringed. "I am sitting right here, and I did not need to know that."

"Sorry, Mom," Holly giggled.

Natalie shot her sister a glare that Charlie had used on her own sister numerous times. "You're a sex therapist. You're not supposed to say stuff like that."

"I'm not sitting in my office, now am I?"

Charlie enjoyed their banter but there was more she wanted to know. "What did he say...when you asked him to teach you?" She needed exact details and also to borrow a little of Natalie's spunk because that's exactly what she wished she could ask Jamie. If he'd just get over the whole orgasm thing.

Jessie grinned. "He's male so he likely didn't say anything. He just started undressing."

Everyone at the table cracked up. Charlie couldn't remember the last time she'd laughed like this, but her fight with Jamie robbed the time of some of its sweetness. She'd shared so much with him in the past two days, and she still couldn't believe he'd told someone else about it. "I'm still mad at him," she informed her new friends.

Jessie nodded. "I'm not sure what he did, but I can tell you what I know about men. They have a goal. Most of their good sense and reason go right out the window of their truck because the goal has to be met. Now, sometimes this is a good thing. But sometimes it's a disaster. I doubt Jamie intended to upset you, but he got something in his head and he wanted to make it happen come hell, high water, or hunting season."

Just then the kitchen door swung open and Ev Camden stepped inside. He was followed by Jamie. Relief that he was right there in her proximity mixed with the volatile anger still residing in her bones and made her uncertain whether she wanted to run to him or slap him. Or both.

He looked like a puppy who'd been scolded, and he opened with, "I'm really sorry." Glancing around the table at all of the Camdens, he cleared his throat. "You wanna go somewhere and talk?"

"I think you've done enough talking," Charlie informed him.

His head fell and so did her heart. "You're right. How 'bout we go somewhere and I'll listen, then?"

Jessie gave her a reassuring nod, and most of the fight bled from

Charlie. He looked devastated, and she couldn't stand that any longer. "Okay."

Holly leapt up and opened the door for them. She grabbed Charlie's arm as they headed out. "If you're always afraid to tell him what you want, you'll never get it. And the thing is that he wants to give you whatever you want, but he's not a mind-reader. He's just a great guy and he feels really bad for whatever it is he did. I can tell." She really didn't know what Jamie had done. Her husband hadn't told her. Something about that bolstered Charlie a little more. She gave Holly a quick hug. "Thank you all...for everything."

As soon as the truck doors slammed, Jamie apologized again. "I'm really sorry I talked to Dec. And not just because you're mad at me. I had no right to do that."

Charlie considered his apology. She'd already accepted it, but she deserved an explanation. "Why did you do it?"

———

Jamie knew this was his moment. This was his chance. If he was ever going to be able to put this back together, he had to take his daddy's advice. He glanced Charlie's way, drawing courage from her emerald eyes even though he had no right to take anything else from her. "Because I've loved you since the first day I met you."

Her eyes goggled. "I didn't think we were saying that yet."

"I shoulda said it years ago. And I suck at saying the right things especially when I most need to, so bear with me, 'cause I'm going to be totally honest with you. It's like...I don't know...it seems like..."

"Like what?" she whispered.

"Like I've been making love to you for decades in every other way but physically. Like our hearts or souls or whatever have been loving up on each other forever, and I wanted so bad to get it right for you physically. I felt like I failed you. I still feel like that." He took both hands off of the steering wheel to hold them up in surrender. "I know you don't want me to feel that way, but I do. I can't help it. I want to make you feel the same way you make me feel when we're together like that. I want to give you that level of release. I want you to feel safe enough with me to let me own that. It's selfish. I get that now. It just didn't feel that way when I was talking to him. It felt like I was doing the right thing or I wouldn't have done it." He stared straight ahead and hammered the last nail in the coffin. He was sure this wasn't the right thing to say, but dammit, he was going to be honest. "I wanted you to... love me the way I do you, I guess."

Suddenly, her fingertips were brushing over his knuckles on the steering wheel. "I was looking for you," she whispered.

His brow furrowed. "What?"

"I kept looking out the window from the bride's room yesterday, and Becca asked me who I was looking for. I was looking for you. On my wedding day, you were the only person I wanted to see. I knew you would know what to do. I knew you would understand why I had to get out of there because... *you* were why I had to get out of there. You always take such good care of me, and I'm so sorry I never appreciated that until now."

Elation exploded throughout Jamie like fireworks on the Fourth of July and the presents on Christmas morning all rolled into one. He never needed anything else but the knowledge that he was who she wanted. "I wish I'd had the balls to speak up long before now. I could've saved you from ever having to endure Ed."

Charlie shook her head. "No. You were right not to tell me. There's so much I haven't told you. So many parts of my life I've never shared with anyone, and you of all people deserve to know everything, even the parts I know no one wants."

"Hey, stop that. There is no part of your life I don't want. I want the good, the bad, the ugly, the parts you think I won't love. I'll prove you wrong. Just stand back and watch me."

Charlie's delicate neck contracted with a harsh swallow. "Sometimes...I can still smell my mom's perfume." Jamie pulled the truck up beside the cottage, shut it down, but didn't move. He took her hand in his own, and for once in his life, just let her talk. "It's so weird when it happens, and it shouldn't ever happen because they reformulated that scent ages ago. It still has the same name, but it smells all different now. But sometimes at my office, and a lot of times at your house." Her chin wobbled, and Jamie eased his handkerchief from his pocket.

"It's...like this hug from her, you know? When I most need it. It's this reminder that she can see me and knows when I need her. I know it sounds crazy."

"It doesn't sound crazy at all, sweetheart. She loved you so much. I know she did." In his line of work, he knew that tears were often the most healing thing a person could ever allow themselves. Painful emotions were an internal churning fire that robbed you of air and of sanity. Water was the cure. He wondered if she'd ever really gotten to grieve her mother. It was entirely likely that she hadn't, not if she'd been rushed to a burn unit hours away from her family. He had so many questions. He wondered if she'd even gotten to attend the funeral, but he wanted her to talk instead of him.

She nodded. "But...the thing is...the thing I don't want to tell you is..." a violent shudder shook through her, and Jamie swore the earth itself vibrated right along—or perhaps it was only his whole world that shook. He wrapped her up in his arms and whispered in her ear, "Whatever it is, say it. I want to know."

She continued to tremble in his arms. He cradled her head in one hand and ran the other up and down her back, desperate to comfort her but unsure exactly how. "Sometimes you smell like smoke," choked from the ashen embers of her throat. He froze. "And," another quiver, "when you do, if it happens to be one of the times I catch her scent... it's like it's all happening all over again. I'm losing her again...in the smoke. I can't have both of you." She lifted her head. "I need her. I have to keep every memory of her because...that's all I have left." She shook her head as if that might somehow fix this. "I've wanted you for so long, but I feel like I have to choose between you. I think that's why I never let myself consider the two of us."

Jamie's response was unplanned, without any kind of calculation. It was automatic and came directly from his heart instead of his mind getting to voice an opinion. "I'll quit," he vowed. "As soon as we get back, I'll quit."

"No. You can't. You love your job. The whole county depends on you. I would never want you to quit something you love for me. I have to learn how to let her go...maybe."

"No." He absolutely would never allow that. "I will not be a person who takes anything else from you. You've lost enough for two lifetimes already. But if you ever want to talk about her, I want to listen. I want to know her the way you remember her." He was trying so damn hard to stop covering his words with his practiced shield of bravado and bravery. And he kinda felt like a pussy for it, but he had to get over it because the broken smile through her tears was like a damn rainbow after a hurricane.

CHAPTER TWENTY-SIX

Charlie tried to think of a time when she'd ever discussed her mother with someone who hadn't known her prior to her death. It made her father so sad, if either she or Becca said anything about their mom, that he forbade them from discussing her or remembering her out loud at all.

That made Charlie internalize every single memory. The first scrapbooks she'd made with childish hands and sloppy cursive were all about her mother. Every photograph they'd had in the home had been turned to ash, so Charlie would try, to the best of her ability, to draw her memories. When that didn't fully capture what was in her mind's eye, she would write and write every single thing, cherishing every single detail. She and Becca would sit up late at night and Charlie would tell her baby sister everything she could remember. She wanted Becca to know their mom as well as she had, even though she was only five at the time of the fire.

She wished she had some of those books with her now to show Jamie. Instead, she decided to tell him a few of her most favorite memories. "My mom wasn't the normal kind of preacher's wife." A grin found her lips. "She scandalized my dad's church with things like wanting to hold a raffle to raise money for the children's home or suggesting that we not have services one Sunday a month so we could work in the soup kitchen instead." She even chuckled over that memory. "This one time, she told a local Jazzercise class that they could use our gym for classes before she'd gotten it approved by some certain committee. Dad almost got fired over that. Oh," Charlie was beaming now, "one time, the wife of one of the church's largest donors saw my mom coming out of a liquor store, because she used to make this whiskey cream sauce that's amazing. I keep trying to remember her recipe, but I can't ever get it quite as good as I remember it being when I was little. All of the whiskey cooks out, of course, but that lady saw her leaving with a bottle of Jack and called her husband. He was kinda like your dad or your uncles in the church. Definitely not people you want to upset, and he was a teetotaler. It was a disaster. They wanted my mom to come in front of the church and ask forgiveness for drinking. It was all insane. I felt so bad for both of my parents. My mom refused to ask for anything from anyone. My dad kept begging her just to do it to save his ministry, but she said the church needed to try her sauce before they accused her of being a lush."

Jamie shook his head. "Just hearing you tell it makes me want a drink," he teased. A wistful glimmer lit the sparkle in his eyes, almost like he loved watching her remember. Maybe he did.

It was such a rush of relief to be able to talk about her that Charlie talked faster. "So, the church bazaar was the next week and my mom baked these cheesecake bars that were amazing and sold them for a dollar a bar. She wasn't allowed to be up there to run her booth, so she sent me and Becca to do it. We made over two hundred dollars before announcing to everyone in attendance that there was Jack in the bars." It felt so good to laugh. "She'd used basically the same recipe she used for the sauce only added more cornstarch to thicken it. The church finally decided maybe they'd judged too harshly. But my dad never really got mad at her. That's how my mom was, you know? Just one of those people who you could tell had the best of intentions and was so kind and so logical that you couldn't be mad because they're almost always right."

"Sounds just like you," Jamie winked at her.

She shook her head. She would never be as wonderful as her

mother had been. That was an impossibility. Her mother had been perfect, at least in Charlie's eyes. "I wish I was more confident like she was, but I'm not. I do think some of the appeal of marrying Ed was that I'd get to be in the same role my mom had. Maybe it made me feel like I'd be closer to her if I was also a preacher's wife." She cringed. "That sounds so stupid saying it out loud."

"It's not stupid. It makes good sense, honestly. Makes me feel better, that's for damn sure." His head angled slightly like he was considering his words before speaking them, which was not what Jamie normally did.

"What?" Charlie prompted.

"I was just curious if you get to talk about her with your dad or Becca? Seems to me talking about people we miss is kinda healing."

"I do with Becca sometimes, but she was so little she doesn't remember things the way I do. Dad won't ever talk about her. I know it makes him sad, so I don't bring her up ever."

"I want to know every single thing you remember about her. I want to help you remember, baby."

Life's breath rushed into Charlie's lungs. Elation filled her soul so thoroughly the boulder in her throat lost a few of its rough edges. "Really?"

"Really. But it doesn't all have to be right now. Whenever you want to talk about her, I'm here to listen, like I said."

"There's so much I remember that I don't get to tell people. I have all these scrapbooks full of things I recalled when I was little."

He grinned at that. "Of course you do. I love the way you remember things. It's so cool, all the details you keep in your head. Most people aren't able to do that."

"I just don't ever want to forget anything good." She turned and looked at him. She wished she could adequately express what this conversation meant to her. "Thank you for letting me talk about her. It means more than you'll ever know." She let her bottom lip slip between her teeth, and then went on with what felt natural. "I want to tell you everything I remember about her, but right now, could we go inside and talk about us?"

"Of course." He seemed surprised she'd asked that, but with the agility and assuredness she'd come to associate with Jamie, he was out of the truck and opening her door for her a second later.

———

———

———

Jamie took two Dr. Peppers out of the fridge and guided Charlie to the couch. He'd talk until all the cows on Camden Ranch showed up at the front door with beer if he had to. He was going to convince her that the two of them were meant to be.

"I want to know what Dec said," was her opening statement. Girl sure as hell didn't beat around the bush about much.

Swallowing down a sip mostly to buy himself a few more seconds, he nodded. "I told him that I couldn't talk about the two of us without your permission." For some stupid reason, he wanted credit for the effort even if he'd divulged more than he'd intended.

"But you did talk to him about us."

"Yeah, I know. I just wanted you to know that I get how badly I fucked up, but I did start out with good intentions." That got him two nods but nothing more. "He said that, for girls, orgasm is about a lot of things and for guys it's, honest to god, really about feeling incredible for a few minutes."

Her lips pursed and she narrowed her eyes. "So, you're actually admitting to the whole *you want to have sex and then have me make you a sandwich* thing? That's all it means to you? To feel good."

"Hell no," he scoffed. "First of all, if you can still walk after you've been in my bed, I haven't done my job. But it means everything to me on top of that."

She was so damn pretty even with water-stained eyes and red-blotched face from her tears. "Could we get back to what Dec said?"

"Right. Okay. Uh, he said that female orgasm is affected by what your religious views are, what your parents taught you about sex, and then what the world tells you is sexy."

Charlie shook her head. "That can't possibly be true because I'm pretty sure there are women who do have orgasms and if all of that plays into it no one ever would."

Chuckling at that, he took her hand and laced their fingers together. "Not everyone grew up as a preacher's daughter, sugar. But all that info is apparently in some lecture he gives at his job or something. About you specifically, he said that if I can prove myself to you, prove that you can trust me, then you might tell me about your fantasies. Or maybe about what you think of when you're able to have an orgasm on your own. He said fantasies are a way to heal from trauma."

"Why does he think I've been through trauma?" She sounded offended.

Jamie let that question hang in the air between them. Surely, surely she recognized that her life had been far from perfect. He prayed she wasn't going to actually require him to say it out loud. Another blink. Another sip of his soda.

Finally she rolled her eyes. "I hate pity. I don't want people to think I'm not okay. Do you have any idea what it's like to always have to be the poor girl whose house burned to the ground and then they had nothing? It's awful. Everywhere we went in Oklahoma City people whispered like we couldn't actively see them talking about us. It's not that much better in Holder County. We're still the poor pitiful Tilson family who lost everything."

Now they were getting somewhere. "People can be assholes. I'll give you that. But did you ever think maybe they're saying stuff because they're in awe of how far you've come under the rough circumstances? Plus, I've never treated you like you were an outsider. I don't think anyone in my family has either, but if they ever have you let me know and I'll put a stop to it."

"I know you haven't. That's one of the many reasons you're my best friend. I just don't want the Camdens to think I'm not able to cope or whatever."

"Honey, anyone who interacts with you for a half second sees how strong you are and how capable too. Give the Camdens some credit. Everyone's been through bad stuff before. Them included. Dec told me he's an addict, and I got the impression he was addicted to some hard shit. You wouldn't judge him for that."

"Of course I wouldn't. That's not something he can control."

"And your family's home burning down isn't something you can control either."

"Touché," she shrugged. "So, what else did he say about fantasy?"

"My basic understanding of it all is that I need to prove to you that you can trust me with anything, and if I can do that you'll let me in a little deeper. Then maybe kind of let me grant you some fantasy wishes so to speak." He'd been trying to break this down into small, bite-sized pieces since he had no idea what she was going to say to all of this. Jamie also didn't know what to make of the look on her face now. Her all-telling eyes were suddenly clouded with what looked like pain. "Babe, you okay?"

She shook herself slightly. "Wishes, huh?"

"For lack of a better term," he pressed from his lips.

She smoothed her right hand over the fabric of the couch like she could somehow align all of the woven fibers correctly. "Want to hear another thing about my mom?"

"Of course." Jamie scooted closer to her instinctively.

"Every single time one of us had a birthday, my mom would take all of the candles from our cake," she choked on that word and he couldn't stand it anymore. Setting his drink on the table, he gathered her up in his arms and settled her in his lap.

"Keep going," he soothed.

She gave him another distant half smile, fractured in places he wished he knew how to find and suture. "She'd take all of the candles and wrap them up in the paper from one of our gifts. She'd tie some of the ribbon around it and give it to us. She always told me to save up all of those wishes and use them on the thing I wanted most." Her shoulders lifted as if they were trying to push off some of the weight stacked upon them. "I saved all of mine in my desk drawer. We never had much money at all, but there wasn't ever anything I really wanted except for my family to be happy and we had that." She pierced him with a fervent gaze. "When I was finally with it enough to really think about everything that had been in the house that we no longer had, I remembered all of my wishes. I remember lying in the hospital bed and knowing that I'd lost every single wish because I never made one. I hurt so bad I just remember thinking that I wouldn't get any more wishes because I wasn't going to survive."

"Baby, my god," he soothed as he tucked her head against his shoulder. "It kills me that you were by yourself for all of that."

"I was kind of okay with it, because I knew I'd get to see my mom again, but I was scared. And then every day I got better, and it didn't make any sense to me. I didn't know how to be better. I'd never expected it. I told my OT that I wished that I'd used all of those wishes to wish that my family would always be safe, but I'd wasted them and I couldn't get them back. She told me that wishes aren't ever wasted and that they don't even require candles, but I didn't believe her until I got to that first day of school in Holder County.

"While all of the counselors were talking to my dad about all of the things I could do and couldn't do because I still had to wear the compression garments, I wished for one friend. Just one. Someone who would talk to me about things that weren't the fire or my injuries." Tears began to stream down her face. "So, see, you've always been my wish. The one that came true and that's why I didn't tell you much about what happened to me because I didn't want you to be a part of that. You were this all-new person who didn't have to know what had happened to me. Plus, I didn't really think I got to wish for more than just being your friend."

He wrapped his arms around her tight enough to hopefully hold them both together. "Well, that makes perfect sense to me because I never believed in birthday wishes until the prettiest girl in the entire world walked into my classroom on my birthday. Hey," he randomly recalled something he'd seen that morning while he was looking for the notepad, "come with me." He set her on her feet and guided her to the kitchen. Carefully cutting a large piece of the coffeecake that Jessie Camden had dropped off the day before, he pulled the box of birthday candles from the drawer along with a lighter. Sticking one candle in the piece of cake, he lit the string and held the plate between them. "Wish for more," he urged.

She stared at the flame for a heartbeat and then looked up at him. "Are you sure?"

"Never been more sure of anything in my life."

Smiling at that, she whispered. "Then you wish with me." Together they blew out the candle.

CHAPTER TWENTY-SEVEN

She knew it was reckless and even a little desperate, but she refused to not take this chance on the two of them. She'd figure out some way to be okay with his job. She refused to ask him to give up anything for her. Besides, it was her pain to deal with. If he could really help her keep all of her memories intact, then maybe she could learn to be okay with the times the scent of smoke robbed her mother's perfume from her.

Her heart thundered out an SOS as she accepted the blown-out candle from Jamie. The wax was still pliable from the warmth. He winked at her. "If I had paper and ribbon, I swear I'd wrap it up for you, but I don't. So, how 'bout I just promise to try to always make your wishes come true."

"You always have," she assured him. "Can I show you something?"

"Sure." He followed her into the bedroom and watched as she dug deep in her toiletry kit. She'd figured if she was going to get to really enjoy any of her honeymoon at all she'd be sneaking into the bathroom to take care of herself on her own. That's how her life worked. But just then, with that candle still burning in her mind and all those wasted wishes in her past, she wanted to give this to him if she was able. Wishes required work. She knew that now.

She retrieved a small silk drawstring bag. His brow furrowed as she eased the top of the bag apart and produced a jet-black butterfly clit massager. When Jamie Holder cocked his left eyebrow upwards and produced that sexy smirk that she was growing rather addicted to, it only bolstered her further. "It's my favorite," she explained. He produced a rumbled sound of male approval which made her giggle. "It always works for me, so…" if her heart would've just settled on some location between her throat and her reproductive organs that would've been extremely helpful, "I thought maybe we could try it together."

Jamie swiped the toy from her hand and set it on the dresser. Then, he crushed his lips to hers. His arms formed a sanctuary of protection around her. He'd told her twice that he had to prove himself to her which was crazy. Until that day, he'd never let her down and even then he was trying to do right by her. It was her who had to prove herself to him. Now, it was her turn to make some sacrifices in the relationship. She had to give him some control, maybe all of the control. And the most confusing part of this was how much the idea of that turned her on.

She drank his passion and his intensity, getting drunk on the way his tongue possessed her mouth. She didn't fully understand how she aroused him the way she seemed to, but for the moment she was just going to enjoy his fervency.

When his right hand gripped her ass with force, she shuddered against him. Instinctively her hips sought his. He ground her body against the steel ridge pressing against his zipper line. Her body rolled from the sensation and the movement broke the kiss.

His eyes were dark now, his irises cloaked with need. "Fucking love how your hungry little body begs for mine. That feels good, doesn't it, angel?" Both hands gripped her ass cheeks now as he slid her mound against his erection. "Tell me," he demanded.

"So good." Her eyes closed so she could memorize this exact sensation. She didn't need to see, only to feel. She wanted to remember every single thing about this moment and all of the ones that were going to come after it. "God, it's so good."

"Now tell me that you know I'll never discuss anything that goes on between us with anyone ever again."

Technically, she was pretty sure that was coercion, but she didn't really care. Letting her heavy eyes open, she tried for a flirty smirk but wasn't certain she'd made the mark. "I know why you did it, and I know you won't do it again."

"Good. Now give me this." He grabbed the tail of her T-shirt and whisked it up over her head. Her breasts were heavy, swollen up over the cups of her bra. This pain was so different than what she'd come to associate with her right breast. It was a pain that could be healed with his touch, with his mouth, with him. It was an ache that had an answer. It gave instead of taking away. "So fucking beautiful. I didn't spend near enough time with these in the shower." He popped the back clasp of her bra with one flick of his fingers. Skilled lover indeed. She found that if she kept her gaze locked on the fervency pinned in his eyes, it made it much easier for her to believe that her breasts really were beautiful, that they were the kind of tits that men would fantasize about even if that was absolutely untrue.

It was almost as if Jamie could hear her internal debate. He flung her bra on the floor and turned her, forcing her to face the dresser mirror. Instinctively she looked away. But he gripped her chin gently and positioned her so that she had nowhere else to look but into her own reflection. With his other hand he pressed her ass back until her cheeks were hugging his erection. She could feel his heat through the denim of her jeans. He thrust against her. "Do you feel how hard I am?" She nodded. "Good. Do you feel how fucking heavy I am all for you?" Another nod. "That is all because of you, because of your body, because I get a chance to show you how fucking beautiful you are, and how fucking long I've wanted to own you like this."

Charlie gave herself over to the persuasion of his hips. The confident sway and the strong, life-giving feel of Jamie surrounding her. "I... want that," she managed in a needy choke.

"What do you want, angel? To be owned? Done."

But she wanted so much more than that. She just didn't quite know how to explain it all. His hands cupped her breasts now, and she stared as her flesh spilled between his fingers. The pulse between her legs intensified to a rhythmic ache. A hunger. Her nipples scraped against his palms as the rope-worn fingertips abraded her tender skin. Every thought was dominated by the rough and reverent caress. He didn't go easier on her right or behave like the dimpled markings concerned him at all. "Don't stop. Please," she begged readily.

"That's what I thought," he growled in her ear. God, she loved that, loved when his own desire turned him animalistic in nature. "Gets my angel nice and wet for me when I get my hands on her tits. There's not a damn thing wrong with you at all, Charlie. Your body is perfect. So damn responsive to me it drives me wild."

How could anyone not respond to him? Everything about him was sure. Her head lolled back on his substantial shoulder. Surely, he was strong and steady enough to keep her most secret desires safe. Jamie rarely made mistakes at all, as far as she knew, and he never made the same one twice. Unlike her who'd spent most of her dating life putting herself in the arms of men who left her unsatisfied, who weren't strong enough to handle what she brought to the bed, who she would never trust. "I'm so wet," she assured him in a desperate whimper.

His left hand skated down her taut abdomen and popped the snap on her jeans. It meant so much to her that he'd not quickly abandoned her right breast, but she didn't have much time to be appreciative. His fingertips teased at the elastic band of her panties. His fingers on her was no longer a need, or some kind of requirement. No, it was now a matter of life or death. The desire arced deep inside of her. "Please, Jamie."

"Love hearing my name on those gorgeous lips. Do you have any fucking clue how bad I want to see my cock between them?"

"I want that," she urged. "I...always..."

"You always what?" churned from deep in his chest.

"Imagine tasting you. Imagine..." but she couldn't do it. She couldn't tell him just how filthy or how detailed her fantasies about him were.

"What, angel? I need you to tell me."

She shook her head. "I can't."

"Can't or won't, baby?"

There was a humming vibration throughout her body. Yearning, pure and raw, coursed through her veins. She swore the butterflies that had been fluttering in her belly broke free and were now wreaking havoc under her skin. "I...don't know how." It was as if the words hadn't yet been invented to describe what she desperately wanted from him.

Jamie's eyes shifted to the vibrator on the dresser and a wicked grin formed on his features. She'd been taught her whole life that sin and temptation came in the most appealing packages, but until that moment she really hadn't gotten it, and it really didn't matter. Her own father might believe Jamie Holder was akin to Satan's stepson, but she'd follow him anywhere. No questions asked.

"Bet I could come up with a few ways to help you tell me," he tempted.

"How's that?" Her voice was nothing more than a few breathy mewls.

He lifted the vibrator in one hand and took hers with the other as he guided her to the bed. "There's only one rule to this game—you tell me if you want me to stop."

She nodded and a thousand scattered thoughts wove together into an erotic tapestry in her mind. Charlie wanted nothing more than to play this naughty game. She shoved the shame she always associated with sex to the furthest recesses of her mind. Maybe, if she was lucky, they would starve there.

CHAPTER TWENTY-EIGHT

Jamie readily admitted that he'd fucked up a lot in his life. All of the times he'd fucked some nameless, faceless woman in the name of trying desperately to get past his love of Charlie had surely done the most damage.

But now, he had a chance to prove to her that he'd stop fucking up in an effort to have her. He'd do the work. He'd listen. He'd prove himself.

Halting beside the bed, he set the vibrator on the mattress and stripped her of the rest of her clothing. Struck again by just how damn beautiful she was, inside and out, he shook his head. "I spent most of my early teen years imagining getting you naked, but I wouldn't have had a clue what to do with you if you'd let me. But now, baby, I know. I still don't deserve to get to see you like this, but I sure as fuck know how to worship you the way you deserve."

Her tender grin revealed more about her than her nakedness did. "I wish I could explain to you what it means to be with you like this. You don't have to do more than we've already done."

But he did. He'd never stop trying to earn her. Letting his actions speak on his behalf, he lifted her in his arms and laid her out on the bed. She was a delectable buffet of femininity. Her breasts were swollen mounds of lush need crowned with her delicate pink nipples, so hard they had to ache. His visual inventory continued as he thanked the Lord for creating her. Her soft belly was pulled taut with her nerves, but he'd take care of those soon. For a moment, he imagined her swollen full of his baby, his lips on the swell, his hands holding his whole world in the two of them.

She spread her thighs instinctively as his eyes appreciated the rise of her mound and the wet satin covering what he intended to own.

"Why are you staring at me?" she whispered.

"Because you're beautiful. Because you're mine." With that he stripped out of his own clothes and climbed onto the bed beside her.

He stroked his thumb over the satin of her panties making her writhe. "Do you remember the rule?" fell from his lips. His tone was thicker than his cock which was so swollen he hurt with it.

"I don't want you to stop," she urged.

"Good." He spread her legs and positioned himself between her thighs. The heat from his breath on the wet panties made her shiver. She was a gift from heaven, so responsive to him he gripped his cock for a moment of relief.

"I could do that," she leaned upwards, but he settled her with a hand on her shoulder.

"We're gonna get to all of that, angel. Right now, you just lay back and let me make you feel good." He stroked his fingers over her swollen lips again just to watch her buck all for him. He'd never been a selfish lover. Yet another thing that hurt him about Charlie's inability to climax with him, but just then there were so many things he wanted her to give him, that he wanted to take all for himself.

Reminding himself that he just had to get her there, to help her work through it, he warmed the clit massager in his hand and then flipped it to its lowest setting. Setting it against the wet spot in those deliciously innocent panties, he smirked as she cried out for him. Her hands moved to her hip bones, whether to stop him or to hold the toy in place he wasn't entirely certain. He circled it over her clit eliciting a hum of pleasure from her. Perfect. "Does that feel good, baby? Do you need more?"

"Please," she whimpered for him.

"Tell me." Those two words were the entire point of this game. He knew she held shame over her body and over sex in general. This was the best way he knew to ease her out of that shame and allow her to own the things she wanted.

A dark fire lit in her eyes as she stared down at him. "*You* tell me."

He was more than happy for two to play this game. "I want you to fall apart on my fingers, honey. I want your pussy cream dripping down my hand. Then I want you on your knees. I want to feed my cock in and out of your mouth, making you take my cum down your throat. I want you tied to my bed, baby, while I take you hard."

"Yes. God, yes, I want that." She thrashed against the sheets now. He'd taken a gamble and won. "I need it," she continued.

He'd had a feeling. She was his every fantasy come to life. Her release was tied to her relinquishing her control to him. And he would do everything in his power to earn that right. "I know you do. I'm gonna give you everything you need to come undone for me."

Abandoning the vibrator for a moment, he slipped her panties down her legs and revealed her pussy, swollen ripe for him. The perfume of her arousal filled his lungs, rendering him weak. He fought his baser nature as the hunger to end the game and fill her with his cock until he was spent crowded his better judgement. Desperate for her flavors, he let his tongue dance along her slit. She slid her fingers into his hair and it was on.

He returned the vibrator to her mound, holding it just above where she most wanted it, until her clit peeked out at him. He rewarded it by removing the vibrator and bathing it with his tongue.

Charlie went wild. She thrashed in his arms as he held her hips in place and rewarded her. "So fucking sweet. I always knew you'd taste like candy made just for me." A newer, more intense awareness settled on Jamie. He wanted her to acknowledge that he was the one who made her feel this way. That her satisfaction belonged to him.

He returned the vibrator to her, circling her clit now. "It's perfectly natural to want to give up control to someone you trust, angel. To someone who knows what to do with it. To me."

———

"Yes," spilled from Charlie's mouth but she couldn't fully explain. There was a fine layer of sweat on her face. Her pulse drummed an erotic beat below her waist, and her body longed to dance to the internal rhythm. But still she couldn't tell him. The shame was too loud. She shouldn't imagine being held with such force…such possession. Her limbs being pinned to a mattress. His voice commanding her.

His tongue and the toy went back and forth working her over, constantly keeping her guessing. And suddenly, she was sliding down a slippery slope of need and pleasure. She couldn't stop it. She didn't want to.

As the vibrator buzzed, she heard Jamie's low thrum. "Because I think what you need is to know that when your pussy is wet and needy that it's a foregone conclusion that it's because of me. That I'll always take care of it. That it belongs to only me."

Her breaths gasped from her. She had nothing to hold onto, nothing but him. He tossed the vibrator aside and replaced it with his tongue. He simultaneously entered her with two fingers and worked her hard and fast.

The entire world spun around her. She couldn't stop it. She was going to lose her grip on everything, and for the first time in her life she was okay letting him hold her world together.

The internal muscles surrounding his fingers began to pulse. He lifted his head from between her thighs and gave her a cocky smirk. "No, baby. You don't get to come until I say. It belongs to me, remember?"

"Oh my god." She clawed the sheets now trying and failing at gaining purchase.

"Not until I say. Not until you beg."

"Please," she complied instantly. He somehow tapped into that inner rebel she kept locked tightly in her soul, the one that would defy direct orders, the one that longed to be a bad girl.

In an other-worldly form of hostage negotiations, he eased his strokes and kissed her inner thighs, continuing the build but denying her the actual detonation. "Jamie," she whimpered, "please. Give it to me."

"Not yet, baby doll. Look how wet you get for me." He dragged his fingertips through the sticky evidence of her need. "Naughty girl."

He buried his face between her legs, drew her clit into his mouth, and began to suck. His fingers stroked to the rhythm set by her heart. Her head pressed deep into the pillow under her and she gave herself over to his power.

The riptide of pure bliss swept over her. Pleasure zipped up her spine and exploded outward to her limbs. The rush swept her up and wouldn't release her until she herself released.

Crying out his name and allowing him to own her indeed, her entire body tensed in wave after wave of exultation.

When the breath finally returned to her lungs and she managed a sleepy smirk, she almost laughed at him outright. The image of male pride hovered over her. She was certain it was taking everything in him not to beat his own chest. "Proud of yourself?" she teased.

"Pretty much feeling ten feet tall and bulletproof, angel. But we ain't done."

CHAPTER TWENTY-NINE

He'd unlocked at least a small fragment of the deep secrets she thought she had to shield from the world. She'd come for him. Come on his hands. Her juices had dripped down his throat. He wanted to drown in them.

His control slipped, but the knowledge that she wanted to be owned remained. "This one's for me, baby," he warned, well aware of what to say now to trigger her deliciously rebellious side. It didn't matter that he'd come with her twice in the last two days. He swore there was two decades' worth of need weighing down his balls, and he was going to make sure she felt every drop of it.

Jamie turned her over and drew her up on her knees. "Arch your back, angel. Put that sexy little ass up on my stomach and give me that tight little snatch."

Her eyes goggled as she turned to stare back at him, but she wiggled her ass in the air daring him to make good on his promises. Gripping her hips, he drove himself deep in one long, greedy thrust. "You feel what you do to me? Feel how you make me hurt with wanting you?"

"Yes. God, yes, I feel it." She pressed back against him and spread her legs further. She wanted him deeper and that was a plea he'd happily answer.

"Good." His sac was heavy and slapped at her with every rapid drive. Her head was lowered, and he watched her tits bounce as they grazed the mattress. He wasn't going to last. Those tight pussy muscles that had just been spasming around his fingers were now taunting his cock.

He palmed her ass, longing to slap it, to know what she'd make of that, but he hadn't unlocked that particular piece of the puzzle of Charlie just yet, so he denied himself the pleasure. "Beg me for it, angel. Beg me for everything I've got for you."

As long as he took her mind off of her own pleasure and focused her on his she'd allow herself to have it. He wove one arm around her and strummed her clit again.

"Please," she choked on her own need. "Please let me...please fill me full."

"Is that what you need, naughty girl? Need me to mark my territory again?"

"Yes," hissed from her. She clawed the sheets now. Sexiest fucking thing right after her titties dancing on the mattress.

Jamie leaned over her and buried his head into her upper back. He wanted to feel her body react to his own this time. He'd been a spectator for the last orgasm. This one was indeed for him.

He groaned as the achy pressure pumped from his balls into his cock.

"Jamie." His name rang out in an almost panicked warning as she brought him to the mattress.

"Greedy girl. This one's for me. I didn't say you could come," he reminded her. And once again he struck gold. It wasn't as strong this time, but she did indeed release again.

He unloaded inside of her, filling her so full she'd drip for weeks with his seed.

Eventually he managed to lay out on the bed and draw her onto his chest. She ran her hands gently through his chest hair. "You know that whole tapping into my rebellious side isn't always going to work." She sounded much too sure of that.

"Oh honey, that isn't the only trick I've got up my sleeve. Trust me."

"I do."

———

Charlie had so many questions, but answers required the guts to ask them. She ordered herself to stop being so tentative. "So...was that... good for you?" Okay, stupid question, but she needed some warm-up time.

He chuckled as he brushed a kiss in her hair. "Good doesn't even come close to describing it, but you're stalling. What is it you really want to know, angel?"

"Why have you started calling me angel? What we just did doesn't seem very angelic." She was getting warmer.

"Because you are an angel. My naughty little angel, which is the best kind. I could call you sugar tits if you like that better." He waggled his eyebrows and she penned a giggle behind her lips. That certainly wasn't something she'd ever even considered as a pet name. "Besides, angels have sex, right? That's how they make more angels."

She propped herself up on her elbow and laughed at him outright. "You didn't pay any attention at all in Sunday School all those years, did you?"

He joined in her laughter, and it struck her how good it sounded when they laughed together. "I paid attention to you. The rest, not so much. I hated school, you know that. I'd rather have been out working the ranch, Sundays included."

"No," she shook her head, "you'd rather have been down at the fire station, which is another reason you are not quitting."

"There was never anywhere I would rather have been than with you, then or now. But you still ain't talking about what you really want to talk about."

"How do you know that?" Another question she already knew the answer to, but for some reason wanted to hear him say it.

"Because I know you. Because I *love* you. I'm lying here watching your mind churn in that pretty head of yours. You know there ain't nothing wrong with you wanting what we did, right? There's nothing wrong with wanting more than we did."

He'd told her he loved her twice now, and not in the best friends kind of way, but she just couldn't say it yet. People she loved got hurt. The person she'd never thought she could ever live without was the person she'd told that she loved most often. "What does 'more than we did' look like for you?"

He shifted in the bed and cradled her face in his hand. "Baby, I can lie here and enumerate kinks for you all evening long, but I think it'd be a lot faster, and probably scare you a whole lot less, if we just focus on our own."

The pounding of her heart urged Charlie onward. "I liked everything you said you wanted to do when we were having sex." Her cheeks flared with heat. "I always felt guilty for imagining things like that."

"Why?" He brushed a few strands of hair behind her ear and she was in awe at how such a small motion could make her feel so incredibly loved.

"I guess it's that thing Dec told you about women developing their sense of what's okay to want from the church and their parents or whatever. Weird to think about my dad while I'm lying here naked with you. Kinda makes me want to puke."

"Well, then we're on the same page there." He winked at her. "So, how about if we try to decide that as long as it's between the two of us and it's what both of us want, then it's fine. No shame. If you want something from me, say it. I can pretty much guarantee you that whatever it is, I already want it too."

Charlie smirked. "So, you mean you also have a fantasy about you wearing a pink tutu and a tiara while we're doing it?"

A harsh laugh exploded from Jamie, but he dialed it down into a smirk of his own in record time. "First of all, I would rock a tutu and crown and don't lay there and act like I wouldn't. I might need to attach it on my cowboy hat to keep it from slipping while I pound that pussy the way you like, but I'm nothing if not adaptable. Fair warning, though, seems like that stuff they make them tutus out of might scratch."

The image he painted so vividly, the easy comfortable way they were with each other—it was all so perfect that it gave her the courage to say, "I like being held down, which I know is crazy, I mean I'm the girl who always wants to know how to get away, so it makes no sense, it's crazy like I said, but for some reason I do," all in one big rushed breath.

All teasing was erased from the air between them. "It makes perfect sense to me," he assured her.

"Why?"

"Because then you don't have to be in control. It's not your responsibility to try to feel anything but what you actually feel. There's nothing wrong with that. And I happen to love holding you down and giving you pleasure, so it's yet another way that we're good together."

Unable to do anything but hide in that moment, Charlie buried her face against his chest. He wrapped her up in his arms, always the person who could restore her when nothing else worked. She mumbled, "Thank you for getting that," into his pecs.

"Come again," he teased.

She lifted her head, certain her cheeks were as red as her hair. "You're so obsessed with that," she tried to joke.

"I'm obsessed with you. The rest just comes along for the ride."

CHAPTER THIRTY

Jamie's phone buzzed on the bedside table. Refusing to do anything that might distract Charlie from what she'd just confessed, he studiously ignored it. But she crawled over him and picked it up.

He pinned her legs open over his crotch as she made her way back. "Put the phone down. I've got a better idea."

"Are you always horny?"

"If you're nekkid, or anywhere in my general vicinity, then yes, I'm horny."

"It's Wes. You should answer it. He might need you."

Jamie's brothers always needed him. That's how the Holders worked, but Wes could wait. The whole damn world could wait until later. Right now, she was his only focus. But Charlie wasn't having it. She shoved the phone in his hand and wiggled out of his grasp. Rolling his eyes, he answered just before it went to voicemail. "What?"

"Nice to talk to you too," Wes sniped.

"Kinda in the middle of something."

"Do you mean in the middle of something or between something? You know like, along the lines of Charlie's legs because if that's what you mean, what the fuck are you doing answering your phone, dumbass?"

Jamie ground his teeth. "Can we just get to why you called?"

"You told me to tell you what goes on down here. I was trying to do my brotherly duty."

Jamie had to admit he was being a bit of an ass. "All right, fine. I'm sorry. What's up?"

"I went into Odell today to pick up some new tires for the feed trucks. Went by The Kettle for lunch and happened by a table with a newspaper. According to the front page, that church out there that Ed's the new preacher of is hosting a meet and greet for the new pastor and his wife tomorrow night. It's a covered dish apparently, so if you wanna go you might want to pick up a bucket of chicken."

It was a testament to how little happened in their corner of Oklahoma that a church gathering made the front page, but it also made absolutely no sense. He held the phone away from his face. "Weren't you supposed to be gone all week on your honeymoon, darlin'?"

Charlie stuck out her tongue and gestured her index finger into her mouth pretending to gag. "Yeah. Why?"

"Wes says the Odell Patriot ran a story today that you and Ed were gonna be at some kind of covered-dish meet and greet tomorrow night at his new church."

"What?" Charlie jerked the phone out of his hands. "Are you sure it was for tomorrow night?" she demanded of his brother.

Jamie couldn't quite make out what Wes was telling her, but he watched her temper rise as she sat beside him in the bed. When he got back to Holder County, he planned to whip Ed's ass just for being a shitlicker but also for making her pissy when Jamie had her naked and sated.

"But why would he agree to that when he knew we were supposed to be out of town? And if it's a new arrangement then he really is nuts. Does he not get that I'm not going to come back and pretend to like him anymore?" Suddenly she grinned and switched on the speaker-phone option. "I'm with Jamie now."

They both heard the delight in Wes's chuckle. "Well, it's about damn time, I'll say that. Listen, you go make my brother smile. God himself knows Jamie's been useless as tits on a bull ever since he thought you were marrying someone else. Be nice if he went back to not being such a pain in my ass."

"You can go piss up a rope, Wes," Jamie retorted.

"Yeah, yeah. I'll see if I can't track down Ed and make sure he ain't had some kind of head injury or something."

"I appreciate it."

"Anytime. And Jamie, don't…"

"Fuck it up, I know," he concluded for him and then ended the call.

"Becca told me the same thing. Why does everyone think we're going to mess this up?"

"It took us a while to get here, so I figure they don't want us to waste any more time."

Charlie settled her head back on his chest. "That's kind of sweet, actually."

"I s'pose. Honey, I know Ed's tighter than a dick's hatband, but are you sure he wasn't having some kind of financial troubles or something? Guy's acting like he ain't smart enough to pour piss out of his boots. Seems to me if he's needing his new job in a bad way, he might not be real forthcoming with them about you leaving."

Charlie shook her head. "Not that I know of. It's like you said, he squeezes pennies so hard they weep. He was getting a paycheck from Pecan Crescent and Dad was paying him for his help around the church, so how could he possibly have financial trouble? His stupid Sebring is paid for and his rent is cheap." She sighed. "I should probably call him and see what on earth he's thinking."

"Fuck that. You wanted a week off. That's what we're doing. You can talk to Ed when we get back, and when I can go with you."

"Overprotective much?" Her tender grin said she really didn't mind.

"Always. And you've known me so long don't even pretend that you were unaware that I'm like this. I'll never apologize for it either. Taking care of you is why I was put on this earth."

She wrapped her arms around him as best as she could. "I don't want you to apologize. I love that you're like that." She loved that he was overprotective, but she hadn't yet said that she loved him. He refused to press her. He knew there was so much tied up in her head right now, he didn't want to further complicate things. For now, he'd just love her enough for the both of them.

"Hey, are you sore?" he asked her suddenly.

She shook her head. "I'm fine. Just trying to process everything. I thought if it ever happened when I was with someone else I would freak out afterwards, but I'm not freaking out. I'm beginning to understand the connection. I didn't really get how much I was missing out on, I guess."

Grinning at that, Jamie rolled her underneath him again. "Good. Now, hush up. We're gonna do some more connecting." With that, he sank his lips to hers and drank the hungry moan from her mouth. He didn't need her to tell him she loved him if she'd just keep making noises like that.

By five thirty the next morning, Jamie was only half-asleep when his phone buzzed on the table beside his head yet again. *In terms of sleeping in, this vacation was sucking so far.* But as he stared down at his baby sound asleep in his arms, he redacted his opinion. Absolutely nothing about this sucked at all. If he got to have her like this every single night, he'd give up his career without a second thought. Even if his stomach continued to twist painfully at the thought.

Rubbing his hands over his face, he lifted the phone. Ford? Realization had Jamie sitting bolt upright in the bed. "You okay?" he tried to whisper for Charlie's benefit, but her eyes fluttered open anyway.

"Uh yeah. I think. Callie's contractions are about a half hour apart, but I don't think we should wait. It's gonna take me an hour to get her to the hospital."

"Did Doc Thompson tell you to wait?"

"Yeah, but...she's hurting and something about waiting don't feel right."

Jamie had been the healthcare go-to for his family ever since he'd become a firefighter. He wondered if that would stop when he quit. "You can go on and take her if you want to, but she's likely to be waiting for a while there before anything happens."

"Better there than here," Ford ground out.

"All right. I'll give Doc Thompson a call. Tell him to simmer down as a favor to me."

"Thanks. Hey, she's several weeks early. You think that's okay?" His brother was officially coming unglued. Jamie tried to keep his smile to himself.

"She'll be great, man. I swear. My nephew's just gonna be like his daddy. Likes to get shit done early."

"Yeah, I guess."

"Hey," Jamie needed to loosen his big brother up. That had always been his role in their relationship. "When she starts really having hard contractions, you go ahead and put your sac in her hands and let her squeeze. Then you'll have some kind of idea what the hell you did to her."

"You're funny," Ford harassed but he was chuckling. "Hey, I know you're finally getting shit figured out with Charlie, but I was really hoping you'd be here for this." Charlie was now sitting up in the bed giving Jamie a deeply concerned look. Jamie had been his big brother's best man in both of his weddings. He'd always been there, bad times and good. Ford was the greatest big brother anyone could ever ask for. Jamie had always tried to emulate him when he was with Wes and Dalton. He hated to miss this birth too.

"Uh, yeah. Let me talk to her and see what she wants to do. Even if we left now, I'm not sure we'd make it back in time."

"Don't worry about it. It's fine."

Ford had guided Jamie through life forever, and that was the first time he'd ever gotten the sense that Ford was lying.

Charlie rubbed her eyes and yawned out, "Is Callie in labor?" Jamie nodded. "Then we're going home."

"Hey, I think we're heading your way."

"Really?" Relief perforated Ford's tone.

"Yeah. You get her on to the hospital, and we'll be there as soon as we can."

Charlie was already up packing before he even ended the call. He didn't want to miss his nephew's birth, but he also wasn't sure they were quite ready to go back. He needed this time to work on the two of them being a couple. "You sure you're okay with this?"

"Of course I'm okay with it. This is your first nephew. And it's Ford. You two have been attached at the hip forever. You are not missing this."

Nodding at that, he considered. "Okay, but what about us? We haven't tried us out in reality yet."

"Everyone knows I left with you. I'm fairly certain everyone suspects that we're now dating. And we are dating, right?"

"I was thinking committed relationship, but dating works too, I guess." He tried not to sound disappointed.

She dropped the shirt she'd been folding and wrapped her arms around him. "I like yours way better."

Grinning, Jamie placed his forehead to hers. "Does that mean you finally wanna be my girlfriend?"

She beamed at him. "Maybe."

"Do I need to take you back to that tunnel thing on the playground?"

"That won't be necessary. I think I've been hoping you'd ask me that again for twenty years now."

"I never said I was smart."

She closed the distance between their lips for a brief moment. Just long enough for him to taste his past and his future. "I was the one that originally said no, so maybe neither of us are smart."

"What do I have to do to get you to turn that maybe into a yes?"

She lifted her head and pretended to consider. "You have to keep on being my best friend, too, and still share ice cream sandwiches with me."

"Done."

"Then, yes!"

Jamie crushed her to his chest. Life just kept getting better and better. He knew they'd have a shit ton of manure to sort through once they got back home but he'd deal. As long as she was his, he'd make it work.

CHAPTER THIRTY-ONE

Charlie and Jamie thanked all of the Camdens for their hospitality and then got on the road. A parade of emotions marched through Charlie as they drove. She was going to have to face her father and Ed. She dreaded both, but she'd also never felt more at peace than she did knowing Jamie was really hers.

She knew she shouldn't want him to quit the fire department, but she also wasn't certain how long she'd be able to encourage him to keep his job. He loved it, but it would eat her alive every time he was on a call. She wasn't certain how long she'd be able to go without telling him the truth either, but he also shouldn't have to give up something he loved for her. That wasn't how things were supposed to work, was it? The war in her mind went back and forth constantly.

"When we go back…" she wasn't even certain what it was she wanted to say. There were so many questions.

Jamie threaded his fingers through hers. "After we go see just how tight Ford gets himself wrapped around his new little plowboy's fingers, we go to my house and you stay. We're still on vacation."

Relieved to hear that, Charlie knew it likely wouldn't be that easy. As soon as they walked into the hospital, word would get around that they were back. She would only really be safe from everyone wanting to know every single thing about the non-wedding, and her and Ed, on Holder Ranch. It struck her how many times in her life she'd only felt safe on Jamie's ranch, and how thankful she was to have an open invitation.

"You might wanna watch out for my mama," Jamie warned.

Charlie adored Sara Holder, so she had no idea why he'd say something like that. She'd been a second mom to her since she'd moved to Holder County. "I love your mama."

"Yeah, I know, and she loves you too. She's getting a grandbaby and I finally got things going with you so she's likely to be so happy she's orbiting the freaking moon right about now. Dad'll have to lasso her to keep her grounded."

"She has wanted grandbabies for a long time now." Charlie was genuinely thrilled for Ford and Callie, but every single time she saw a newborn, a twist of unwelcome jealousy turned in her stomach.

The unspoken question of whether or not the two of them would ever eventually have children hung between them, and she swore if he proposed to her right then and there in his truck in the middle of Kansas she would've said yes. That was thoughtless and stupid. They still had dating to do, and things to work out, and...well, she was sure there were other things. All those things she'd never done with Ed, she wanted to do with Jamie. If they were going to make this work, she wanted to build a strong foundation and all that other stuff her father talked about in the premarital counseling he did with newly engaged couples, the ones she'd brushed off with Ed.

"What's going on in that pretty head of yours?" Jamie took a sip of the tea he'd gotten at the drive-through where they'd gotten burgers.

"Just how much has changed in the last few days."

"Things have changed for me too, babe, so if you wanna talk about it I do seem like the ideal candidate for that." He winked at her.

They talked for hours, just like they always had. Jamie finally said, "I don't feel like we got to finish our talk last night before Wes called. I want to always be in the business of making your wishes come true."

"So, you want to be my genie in a bottle?"

"Hey, if you rub it the right way, good things happen is all I'm saying."

Charlie dissolved into giggles, but eventually they were back to her having to verbalize things she wasn't sure she could. "I like everything you said you wanted to do to me last night. Couldn't we start there?"

"Yeah, but I was looking for specifics."

She owed him that much. Actually, she owed him everything. "I think maybe that people have always been so careful with me. They see my scars and know my story and they're afraid to touch me, like I'll break or something. Do you know one of the best parts of us skipping class on my first day at school?"

Jamie smirked. "Other than you getting to spend it with me?"

"You're hilarious."

"I am aware."

She rolled her eyes. "It was that we had to run fast to get away before any teachers saw us. I loved that I got to run. My dad always freaked out if I got winded at all after the fire. I know why, but I always felt like a flower in a vase."

"Interesting analogy."

"It's the truth."

"I get it, baby. You were cut and shoved into a glass cage to be admired but not to really live."

"Exactly, and that's what Ed wanted from me too. I want to not be afraid, but I also really want people to stop being afraid for me on my behalf. I want you to be rough with me. I liked when you...you know, popped me on the butt that time. It took me a little while to understand that you might be okay with that. You're so protective of me, but not in a smothering way. It...was an unexpected juxtaposition, I guess."

"If you like it rough, and I already know you do, then part of my job in taking care of you is to fulfill those fantasies. Don't seem like a juxtaposition to me. Seems like it falls right in line."

"That's usually what I think about when I'm alone. You...using me." There. She'd said it. Maybe not the specifics he'd likely wanted, but it was a start.

Jamie adjusted the seat belt strung across his lap. "Gonna have to unsnap my jeans here in a minute."

"I could take care of that for you," she offered.

"I've worked way too many wrecks to ever do that while I'm

driving, but you can be damn sure that's what I'll fantasize about next time I jack off, which I'm hoping ain't for a long while."

"Why?"

He chuckled at her. "Because, honey, I plan to have you in my bed day and night."

Before Charlie could respond to that, her cell phone rang. She'd called Becca to tell her why they were coming home early but hadn't alerted anyone else to the news. She glanced at the screen. "It's work." She answered on the third ring and tried to plan out what to say to get her job back. But before she could launch into her spiel, the new director cut her off.

"Hi, Ms. Tilson, we have a bit of a problem that we're hoping you could help us with."

"Sure. What's going on?"

"Trisha can't seem to find your laptop with your patient files on it. We were under the impression you were leaving it in your office, but it doesn't seem to be there."

Trisha was the other OT at Pecan Crescent, and a good friend of Charlie's. "I did leave it in my office. It was on my desk, still plugged in and everything. It should be on the facility's mainline. All of my patient files are there with the Pecan Crescent passwords."

"Trisha insisted that you wouldn't have left us in a lurch. She says you've always been professional, but the laptop isn't there."

"Is it possible that someone else needed to use it?"

"I have no idea. I'm still trying to get my new office sorted."

Charlie knew the timing was bad, but she wanted her job back badly enough to plow on through. "Um, Ms. Billingham, since we are talking about me always being professional, I would really like to speak to you about perhaps getting my job back." The line went silent for too long. "I could come in tomorrow, maybe, and help you find my laptop. It has to be there somewhere."

"I'm going to need to give that some thought. I'm not certain it's such a good idea."

"Oh," Charlie hadn't known what the reaction would be, but she hadn't expected an automatic no. "Well, if you change your mind..."

"To be frank, I wasn't very impressed with your irresponsible, downright senseless decision or the way you've treated Chaplain Weaver. He's been so helpful to me since I started here."

Charlie's mouth dropped open, but she couldn't produce any words for several seconds. "Irresponsible?" finally spluttered from her.

"And cruelly embarrassing if I'm being honest. Ed was devastated."

Never, in her entire life had she ever been accused of being any of those things. She'd worked for Pecan Crescent for over a decade. Ed had only worked there for two years, and he was starting a new job in a week. How was this happening? "My reasons for doing what I did are personal, but that doesn't mean that I don't have them or that they are senseless."

"Yes, well, that isn't what it looks like from my desk."

Those words turned directly into flint on steel. Charlie's temper flared, "And just what does it look like?"

Jamie patted her thigh as if that would help her simmer down. It did not produce the desired effect.

"I don't have to answer that," the director countered.

"But you will." She'd only been there two weeks, and had rejected help at every stage, but Ms. Billingham always liked to have the final word. Charlie was likely digging her own grave, but she no longer cared.

"Fine. I will then. It looks to me like you left a good Godly man for the frivolous pursuit of becoming another woman in the lengthy list of Holder conquests. Have a nice evening, Ms. Tilson. I'm sure we'll be able to find the laptop without your aid."

She ended the call and Charlie considered tossing her phone out the truck window yet again.

"What'd she say?" Jamie finally asked. "When you go silent, I know you're pissed."

"Basically, that I can't have my job back because they like Ed better than me even though I've worked there way, way longer and he barely shows up for his own Sunday services."

"Damn."

"Oh, and my laptop is missing or something. Ms. Billingham couldn't find her butt cheeks with a mirror so it's probably still sitting on my desk."

Jamie was chuckling at her analogy. "You are so fucking cute when you're mad at someone who's not me. Trust me, honey, men will always show you their true colors. Sounds to me like he's been showing them at work for a while, but people gotta sit back and pay attention. Once they do that, they're likely to be begging you to come back."

"Maybe, but his last day was Friday, just like mine. So, neither of us have been there. Plus, he hasn't really done anything wrong. I just didn't want to marry him, which technically isn't his fault. Meanwhile, I'm out of a job. I can apply other places, but I'd need a recommendation from Ms. Billingham and I'm not going to be able to get that."

"They ought to take recommendations from your patients, not your boss. They love you."

That wasn't a terrible idea. Maybe she could make that work. "I do miss them. I want to go visit them even if I can't get my job back. Mrs. Garcia especially."

"You know, there's a decent chance that they'll let the wedding thing blow over in a week or two. Let them get to needing you, then they'll be calling."

"I can't go on too long without work. I'm going to have to renew my lease that I was going to let go."

Jamie glanced her way as he took the exit that would lead them home. "Move in with me."

"What? You cannot be serious."

"I'm dead serious. Let the lease on your house go. Move into mine."

"We've been dating for two days."

"Yeah, and best friends for two decades. Even if you decide you hate me, you can stay there until you find somewhere else."

"I would never hate you."

"Then why not?"

"I don't know. I'll think about it."

By the time they were pulling into the hospital parking lot, Charlie still wasn't sure what the right decision was. She decided to think on it later, so they could be there to celebrate with Jamie's family when the baby finally came. According to Wes, Callie was progressing slowly, and Ford was fit to be tied that she was hurting.

But the whispering began as soon as they passed the admission desk heading to the maternity floor. All of the Holders were highly recognizable in Odell. Everyone in a hundred-mile radius of Holder County knew Ford was going to be having a son soon. They'd been waiting on the birth of this child ever since the oldest kids had graduated from high school. To the citizens of Holder County, it meant Holder Ranch would live on another hundred years or more and would remain under Holder family control. The entire community's economy would remain healthy. All of the hospital staff knew Charlie's father because he visited patients up there all the time. They knew her by proxy and, based on the number of hushed whispers as they walked by, they all had an opinion on her life.

Great.

CHAPTER THIRTY-TWO

Jamie tried to keep an eye on Charlie's expression as they got on the elevator. Just like always, gossip about the Holders moved faster than two nekkid teenagers who just got caught.

When a couple in their thirties both leaned into one another and started whispering, Jamie cleared his throat rather loudly and shot them a glare. They hushed up, but he knew that wouldn't be a permanent solution. Dammit. He'd been hoping to ease Charlie into the churn of the rumor mill that ran constantly about his family instead of tossing her in headfirst right off the bat.

They exited on the third floor and headed toward the familiar sounds of his family.

"I feel bad for the baby," Charlie whispered.

Of all the things he thought she might say, that sure as hell wasn't one of them. "Why's that?"

"It's a lot of pressure on his little shoulders. He's not even here yet and people are expecting him like a royal birth or something."

Jamie debated. Did she think people were whispering and giving them odd looks because of Ford's kid? Surely not. "I don't...think people are talking about the baby yet."

"I know. It just occurred to me that it's a big deal to be born a

Holder here. I'm trying not to care what they're saying about us. They'll get over it. Believe me, I have plenty of experience with people talking about me wherever I go. That was my whole life after the fire."

Jamie tucked her closer to him and guided her into the waiting room that was packed with his family. They received a hearty welcome from the entire Holder clan.

His mother beat a path to them before everyone else. "I didn't expect y'all back so soon." She gathered them into a three-person hug and squeezed so hard Jamie was mildly concerned she was cutting off Charlie's air supply. When she finally released them, she took Charlie's hands. "Now, I have to tell you, I'd almost lost hope when I got your wedding invitation, and I am so thankful that you two have finally come to your senses. I know it'll be you two I'm up here waiting on grandbabies from soon."

"No pressure though, right, Mama?" Jamie shook his head at her. Charlie had folded her lips under her teeth to keep from laughing. He got several handshakes and slaps on the back from his cousins. His daddy and his Uncle Gentry were seated in a back corner and both smiling at him, so Jamie joined them. He pulled Charlie down in his lap to save his cousins from offering up their seats since there were no others available.

She seemed uncomfortable at first but relaxed a minute later and grinned up at him. Barrett chuckled. "I see you might've gotten a few things figured out since we last talked, son."

"Yeah, but we're still taking it a little at a time despite Mama wanting us to make good use of an empty gurney and then head on down to the justice of the peace right now."

His dad and uncle both laughed.

Charlie shook her head at him, but her smile had widened. "Shouldn't it be the other way around?"

"I was just saying for efficiency since we're already here with the gurneys."

"Don't ever be efficient in that area, son," Uncle Gentry said. "Always take your time."

"Amen," Barrett agreed.

"Is Ford still trying to strangle the doctor?" Jamie quizzed.

"Your brother, just like all of my boys, got a hearty dose of overprotectiveness from me. I've tried to simmer him down every time I've been in there, but only Callie has succeeded. I hope that kid makes an appearance soon. She finally agreed to the epidural, so he's been better since that went in."

"They give it to him or to her?" Jamie laughed.

"For a minute, I thought we might have to give it to both of them," Uncle Gentry agreed.

As the night wore on, Charlie eventually fell asleep curled up in Jamie's lap which suited him just fine. Most of the Holders who hadn't headed back to the ranch for morning chores were dozing in chairs.

"What did you do to make this a reality?" Gentry softly asked as he gestured to Charlie.

Jamie grinned down at her and whispered. "I finally said a lot of things I should've said a long time ago. And then I shut my mouth and listened. I decided to quit the fire department too. I think that helped."

Gentry shifted in his seat. "Are you sure that's a good idea?"

"If I have to choose, I choose her. I'll choose her every time."

"I understand that, kiddo. Did she ask you to quit?"

"No," Jamie shook his head. "She just explained what it was costing her when I'm at work and it's too much. I can't expect someone who went through what she went through to ever be okay with my job."

Gentry had his Stetson balanced on his bent knee. He placed it in his lap and thumbed the rim. "I hear you. Only problem is that taking a man who loves his job the way you love firefighting out of his profession often works about as well as pulling skin from bone. It's a part of you."

"I'll figure it out."

"Seems to me you might be selling your horse to buy a saddle. That ain't ever gonna work itself out."

"I'll work the ranch. It's what everyone's always wanted me to do anyway."

"You haven't ever loved ranching the way you love fighting fires. You know it and I know it. The thing about quitting something you love for her is that resentment don't usually come on all at once. It sneaks its way in real slowly over time. Sometimes you can stop it and sometimes it's taken over before you even realized you opened the door for it. It's mighty hard to get it out once it's in too. Think on it a little before you go talking to the chief."

Before Jamie could agree, a weary Ford appeared in the waiting room. He was beaming. "Eight pounds, six ounces. Poor kid looks just like me."

Soon everyone was up and congratulating the happy, sleepy couple and taking turns holding Ezra James Holder. Jamie had no idea he was going to be the kid's namesake, but he was thankful he hadn't missed his arrival.

When the little guy began to wail to be fed again, Charlie and Jamie headed back to the ranch.

"He's so tiny and adorable," Charlie gushed.

"He does look like Ford. Doesn't even seem like Callie had a hand in it."

"Your mom is over the moon."

"Yeah, listen, I'm sorry about her. She gets ahead of herself."

Grinning at that as she stared up at the star-strewn night, she squeezed his hand. "I definitely wouldn't mind having your babies. I just want to make sure we do all the right things so nothing goes wrong."

Exhaustion made the miles between the hospital and the ranch feel endless, but Jamie roused at that wish. "I'm not sure that's how life works, angel. There will always be some good and some bad. As long as we face it all together, that's all I think we can ask for."

"I know. I just want to feel totally prepared. I want to take it slowly like you told your dad."

"I'm fine with slow as long as we keep moving."

"I'm exhausted but I'm ready to finally start doing things that are right instead of only doing the things that don't scare me. Maybe if it doesn't scare you a little it's not worth going after."

"Sounds about right to me." They pulled under his carport, grabbed their makeshift luggage, and headed inside. "I'm beat, but I'm never too tired to make you moan out my name."

Charlie brushed a kiss on his cheek. "It's almost four in the morning. I got a nap and you didn't, so if anyone is going to be making someone moan it's me." She tripped over the empty bottle of Crown on his floor. When he caught her, she leaned down and picked it up. Concern dampened the intrigue in her eyes. "Do you have some kind of problem I didn't know about?"

"I don't have the problem that caused that to be on my floor anymore," he assured her.

"What was the problem?"

"That the woman I love was supposed to marry someone else."

Her exhausted eyes softened even further. "Jamie," she shook her head. Setting the whiskey bottle down she wrapped her arms around him. "I'm so sorry I was so stupid."

"None of that. Let's get some sleep."

She flung off her clothes and crawled under his quilts and blankets, and he was astonished with the ease at which she allowed herself to be naked with him. "I've always wondered what it would be like to sleep in your bed."

"What do you think?"

"It's cozy, but I'm really hoping you've washed the sheets since the last girl slept here."

"Been months since that happened. I washed the sheets last week."

"Come here," she beckoned. He toed out of his boots and flung off his clothes as well so he could join her. "Thank you for rescuing me, and thank you for always being there for me. I promise I'll figure out how to be your girlfriend and even your wife. I just need a little time."

"You take all the time you need, but you've already got it all figured out. We don't have to do everything perfect. We just have to try."

CHAPTER THIRTY-THREE

There were so many things that Charlie wanted to give him. Reassurances, satisfaction, and most of all love. She let her hand skate down the firm planes of his chest and her fingers ripple over his six-pack. Being able to touch him like this was something she wasn't certain she'd ever understand. It still felt oddly forbidden, something surely she would never be lucky enough to have. And yet, he was right there, tensing under her touch.

As her hand neared his abdomen, the heat pouring off of his erection greeted her senses. She wanted to absorb every moment of this. To memorize the heady sensation of his rampant desire for her. Using her thumb and middle finger, she traced the sides of his cock and reveled in the needy growl it produced. He sounded like a wounded animal trapped in a cage, and only she could save him.

"I want to taste you," she whispered as she let her fingertips trace and tease the steel-hard length of him. With a smirk, she said, "I want to suck your star-spangled firecracker."

They both laughed. His fingers wove through her hair as he angled her face up to look at him. "If you put that sexy little mouth on me, angel, I'm gonna come down your throat. I won't be able to pull out.

I've dreamed about it too many times." His warning was drenched in aching need.

"Good. That's exactly what I want."

"I'll be rough with you." This particular warning was a choked moan that did things to Charlie she couldn't fully explain. Her body reacted on behalf of her mouth as she bucked against his hip and shuddered as his hip bone taunted her clit. "You like that, don't you, naughty girl? You like knowing that you drive me so fucking wild I lose control with you."

She kissed her way under the covers until he flung them off. Spinning her tongue around his navel, she watched his eyes flare with desperate hunger. "If you want a taste, you have to earn it, angel. Wrap your hand around me and get my cock between those titties. Let me fuck them first. I ain't got patience for your teasing right now."

Her breasts being a part of giving a man a blow job had never even entered her mind. She'd become so accustomed to removing them from the equation altogether. Jamie had united them back to her in their sexual encounters, but this was almost as shocking as it was confusing. Yet, he did not appear to be kidding.

If that's what he wanted, then she'd do her best. She wanted this to be all about him. And the best part of that was—meeting his desires aroused her own. His satisfaction was the crown that led her to climax.

Her nipples were drawn to stiff peaks of want, and her breasts themselves were stacks of swollen need. Even the scars that night seemed slightly less pronounced somehow. She followed his instructions and held his length between them.

"Jesus, that's good. Feeling those nips press into me. Such a good girl," he grunted. "Do you feel how fucking slick I'm getting just thinking about being in your mouth, baby?" The pearlescent precum weeping from his slit had her grinding herself against his mattress. She did that to him.

Charlie nodded and licked her lips, pouring lighter fluid on the flames of yearning in his eyes. Such a dangerous and simultaneously thrilling thing to do for a girl who'd lived the life she had. But the fire in his eyes would never hurt her. It would never take anything away.

"Clean me up," was his next command.

"Yes," she let the whispered word caress over his cock before she complied. She wrapped her lips around his head and indulged in the earth and salt flavors of Jamie. He tasted like hers. She fluttered her tongue over his slit, trying to coax out more of his need, and listened to him roar out his pleasure.

"So damn good. Who the fuck taught you to do that? I'll fucking kill them."

Trying not to laugh at that, she shook her head. "I've never done this before, but I've read a lot of books."

"I'm the only one who gets to see you like this. Do you understand that? This is for me."

She nodded and then indulged herself in a few gentle sucks of his head and crown. He gave several ragged thrusts set to the rhythm of his hunger. She pressed her breasts together tighter instinctively and suckled at his head when he brought it near her mouth.

"So fucking good," he ground out and picked up pace. "Your tits feel like some kind of goddamn heaven I'll never deserve against me. And that tongue, baby, that tongue needs a reward."

"I love how you taste. I want more."

Jamie's hand tightened in her hair and lifted her face away from him. She pouted, which seemed to please him more. He swung around and steadied himself up on his knees. She was unable to keep her breasts on him in that position, so she wondered what was coming next. The fact that he kept her guessing only further amped her own arousal.

Keeping his hand in her hair, he guided her face back to his cock. "The deeper you can take me the better your reward gets, honey." Challenge accepted. She traced her tongue up and down his cock, making him groan. And then as she drew him deep into her mouth and adjusted for his size, he extended his arm down her body and gripped her ass with punishing force.

His fingers brushed along the center making her shiver and clench. "Relax for me, baby. Arch your back. Let me show you how good I can make this feel." Allowing him to lead her, she did as she was told. She took his cock deeper into her mouth and arched her ass up higher in the air. "That's it."

She began sucking in rhythm as he strummed the center of her ass. He throbbed against her lips. The forbidden sensations filled her with some kind of primal femininity she hadn't expected.

"Someday, I'm gonna make this little rosebud mine, angel. All mine. Fill it full of me," preceded his next half-starved groan. He sounded like he was half in agony and half in ecstasy, and she had done it all. "So tight. I won't make it one thrust before I'm pulling out and coming all over that sexy ass. Spilling down between those pussy lips."

Lost in his filthy words and in the pure erotic bliss he was conducting with his fingers, she moaned over his cock.

"Fuck. That's it. Tell me how good I taste." A shudder rippled throughout his body and that heady sense of power filled Charlie again. She craved more attention on that forbidden spot he kept flirting with. She pressed back slightly to meet his fingers and then took his cock deep again desperate for friction on her ass. She was desperate for more of this particular illicit reward.

She had no idea how this man that she'd craved for years, so secretively she'd kept it from herself, was the sin and the sinner, the savior and her redemption all tied up in one beautiful package. But she wanted every side of him to belong only to her.

Sucking him harder, she relaxed her throat and let the sounds he made, the scents of him aroused, and fullness of her mouth absorb her every sense. She focused on the sensations between her ass cheeks. How did that feel so good? How had she never heard of this?

Another rushed moan spilled from her lips and ran the length of him.

"Fuck baby, if you keep doing that I'm gonna come. If you don't want to swallow me, I need out now."

But she did want to swallow every drop of him, wanted him to flood her mouth. She sucked harder and he lost his rhythm teasing her rosebud. A lengthy line of expletives flew from his mouth as hot cum flew from his cock. She drank him down through the first few spurts and then pulled her head back. The next landed on her breasts. It was the first time in her life she'd ever thought of them as sexy.

He gasped for breaths and then cradled her face in his hand. With his other, he dragged two fingers through the cum on her chest and brought them to her mouth. Obediently, she spun her tongue over his fingers the same way she had his cock.

"So goddamn perfect. I love you so fucking much." He grabbed some tissues from a box on his bedside table and scrubbed her clean. "I have no idea what I did to deserve that but give me a minute and I'll make it up to you."

He collapsed on his back and drew her up on his chest. "You don't have to do anything for me. It was perfect just like it was."

"That ain't how this works," he insisted.

"But sometimes it's how I need it to work." He'd stripped her of so many guards, done things she'd spent a lifetime thinking were sinful until he'd convinced her otherwise. She just wanted to sleep in his arms and deal with the deluge of thoughts later.

"You sure, sugar?"

She nodded against his chest.

"You want to talk about any of that?"

"Why did what you were doing to me feel so good?"

A sleepy chuckle shook his chest. "You have a whole lot of nerve endings down there. Plus, sometimes things that we've been told are forbidden feel even better than they would if we'd never been told that."

Thoughts of forbidden fruits, and Eve, and temptation and then... her father flitted across her mind. Cringing at that, she squeezed her eyes shut and forcibly pushed those thoughts away. Ugh, who thinks of their dad after *that?*

"You okay, sweetheart?" Her tender, caring, overprotective Jamie was back.

She grinned. "Lots of weird, random thoughts."

"I'm here for weird thoughts. They're also totally normal."

"Let's go to sleep. We're exhausted."

"I won't argue that, but if you need to talk, wake me up."

CHAPTER THIRTY-FOUR

The next evening, Jamie tried to shake off what had happened in the shower as he wrapped a towel around his waist. He'd fucked her in the shower again, and again she hadn't climaxed. Maybe she didn't like shower sex. But what he thought was far more likely was that he'd pushed her way too far, too fast the night before, and she still wouldn't really discuss it with him.

"It's not going to happen every time," she reminded him as she carefully combed out her long auburn curls. "If I feel like you expect it to, then I'm really not going to be able to."

"I'm not trying to put pressure on you, honey. I just want to make sure I always do right by you."

"You do." She disappeared into his bedroom and started to get dressed. They'd quickly snuck over to her house, in one of his brother's trucks, and she'd grabbed a bunch of clothes and other things she wanted to keep at the ranch for the week.

They'd gone to such lengths that morning not to face anyone yet, Jamie was confused by her afternoon announcement that she wanted to go out. *Women.* Why did they have to be so damn confusing?

When he finished dragging his comb through his hair and putting on deodorant, he joined her in the bedroom. "You're sure you want to go out tonight? You know this whole town is gonna be all over us."

"As much as I always thought I would love to hide away on Holder Ranch every day for the rest of my life, I don't want that right now. I want to go live my life with you. We're dating so we should go out and date, right? People will get over it. The sooner they get over it the sooner I can start applying at other eldercare facilities. I want to work."

"If you're sure."

"I really don't think you get how accustomed I am to having people talk about me behind my back or directly to my face, even. You don't get to grow up being the preacher's daughter and not get judged constantly. So, add that on top of being the girl whose house burned down and her mother died and the sheer amount of pity—that's really just gossip in a Halloween costume—that gets heaped on top of you, and believe me, I can more than handle people thinking whatever they're going to think about the two of us."

"I do get that. It's my job to keep you safe. I don't like the idea of you hurling yourself from the skillet to the fire, so to speak."

She wrinkled her nose. "I know you don't, but we can't stand outside of it forever."

Jamie shrugged on a clean, white button-down mostly to watch the way her eyes flared when he did that. He still wasn't certain that she really understood what would likely come from them showing up officially together down at Rusty's Spur—Holder County's only loud and proud honkytonk—but he'd protect her until his dying breath. If she wanted to go, he'd take her.

"Besides, Becca said she'd come by."

And there it was. She wanted to go see her sister. "You know we could just go to Becca's house and hang out."

"Becca is never at her house. I'm not sure she even remembers how to get there. If she's going to be at Rusty's tonight, I want to go see her. I need her take on how my dad's acting about this before I talk to him."

Jamie lifted her cell phone from the front pocket of her purse. "There's like fifty-seven different ways to talk to her on this thing. But

I draw the line at you communicating via those Tik Tok videos. What the hell are those even?"

Charlie giggled. "I want to see her. I miss her, and..." she gave him a deliciously naughty grin.

"And what, baby doll?" Unable to resist that expression on her face, he moved to her and wrapped her up in his arms.

"And I kind of want everyone to know that you're mine." He could feel her cheeks heat through his shirt.

"Now that is a plan I'm on board with. You shoulda started there." He released her, waited on her to slip into a pair of ballet flats, and guided her out to his truck.

The Spur was packed that night as usual. Jamie kept his arm wrapped tight around Charlie. If she was out to make a statement, then he'd do everything in his power to hand her the proverbial microphone. He brushed a kiss on her cheek for good measure as they headed toward an empty table near the back.

He tipped his hat to his cousins Jace and Boone who were seated at the bar. They returned the gesture. "Glad you finally got your shit together on her behalf, man," Jace slapped him on the shoulder as they passed.

"Better late than never, right?" Jamie offered for lack of anything better to say.

Every eye in the bar was on them. Why people cared what the Holders did still didn't make any sense to Jamie. But apparently everyone did. He pulled her into the booth beside him. If they were gonna make a statement, they might as well leave no room for doubt. "I'll never get why so many people care what me and my family do," he whispered.

She offered him a sympathetic gaze. "You're Jamie Holder, and you're out with the preacher's daughter. It's only going to get worse. Are you okay with that?"

"I'm down for whatever you want. I just don't get the fascination with us. We've been running the ranch for hundreds of years now. Ain't nothing about that going to change."

"You're kind of cowboy royalty," she informed him. "I know you don't want that, but you are."

"Yeah, well, you can call me the king of Fuck that Nonsense."

The waitress made a beeline to their table. "What can I get y'all?"

"I'll take a Crown and Coke," Jamie ordered then turned to Charlie. "You want a glass of red?"

Charlie glanced around the room at all of the people, trying and failing to pretend that they weren't staring. "Uh no, I'll just have a club soda, please."

"Sure. No problem. We heard you two were back in town this morning. You running from your wedding is all anyone can talk about. I keep telling people, look, if you get the chance to get yourself a stallion you don't walk down the aisle to meet a donkey. It's simple as that."

Charlie choked back laughter while Jamie made no such effort. He laughed at her outright. "Could you hurry it up with our drinks?"

The waitress sighed. "Yeah. Sure. You want it on the Holder tab?"

"No," he reached for his wallet. "I got it."

"Such a stallion," Charlie harassed as she whispered a kiss on his jawline.

"Don't you forget it."

When the waitress left, Charlie scooted even closer to him. "I don't get why everyone is shocked I'm with you. They've seen us together before. We've been hanging out together for decades. I get that brides don't run all that often, but it can't possibly be this fascinating."

"Are you not drinking because of your daddy?" Jamie asked.

"Yeah. People tend to call and rat me out, and that's a pain for him. It's just easier not to drink in public. Plus, I kind of like soda."

"Right. It's easier not to. I think both of us have grown up doing a lot of things because of who our daddies are, and I think for the most part people are so interested in us for the same reason."

"What does us going from friends to lovers have to do with our fathers?"

"Baby, don't you get it? My family has a reputation of being way more sinner than saint, and I ain't saying we didn't earn it, but you're Reverend Tilson's daughter. I'm ruining your reputation with mine."

She shook her head at him. "Well, now I'll be the queen of Fuck that Nonsense."

"See that, I've already got you cursing like a cattle rancher. Half the people in here are worried over you, and maybe they're right. But the other half want to come over here and shake my hand. Whole damn town drives me nuts."

"I do not need anyone to worry over me. You're the best person I've ever met. So, if some of the Holders are more sinner than saint, you're still not."

Jamie made certain no one could hear them and lowered his voice another few decibels to be safe. "Pretty sure saints don't talk women into doing what I had you doing last night."

"I don't really want to have this conversation with you in here, but I will say this—I loved what we did last night. I love being with you like that. I love being with you no matter what we're doing, but no one has ever made me feel the way you make me feel. That's why I'm sitting right here beside you. I'd really appreciate it if you'd get over your own self-imposed guilt and stop obsessively worrying about me. I'm not a dried flower. I won't fall apart if you shake me."

Well damn. All right. Maybe he had gotten too caught up in his own head. "Sorry," he offered quietly. "I'll get over myself."

But she wasn't finished. "I also don't care what anyone in here thinks. That's why we needed to come out tonight. People can see us together and move on."

"You cared enough not to drink," he couldn't help but argue.

"I don't care what people think about me and you. Not wanting to get my father in trouble with the church board is a whole different thing. Besides, you didn't put our drinks on the Holder tab because you don't like the idea that your father pays that bill."

Jamie couldn't argue that. "I don't need people taking care of me. It's my job to take care of them."

Suddenly Becca spun into the booth seat across from theirs. "Hey, Sis. You look good and fucked," she goaded her sister.

Delight sparkled in Charlie's eyes and her megawatt grin at her sister made Jamie feel guilty for trying to keep her at his house. "You're here!" She all but applauded. "And being supremely crass, as usual."

"I am not crass. I'm just calling it like I see it."

"I want to know what Dad did and said after I left"

Becca rolled her eyes but managed a smile for the waitress who delivered their drinks. "Dad is going to be Dad. I don't get why you worry so much about what he thinks." In a distinct juxtaposition to her big sister, Becca proceeded to order a martini with an extra shot.

"What did he say?"

Becca shifted uncomfortably, and Jamie tucked Charlie closer to him. This was going to be ugly. He could feel it.

"Just tell me," Charlie prompted.

"That he was hurt and disappointed...in you."

But Charlie didn't seem rattled. "Is that it?"

"Louann tried to talk to him and explain that you'd been in love with Jamie forever and that you'd only agreed to marry Ed to make Dad happy. But Dad went on for most of dinner about the sacrament of marriage, and honoring vows, and seals on your heart or some jazz like that. Honestly, I don't know. I zoned out for like half of it. You know I can't pay attention when he starts in on all the Johns. I mean, how many Johns were there in biblical times? Or are they all the same dude? Why couldn't there have been sexier names back then? Like Zeke, maybe."

Charlie gave her sister a withering glare. "You do know there is a book of Ezekiel in the Bible, right?"

"Seriously?"

"Yes."

"Who knew?"

Jamie cut in, "Even I knew that."

Becca gave them both a sweet but defiant grin. "I'll look it up. Anyway, Daddy wants us both to come to breakfast with him and Louann at their house tomorrow at seven o'clock. And he wants you to come alone." She wrinkled her nose which was a duplicate of her sister's. "On the plus side, Louann is making her bacon strata so at least that will be good."

"I'll come. I have a few things I'd like to say to our father."

Becca gave mock applause. "My big sissy really did finally find her balls."

Jamie was just about to inform both of them that Charlie wasn't going alone. He'd be there. But Becca's proclamation gave him pause.

He didn't want to be overbearing or make Charlie feel like he thought she couldn't handle herself. Negotiating that, he decided on, "If you want me to come, welcome or not, I'll be there."

Charlie grinned at him. "I've got this. You sleep in. You're still on vacation, remember?"

"Yeah, like my daddy isn't gonna have my ass up on a horse first thing in the morning." He downed another sip of his drink.

"Have you talked to Ed?" was Charlie's next question for her sister.

"I drove by his house last night just to do some spying on your behalf. His car was there, but as far as I know no one's seen him in town lately."

"He tried to access my checking account and he told his new church that I'd be at a covered-dish dinner last night."

"I told you he was a twat-waffle."

"But why would he do that? Wouldn't he not want to make promises he knows he can't keep, especially to his new employer?"

Becca considered for a moment. "I don't think that's Ed's game. I don't think he cares anything at all about promises. I think he wants to control you. I think that's what he's always wanted."

"That still doesn't explain why he'd do what he did," Charlie pointed out. The gnawing in Jamie's gut over Ed's actions hadn't let up in days, but he wasn't able to come up with a logical answer either. What was the guy up to? And why?

Becca swiveled in her seat when a contagion of gasps worked through the bar crowd. She turned back with her mouth hanging open. "Uh, well, you could ask him I guess because he just walked in."

CHAPTER THIRTY-FIVE

Jamie's chest expanded with a deep breath. His muscles contracted of their own accord as he stared down Ed who was heading their way.

Jace and Boone were right behind him and looked way too eager to leave a Holder brand on Ed.

"Fucker does not want to do this," Jamie spat through his teeth.

Charlie shot him a pleading look. "Don't hurt him. Please. He's just being stupid."

"Not gonna start anything, but if he does, I guarantee we'll finish it," he quickly explained the way the Holders fought before he stood up out of the booth. "You lost, preacher boy?" He gestured to the bar. "Not your usual digs, now is it?"

"Jamie!" Charlie huffed. Much to his dismay, she stood and positioned herself between him and Ed. "Why are you here, Ed? This is ridiculous."

"I'm here to take you home," Ed informed her like she was some kind of insolent child.

An almost inhuman snarl sounded from Jamie. "You are fucking my last nerve, boy, and that ain't gonna end well for you."

"We'd love to see you try to make her go with you," Jace laughed in

Ed's face. "None of us take too kindly to assholes who try to make women do something they don't wanna do, especially one of our own."

Charlie was still standing in the center ring of this shitshow. Jamie had to get her away from Ed and away from his cousins before she was in the middle of the flying fists. Jace was a bronc rider by trade, and his temper was even shorter than his worst rides. Boone had only slightly more logic in the head on his shoulders, but he'd come out swinging in the name of Holder pride quicker than a lightning strike.

"Let's go, Charlie. I think you've made enough of a fool of both of us," Ed sneered.

A blood-red haze of fury flared in Jamie's vision as he lunged to yank Charlie out of the way, but she held her ground. "You, calm down," she ordered Jamie. "And you," she spat at Ed, "are obviously delusional. I'm really not sure how to make it any more obvious that I want nothing to do with you than leaving you at the altar. I don't have to make you look like a fool. You do that all on your own. I have no idea what your game is but telling your new church that I'm going to be attending events with you is borderline insane, and stay the hell out of my checking account. Walk away. I never want to see you again."

Ed's beady eyes flipped from Charlie to Jamie and back again. And then he dropped the lit match on the soaked fuse. "That's not how this works, Charlotte. I do have some say over the fact that you're perfectly happy to just lie down and become another Holder whore."

A quick gasp echoed from Becca as she yanked her sister out of the way. Jace caught Ed from behind and held him in place. Like an over-pumped shotgun, Jamie burst forward, but before his fist connected with Ed's vile face, someone caught his arm and pushed him back.

Everyone gathered around the fight took several steps back as Barrett Holder entered the ring. "Simmer down, son. He's not worth it. Jace, let him go." Terror rode hard in Ed's eyes. Having been robbed of a brawl, Jace shoved Ed forward much harder than was necessary.

The adrenaline rolling off of Jamie was palpable in the air surrounding them. "If you ever call her another name, my father won't be able to stop me," he spat.

"He's not going to ever say anything like that again, because he's not nearly as stupid as he looks," Barrett spoke calmly and with the authority of the man who called every shot in that county. "Ed, I get that your pride is hurt, but don't be a fool. Stay the hell away from my kids and away from Charlie. Don't press me. I pack an even bigger punch than my son, but I won't be here to save you next time."

CHAPTER THIRTY-SIX

"I'm taking you home," Jamie informed her as he slammed his truck door.

"I'm sorry, what?" she huffed.

"You don't want to be around me for a while."

"Why is that?"

Instead of answering that question, Jamie exploded. "Who the hell does my father think he is getting in the middle like that? I don't need his help. I don't need anybody's help."

"That's right. You're the only one who gets to be a savior, right?"

"What the hell is that supposed to mean?"

"You're just fine as long as you're the one cast as the hero in every situation, but man, as soon as I or anyone else wants to step in and help you out, we become the villain fast."

"I didn't say that."

"You don't have to say it. I know you. You taking me home because you're in a bad mood is not how relationships work, and maybe your father stepped in because you were letting your ego make all your decisions."

Jamie gripped the steering wheel so tightly he was mildly

concerned he was going to rip it from the console. "I like making things better, okay? Is that such a bad thing?"

"Not unless you ruin relationships in the process. It's okay that you need some help sometimes. You want me to be your wife, but you don't want me to really have an equal role in the relationship. I don't want to always be the one who needs to be saved, Jamie. I'm not a damsel in distress. Your father had every right to keep you from being an ass tonight."

Since that sounded a lot like what his father had told him the last time he and Charlie argued, he dialed his temper down a notch or two. "I do want you to be an equal partner, and it doesn't seem like it should be a freaking crime that I like saving people, especially people I love. But for the record, I never thought you were ever a damsel in distress."

"Prove it."

"And how do I do that?"

"Tell me what you're scared of, and then tell me what you'd do when we get to your house if I was just some random girl you were blowing off steam with."

"I'm angry, not scared."

"Trust me, they're always one and the same."

Jamie shook his head and refused to comment. He was driving under the Holder Ranch sign on his father's side of the ranch before it occurred to him that he hadn't made good on taking her home. He didn't want her to spend the night away from him, but he was afraid to show her the way he could be when he was pissed like this. Holy fuck. She was right. He was scared. "I'm scared for you to see me angry, okay?" And somehow that confession led to others. "Everyone keeps telling me not to fuck it up like they're sure I'm going to. I'm scared that I won't always do right by you. And goddammit, I'm..."

"Just say it," she soothed.

"Scared if I quit my job I'll end up resenting you. I'm scared I'll never be good enough for you. That I'm gonna somehow turn you into exactly what Ed called you. That's all I know how to do. That's all I've ever done."

By the time he finished his diatribe, they were at his house. Somehow, she didn't even look offended. "Nothing about you being angry scares me," she whispered. "It would scare me more if you stuffed all of that away and never told me any of it. I don't want a relationship where we're not allowed to feel how we feel."

"Yeah, well, I don't want to feel like this."

"We don't always get a choice in that. Do you plan to *really* use me and then move on in a day or two instead of that just being a fantasy?"

"Of course not."

"Do you get that you don't get to decide how other people see me or you? If people want to think that I'm a *Holder whore,* then that's their problem, not ours."

Jamie let his head fall forward onto the steering wheel. "Please stop saying that."

"Sorry. But it's true. You have been the very best person you could ever have been to me for the last twenty years, so you thinking you're somehow not good enough is ridiculous. You seem to have me put up on this ridiculous pedestal that you somehow don't think you can ever reach. I don't want to be up there. I want to be down here right beside you. I don't know how many different ways to show you that. You don't have to do anything to earn me. I'm right here, right where I want to be."

That just couldn't be true. All the shit people said about his family...some of it was accurate. He had to always be the hero because that was the only way he'd ever deserve to be hers. "I don't want to ruin you," choked from him.

"But that's exactly what I want."

She climbed out of his truck and headed into the house. He followed after her, tracked her to the bedroom, and watched intently as she spun back to face him. Stubborn defiance lit in her eyes as she stared him down. Her fingers flew to the top button on her blouse and slipped it seductively through its closure. She slowed with the next, only amping up the ravenous need running rampant through his veins.

A rumble of frustrated hunger curled up from low in his throat as she tossed the shirt away. "Use me," she demanded.

"I...can't."

She popped the snap on her jeans. "Can't or won't?" He stared as she slipped them down her shapely legs and stepped out of them. His eyes zeroed in on the wet satin panties she was wearing. "I hurt," she cooed. His fantasy come to life. A walking wet dream standing before him asking him to be rough. "Make it better. You're the only person who can."

Fuck him. He lost all ability to talk himself out of this. Diving across the few feet that existed between them, he ravaged her mouth with his own. She was so much more than just one of his conquests, and he was desperate to prove that he was more than testosterone and muscle and bad judgement.

But there was knowledge in the way she kissed him. The familiarity drained him of a little of his outrage. He didn't have to prove himself to the county. He only ever had to prove himself to her. She'd told him exactly what she wanted.

It wasn't her that needed to be saved. It was him, and she was holding out her hand and telling him to take it.

He yanked his own shirt off and then turned her so she was facing his footboard. He used the shirt to bind her hands to the bed. She shuddered from his force. "Yes," she whimpered. "Please don't stop."

"I'm just fucking getting started, honey," he assured her.

He toed out of his boots and shed the rest of his clothes. He gripped her ass hard and rough, ashamed but unable to keep himself from her flesh. She wiggled that sexy as sin ass all for him. He swatted her twice and then pressed his fingers to the crotch of her panties and growled out, "Such a good girl. So nice and wet for me."

Her breaths disintegrated into vibrations, and her moans were half-starved for more.

Dropping to his knees, he hooked his fingers in the panties and slowly slid them down her legs but left them as a strap for her ankles. He raked his teeth over the thick globes of her ass and then nipped until he was certain she'd have marks. The cream of her arousal soaked the tender curls between her legs, and her scent made him savage.

He spread her cheeks and feathered his tongue over that puckered little rosebud almost as pink as her pussy.

"More, please, please more," dissolved into a deep, throaty moan. He spread her legs further, testing the panties, and devoured the honey he'd just gotten her to produce. Pressing the palm of his hand against her clit he gave her something to grind against as he fucked her with his tongue.

When he could feel her lips tensing as she pulled at his tongue, he dove deeper, walking her to the cliff's edge of arousal. He replaced his tongue with his fingers a moment later. "You don't get to come until I'm buried deep inside of you. Do you understand that?"

A whimpered groan was her only answer. He fucked her hard with his fingers and slapped her ass with his other hand. "Not until I'm inside of you. If you come before I say, I'll turn you over my knee and make you count the strikes."

She pulled at her makeshift binds and moaned constantly. "Please. Please, I need to."

Jamie longed to roar out his dominance as she begged for release now. He stood, unable to wait longer, gripped her hips, and fucked her like rag doll. She fell apart on his second thrust.

"Good girl," he growled. "You come because of me. Understand? You're mine. Say it."

"Yours," echoed from her.

He pounded inside of her, burying everything everyone else thought he was and letting her atonement make him whole. Every accolade, every admiration, and every failure ever associated with his name turned to ash in her heat. She washed him clean.

His right thumb strummed her rosebud again. She trembled against the bedpost. He continued his rhythmic pounding and eased his thumb gently inside of her ass.

She screamed out his name.

"I know now, don't I? I know when you want to run away what you really want is to be tied down and for me to take care of this pussy. Isn't that right, angel?"

"God, yes," she gasped.

"It's my job, baby. My privilege. You don't have to run away. You just beg me like a good girl."

———

The buildup of fears and frustrations she'd clung to her entire life shattered at his hands. The bindings had freed her of every expectation she ever had of herself. Charlie swore her orgasm was blinding. Wave after wave of pressure released and washed her clean. It stripped every piece of herself that someone else had pinned on her. No longer the preacher's daughter. No longer the pitiful girl. No longer the function of some male's title. She was all her own and, in turn, all his.

The muscles in her pussy cinched along with the ones in her ass. He roared as he filled her full of him. Feminine pride welled from deep in her soul. He was all hers as well.

His pumps were ragged and desperate. No rhythm. Only love and satisfaction.

When he finally stopped and they caught their breath, he untied her. Fear still played cruelly in his eyes when she stood. She threw her arms around him. "Thank you."

"I don't know how I fucked up so badly when I love you so much. I didn't mean to keep all of that from you."

She lifted her head from his shoulder. "I love you too."

He crushed her to him. "Really? You're sure? You love me like that?"

She nodded against him. "I always have."

Eventually he went to the bathroom and returned with a warm, wet cloth to clean her up. He carried her to bed and laid her gently on the mattress. She crawled up on his chest and refused to acknowledge the anxiety of what might happen now that she'd said the words out loud.

CHAPTER THIRTY-SEVEN

Still rather enjoying that delicious rubbed sensation between her thighs, Charlie slipped her jeans up her legs. Jamie watched her from the bed. She knew there were a thousand things he wanted to say, but he kept each word locked tight behind his tightly sealed lips.

"I know you don't want me to go without you, but I'm a big girl. I have a lot I want to say to my father."

He climbed out of bed and cradled her face in his hands. "I have no doubt that you've got this. It's just...I have a weird feeling. I like knowing you're safe here. Something's riding me weird."

Charlie remembered having a weird feeling the morning of the fire. She took intuitive feelings seriously always, so she considered his words. "Okay, I get that. Do you want to drop me off over there? Would that make you feel better?" She couldn't feel much beyond her nerves and her irritation with her dad, so if Jamie was feeling something, she wanted to hear him out. She vividly remembered her father brushing her off that morning when she'd told him she was sure something bad was going to happen.

"Maybe."

"You can. I hate for you to have to come back out there and pick me up later, though. I have no idea how long I'll be there. And I kind of wanted to go to the nursing home afterwards and have a face to face with Ms. Billingham. Plus, I want to prove to her that I left my laptop on my desk right where I said it was. If she's really going to refuse to give me my job back, when there's no one to even replace me yet, I want to see her do it in front of the rest of the staff."

Jamie studied her. "I love you."

"I love you too," she whispered.

"Just making sure you haven't changed your mind." He beamed.

"Never."

He leaned his forehead against hers. "I'm being crazy. I'll be fine. You go." He considered for a split second. "Maybe text me when you get there."

Charlie brushed a tender kiss on his soft, eager lips. "You got it."

"Tell me one more time before you go," he urged.

Beaming at that, she gushed, "I love you, Jamie Holder."

"I'm probably gonna want you to say that about fifty million more times."

"Anytime. Now, I need to go because I do not want to be late. I don't want to give Daddy any leverage."

He patted her backside. "Go on. Be careful. Tell your old man that if he needs help getting that corncob out of his ass, I've got a thousand-pound fence pull bar he can borrow."

Charlie shook her head at him. "I'm probably not going to tell him that, since my goal is for him to eventually not hate you, but we'll see where the breakfast conversation goes."

"I might go by the fire station," he stated hesitantly.

"To do what? I thought you hadn't decided yet."

"I don't know. Just...kinda want to talk things out with the chief. He's been married longer than I've been alive. Maybe his wife will have some advice. Or maybe he'll tell me I'm right and to go on and quit and cowboy up about it."

"Promise if you quit, you're not quitting for me." She knew she was obviously the only reason he'd quit, so she was hoping that would buy them some more time to discuss this. He had a determined look in his eye that bothered her. She knew when Jamie Holder was bound and determined to make things happen he didn't let much stand in his way.

"I'll be fine. You go," he urged.

A little while later, she sat in her car and checked her makeup again, though she had no idea why. In a moment of pure rebellion, she'd smeared on a deep red lipstick she knew her father would hate. She was debating wiping it off, but finally flung herself out of her car. She was tired of letting his wishes dictate her life.

The door swung open before she could knock. Louann beamed at her. "I'm so relieved you came." She swept her up in an all-encompassing hug. "And you look so happy. I'm so glad you're back home." Charlie hugged her stepmother but wasn't really comfortable with the huge display of emotion. "We just weren't sure what to think when you didn't come down the aisle."

"I'm sorry I left everyone hanging. I never meant to hurt anyone. I just knew marrying Ed would be a huge mistake, and I had to get out of there."

"I understand that." Louann led her into the kitchen where there was a huge casserole dish of the delicious egg, bacon, and mushroom strata and a basket of fresh croissants. She hadn't cooked the strata since her father's heart attack, so this was a special treat. Charlie's mouth watered. "Your father, on the other hand...well...it might take him some time to come around."

"He can take all the time he needs, but I'm very happy with Jamie. It's the way it always should've been." With each truth she spoke, the more solidly she stood on her own two feet. "I won't apologize for that."

"You shouldn't have to, honey," Louann assured her. "Your father loves you so much. He just struggles with how to show you sometimes."

"Where is he?"

"In his office. I'll go fetch him in a minute."

A knock on the door signaled Becca's arrival. Charlie noted that she was still wearing the dress she'd had on at Rusty's the night before. She wondered who her sister had gone home with and whose bed she was rushing out of this morning.

Becca waltzed into the kitchen, snagged a croissant from the basket, and pinched off a hunk of the warm bread. "Where's Daddy? I'm ready to get this show on the road."

Louann shook her head. "You've been in a rush for as long as I've known you, child, but I still don't think you know where it is you're rushing to."

Before Becca could make a retort about that, Reverend Tilson joined them in the kitchen.

Charlie forced a smile. "Hey, Dad."

He gave her a slight nod and took his usual seat at the table. Charlie decided there was nothing more annoying than passive-aggressive pastors and then remembered that she'd been about to marry one. She shuddered at the thought.

The girls helped Louann bring the food to the table and bowed their heads as their father said grace. Charlie caught the digs in the prayer. The quotes from Proverbs about rash judgement and not considering one's vows. She and Becca shared a quick eye roll while their parents' eyes were closed.

They ate in silence for several long moments while Charlie debated just leaping into everything she wanted to say. She'd envisioned her father starting the conversation, so she needed a new plan.

"Do you intend to marry Jamie Holder?" erupted from the other end of the table. Yanking herself out of her own head, Charlie wiped her mouth.

"Jamie hasn't asked me to marry him yet, but if and when he does, I will say yes."

Becca did a quick little dance in her seat.

"Rebecca," her father scolded.

"Dad," Becca came right back. "I can be happy for them. You don't have to be. I'll do it for you. That's what I've always done."

"What do you mean by that?"

Charlie leapt in. This was her fight and she wasn't going to let Becca go to bat for her anymore. "She means that no matter what either of us does, you're not happy for us. Nothing is ever good enough for you. It doesn't matter that it makes us happy. That means nothing to you. You spent our whole lives trying to force us into some kind of perfect preacher's kid mold. We're our own people with our own wants and our own dreams. And there is nothing wrong with us being who we are. But Bec and I have always had to be excited for each other, because you never were."

Becca gave her two discreet thumbs up, but then there was a knock on the front door.

"What now?" Reverend Tilson lumbered from the table and headed to the living room.

Louann's lips drew to a thin line. "I hope it's not Mrs. Thomas again. She's been driving your father crazy about the youth carwash lately. She's stopped by four times in the last two days. You all need to have this discussion."

But it wasn't Mrs. Thomas from the church. When her father returned to the kitchen, Ed was with him. The few bites of strata Charlie had gotten down turned to a brick in her stomach. "Why are you here?" she demanded. "I have absolutely nothing left to say to you, and I'm fairly certain that none of the Holders would hesitate to make good on their threats from last night."

"I deserve to have a conversation with the woman I was going to marry," he sneered.

"That doesn't seem like he's asking too much," Reverend Tilson agreed. Of course he did.

Charlie pursed her lips and gestured to the empty seat at the table. "Fine, if you want to talk, then let's talk. Why were you trying to access my bank statements?" Ed gaped at her question. Good. She wanted him off balance. "And why on earth did you tell Trinity Church that we would be at a dinner when we were supposed to be on our honeymoon? And along those same lines, why didn't you tell them I would not be coming after I left?"

"It was my right to see how frivolously you've been spending your money since we began our engagement. I also needed to make certain that you'd quit your job as I told you to. I wanted to check when your last paycheck went in. And you didn't deserve a honeymoon. I cancelled our trip weeks ago, right after the last time I found out that you'd gone back over to Jamie Holder's house, despite my orders not to. It was high time you learned a lesson. I intended to teach you to be obedient."

Unmitigated rage ignited in Charlie. "To be obedient?" She spat every syllable of the last word. "You know, I really didn't want to have to spell it out for you, but if that's what you want, here goes—you are a pitiful excuse for a man. I can't even stand to be in the same room with you much less to be your wife," she gagged on the word. "I do not love you. I didn't ever love you. I will never love you. I'm sorry that I didn't end things between us before the wedding. I do take full responsibility for that, but I am not sorry that I did what I did. Being miserable for a few weeks until you get over your stupid ego trip is better than being miserable for a lifetime."

"Trinity won't hire me without you," he raged.

"That is not my problem." Those words were every bit as freeing as the bounds Jamie had tied her in the night before. It wasn't her job to make everyone happy. It wasn't her responsibility to fix everyone's problems.

Sinister reprisal tensed in Ed's eyes as he leaned across the table. "I meant every word I said last night. You are nothing but a filthy notch on one of the Holder bedposts now, and you will never live that down. I was trying to save you from becoming what you're so determined to become, but it's too late for you. You're no longer good enough for me. I should've known after what happened to your mother. God himself tried to correct your spiteful, willful ways, but you still remained sinful. I have no idea why I thought I could do anything with you at all."

Charlie leapt from the table sending her chair careening backwards into the hutch. She didn't care. "What the hell is that supposed to mean?"

"The Lord giveth and the Lord taketh away," he sneered.

The satisfying slap of Charlie's hand flying across Ed's cheek echoed throughout the room. The sting on her palm throbbed upwards to her fingers, but she didn't care. There was an outline of her fingertips in deep red across Ed's stupid face.

"Get out of my home," Reverend Tilson roared as Ed stumbled backwards in shock. "You were wrong about Trinity not hiring you without Charlie. They won't hire you without my recommendation, which you no longer have. If that's really how you believe God works, then you don't deserve a church, or to be a chaplain, or anything at all, most certainly not my daughter's hand in marriage. Get away from her and do not ever come back. I was blind and chose to only see what I wanted to see in you. But Charlie is so much smarter than I am. She saw you for what you really are just in time—a self-righteous fool."

"If you take away my recommendation, I'll make you sorry," were Ed's final words before he stomped out of the house.

CHAPTER THIRTY-EIGHT

Jamie's father had been right. He sucked at taking time off. It made him anxious. He needed something to do. Correction, he needed Charlie to come back so he could soothe whatever her father had inflicted on her this morning. He swore if the good reverend told her he was disappointed in her, Jamie was going to have plenty to say about it.

She'd texted when she'd gotten there, but he hadn't heard anything since, and he still couldn't shake the feeling that something was wrong.

He turned his horse back out in the pasture after he'd checked his cattle and then stumbled up on his father and Wes in the barn. He batted away a few gnats as he entered. The beams of sunlight breaking through the slat boards lit the path. "Hey, listen, can we put off spring burning for a week or two still? I'm trying to get Charlie comfortable living here. Us setting shit on fire is probably going to be rough on her." Every spring, cattle ranchers in the area burned back dead grass and brush to bring out the nutrients in the pastures for the newborn calves.

Barrett nodded. "I think it's still a little too wet to burn now, anyway. Winter went on so damn long. We need another few weeks at least. Shouldn't be a problem. And I am sorry I got between you and

Ed last night. You may not believe this now, but someday you'll know why I did it."

"Why don't you just tell me now?" Jamie hadn't meant to come off quite as pissed as he sounded.

"I did it because of Charlie. Do you remember me telling you about the other man your mother was set to marry?"

Jamie nodded but Wes's mouth hung open before he managed a confused, "What?"

Their father stared out at the endless prairie just outside the barn, but Jamie knew he wasn't seeing their tallgrass fields. The memories almost danced in his eyes. "I decided I needed to show him that Sara was mine, and to make sure I left a mark. So, he came into Rusty's one night forty-some odd years ago, and made a ridiculous remark, and I took the bait. Your uncles and I went after him. He went out on a stretcher, but I went home with the shame. I'll never forget the hurt and disappointment in your mama's eyes that night. I just...I didn't want you to have to go through disappointing Charlie the same way I did your mother. If I could go back and do it all again, I never would've lifted my fists that night. I was trying to save you from living my mistakes."

Damn. All of the fiery gall Jamie had saddled up and ridden with that morning dissipated in the dusty air.

"The worst part of it was," his father continued, "I was hurting too bad to love her that night. I decided then and there that there wasn't anything worth doing if it kept me out of her bed. I've kept that vow to myself every day since."

Jamie chuckled. "So, you're basically saying make love not war?"

Barrett tipped his Stetson to his son. "One will always make you a whole lot happier. I can promise you that. Where is my future daughter-in-law this morning?"

"Over at her daddy's. She wanted to hash things out with him."

"And it's driving you crazy that you're not with her," his father stated.

"A little. But she wanted to do it on her own. I respect that. I just don't like not being with her. I never have."

Barrett and Wes shared a quick grin. "We noticed that a few times over the last twenty years. You know, if you wanted to run into town for me, your mama's determined to plant a garden again this year. They got some tomato plants in down at the feed store. You could swing by the good reverend's house on your way."

"You just trying to get me to do your honey-do list for you, Dad?" Jamie teased.

"I figured I could kill two birds, so to speak."

"The cows have eaten every garden Mama's ever planted," Wes reminded them.

Barrett chuckled, "Your mother doesn't give up easily. That's why all of us turned out as well as we did."

Jamie shook his head. "I'm not gonna go check on Charlie. I don't want to be that guy. Ed was like that, and I sure as fuck don't want to do anything that might remind her of him. But I do think I'll head into town. I need to go talk to the chief."

"I wish you wouldn't quit the station yet," his father urged. "Give Charlie a little time. She'll come around."

"I'm not so sure she will. I want to put a ring on her hand sooner than later. I have to pick, and I pick her."

"Patience never was your virtue," Barrett sighed.

Jamie headed back to his truck and mentally rehearsed what he planned to say to the chief.

As he was heading into town, a late-model Sebring flew past him going the opposite direction. There were only a handful of people in all of Holder County who drove sedans at all, and there was definitely only one who drove one that old and that ugly. Ed had to have been doing eighty in the thirty-five zone with cattle crossing signs everywhere.

Jamie brought his cell phone to his ear. His father was right, he didn't want Ed leaving on a stretcher after a fight, but he also wasn't above getting a little revenge for what he'd said to Charlie.

He called his buddy Nate Wilcox's direct line at the sheriff's office. "Hey, man. Nice job with Charlie Tilson. I always figured it'd be you two."

"Thanks. Listen though. I just passed a Sebring doing at least eighty out on Country Road 5290 heading toward Odell. Do you have any patrol cars out in the trap today? Guy's gonna get someone killed." There was a speed trap about a mile past the last entrance to Holder Ranch. Everyone who lived in town knew all about it.

"Eighty, huh? Let me see who's out there today." Jamie heard him typing on a keyboard. "Yeah, I've got a patrol car just a mile past the last entrance to your ranch. If he's heading into town, he's gonna fly right past him. I'll let 'em know to be on the lookout."

"I appreciate that."

"No problem. And if we bring Ed Weaver in, do you want us to give you a call?"

"Was I that obvious?"

"I'll keep my mouth shut about who tipped us off."

"You're a good man. I owe you one."

"Never a bad thing for a hose jockey to owe me a favor." Nate chuckled.

"Careful now. Next time you call us out because Chester Regis is three sheets to the wind and has his truck down in a ditch, we'll turn the hose on you." There'd been an odd ache in Jamie's chest ever since he'd left the barn that morning. It continued to expand to incorporate vital organs the longer he talked to Nate. He was gonna miss this. Miss all of his friends at the sheriff's and fire departments. Miss every single thing, even the endless nights that resulted in heart-piercing pain for what victims went through. He hated this, but the right thing and the easy thing almost never walked the same road. He knew he was doing the right thing. Charlie was worth it.

He parked his truck in the lot and let the ache consume him for a minute. He stared at the old brick building that had been his second home for decades. Trying to shake that off, he headed inside.

Brady Mitchell and Kane Kincaid were polishing the ladder truck —Jamie's ladder truck. He walked through the gathered water under the engine from the wash it had just received. "Nice job, gentlemen. What'd I do to deserve this?"

Brady laughed. "Look who dragged his face out from between Charlie Tilson's thighs to come pay us mere mortals a visit. Your tongue get tired or something?" He tossed the rag he'd been holding in a nearby bucket and offered Jamie his hand. "We missed you. Chief's a bear when you're not around."

"That's because you're all fuckups and he knows I can keep you in line."

Kane joined them. His dark eyes were alit with mischief, as usual. "You never answered his question," he harassed. "Your dick better be chafed 'cause that's the only acceptable excuse as to why you're here and not in bed with Charlie. Don't y'all have to make up for lost time or some shit like that?"

Jamie flipped him off, a sign of love between two firefighters. "If your dick's getting chafed, Kincaid, you ain't doing your job right. Might want to go back to the five-knuckle shuffle until you learn your way around women."

There was a rhythm to their joined laughter. A steady pulse of humor combined with a readiness, an assuredness that they could handle whatever the day brought them. Jamie was worried that pulse was what kept him sane. "Hey, is Chief inside?"

"Yeah, he's in the kitchen trying to convince Yeager that the coffee he makes tastes better than burned fuel. Yeager ain't buying his cold-hearted lies. Kid's got potential."

"Who the hell let Chief make coffee?" Jamie scoffed.

"You ain't around," Brady stated as if that was the obvious reason.

Diesel fuel laced with the faint smell of smoke ushered Jamie past the turn-out gear locker. He paused for a moment to inhale the memory. An American flag the approximate size of his barn hung on the concrete brick wall, with a random collection of memorabilia and firetruck license plates all older than Jamie.

Following the scent of frying bacon, he found Jared and the Chief in the small firehouse kitchen. "You convince him to try your motor swill coffee yet?" he teased. "Think of it like an induction ceremony, Yeager. Or maybe a hazing."

Jared laughed. "I'm not drinking that." He pointed to the high-end coffee maker Jamie had purchased for the station. "Pretty sure we could clean the battery leads on the engines with it, though."

"You're on dish duty, Yeager," the Chief sniped.

"When am I not?" He sighed and took his spot at the old kitchen table.

Chief continued on with his commands. "Sit, Holder. I made enough sandwiches for you too. You better not be here to tell me you fucked it up with Charlie Tilson."

Brady and Kane both scrubbed their hands and took their seats at the table as well. Jamie knew he shouldn't accept the invite. He was only putting off the inevitable, and that was only going to make what he'd come there to do a thousand times more difficult. But one more meal with the guys was too much to turn down.

He settled at the table. "I didn't fuck it up," he informed them. "But I doubt you're gonna like how I made it work."

CHAPTER THIRTY-NINE

Charlie stood nearly paralyzed after her encounter as she heard the front door slam shut. Her hand hurt badly, but not nearly as badly as her soul. How could she possibly have been about to marry *that?*

Bile-soaked shame singed a path from her stomach to her tongue. She was going to vomit.

"Here," Becca offered her something, but Charlie couldn't concentrate enough to understand what it was. Her sister took Charlie's right hand in her own and wrapped it in the cloth-covered ice pack. "I've slapped a couple guys before. Hurts like he... uh Hades." She offered their father a quick apologetic glance.

"Are you all right, sweetheart?" He approached them both cautiously.

"I'm...not sure."

"Come sit down in here. There's quite a bit I need to tell you." He gently guided her to the living room sofa. Still horrified at what might've been, Charlie took in the room in pieces, like some kind of Picasso artwork where things might fit, but she couldn't make out how.

Becca settled beside her. "He is why you have to stop doing things because you're afraid," she whispered.

Charlie knew that now. She didn't need the lecture anymore, but she also didn't blame her sister for reiterating the point. How many mistakes had she made because she acted out of fear? Twenty years of not being with Jamie was definitely the biggest, most unforgivable loss.

Her father gave an audible breath. "I owe you an apology."

Those words cleared a little of the wreckage from her mind. "For which thing?" she managed.

Her father nodded his acceptance of that. "Several things, but I'd like to start with Jamie. You remind me so much of your mother."

"Why do you always say that like it's a bad thing?" Her whispered question was half-haunted with memories.

Her father wrapped his arm around her and pulled her closer. "It's a wonderful thing. She was everything to me. You know that. But it also frightened me."

"Why?" Becca asked on Charlie's behalf.

"There's a lot about your mother's and my relationship that we never told you girls. But I think you have the right to know. I haven't always been very good about admitting my flaws, but that doesn't mean they don't exist. I met your mother when I was serving as the brand-new youth minister at the Pilot Methodist Church out toward Prosper, Texas. I was still in seminary, but I needed the money so I took the job they offered me. First time I saw her, I swear I fell in love with her. That red hair and those freckles did me in. She was only sixteen at that time. She was in my youth group. I knew it was sinful, that I was giving in to the temptation of lust, but I asked her to date me in secret."

Charlie was enthralled. "Why did you never tell us this? It's so romantic...kind of. We wanted to know, and you kept it from us."

"I was ashamed. I asked your mother never to tell you girls. I used to meet her out near the back gates of this old horse farm, right on the banks of the lake. She'd," he choked, and Charlie took his hand in her good one.

"Keep going. Please. Even if it's hard."

Her father nodded. "I intend to. Just give me a minute. I can still see it all like it was yesterday. Memories can be cruel, Charlie."

"They can be, but they can also be healing."

"If you say so. She used to come running right into my arms late in the afternoon when school got out. She'd make up some lie to tell her parents about where she was going to be, and we'd stay out on that lake shore until she had to leave to make it back for curfew. I couldn't even see her home safely without losing my job." He shook his head. "I hated it, but I loved her. I told myself it was the only way. Until...we got caught."

Charlie squeezed her father's hand. She could feel his agony through the palms that had raised her. "I take it that didn't go well."

He shook his head. "She'd told her mother that she was going to the library that afternoon and then to see a movie with some friends from church."

Becca piped in, "At least the friends from church part was kind of true."

Louann rubbed her temples. "Becca honey, what are we going to do with you?"

Their father gave Becca a slight headshake and continued on with his story. "Her parents decided to have supper in town that night at the diner across the street from the library. They went in to see if your mother and her friends might like to join them before their movie. Of course, they weren't in the library. This was long before the days of cell phones, so her mother searched for her. She wasn't in the movie theater either. There were only three cinemas back then, so it was a quick search. They tried calling the police, but she hadn't been missing long enough. Small Texas town. Police weren't too worried. Said to let them know if she didn't make it home by curfew. But your mother's parents were very strict, and they were not only worried, but angry. They phoned the church, and the pastor there—my boss—called the parishioners to search for her. And...they found us."

Charlie tried to memorize every detail of the story. She never wanted to forget a single word. "Did you get fired?"

"That very night," her father's voice held echoes of his pain. "Her parents came down hard on her. She wasn't allowed out of their sight other than for school. Her seventeenth birthday was the next week. I managed to slip a birthday card in the mail to her from a different address. Tried to disguise my handwriting. It must've worked because I'd put a train ticket in that card to Oklahoma City where I planned to transfer the rest of my studies to. The train left the night of her birthday. She managed to sneak out one more time. That was the last time she ever saw her parents or any of her friends. I'll never forgive myself for that."

"Are you telling me that her parents never forgave her?" Charlie leapt. She'd never known her maternal grandparents. She'd ask about them occasionally, but her mother never said much.

"Never." The pain in her father's eyes was unbearable.

"That's ridiculous. She loved you. Why couldn't they see that?"

Her father's eyes closed. "They saw only what they wanted to. The very same way I was about Ed and about Jamie. You see, sweetheart, the way you always run to Jamie...it reminded me so much of the way your mother ran into my arms those afternoons after school. I knew you loved him before you ever did. I could see it. You looked at him the very same way she used to look at me. It terrified me."

"Why?" Her voice faltered. "Why wouldn't you want me to have what you and Mom had?"

Tears pricked her father's eyes. "I do want you to have that. I want both of you girls to have that. But honey, remember, if I'd never sent your mother that ticket, she'd be alive. I was the mistake that not only took her family away from her, but ultimately I took her life as well."

Charlie's nostrils flared and the rock-like enclosure in her throat continued to expand. The longing for her mother and the heartbreak for her dad consumed her. "That isn't true. That...isn't how life works."

Her father kept speaking like she'd said nothing at all. "I know it was wrong of me to keep you girls from talking about her, but I was so worried that you'd make the same mistakes we did. When you came home from your first day of school here telling me about Jamie, I saw every gruesome detail of my life repeating itself over with you. I couldn't have that. I had to protect you." He shook his head. "The Holder family...they bear a tremendous amount of responsibility in this town. I know that. But the way those boys are able to take off that mantle and...cut loose—it seemed they always got away with whatever they were doing. I don't know. I resented it. I resented the relationship you had with Jamie. You went to him instead of coming to me. I have spent the rest so many years resenting the Holders, blaming them for winning the hands they gambled on when the one and only time I'd knowingly done something wrong, I'd lost everything."

Charlie threw her arms around her father. "You didn't lose everything," she choked. "You never lost us. But please, stop pushing me away."

"I'm sorry I did that. It was never my intention. I was only ever trying to keep you from following someone down a path you couldn't come back from. The way your mother did. I didn't want you to live her mistakes. I was so afraid you'd die by them."

"Daddy," Charlie placed both hands on either side of her father's face. "You listen to me. You were never a mistake, and neither is Jamie. That isn't how life works. We all make a thousand decisions every single day that affect everything else. Mama met you that night at the train station because she loved you. She was a little young, but that doesn't change the fact that she did. It is not your fault that she died. It's not any of our fault. She went with you so she could live the life she wanted. And she did that. That's all that matters. She would never have chosen not to have the years she had with you and with us even if it meant she would've lived longer. I know she wouldn't have. You don't give up love because you're scared. You don't gamble on some completely uncertain future just because you're scared of what happened in the past." Realization struck in Charlie's head like lightning. It sizzled through her brain. "Oh my god. I have to talk to Jamie. He can't quit. He can't give up something he loves just because I'm scared. I'm sorry, Daddy. I love you so much. Thank you for telling me all of this. I want to hear every single story you remember about Mama, but right now I have to stop Jamie from quitting the fire station."

CHAPTER FORTY

They'd just taken the first bites of their grilled cheese and bacon sand-wiches when the sirens split the station and the radios started crack-ling. Wasn't that always the way? Jamie wasn't certain how to proceed. He'd come in with the intention of quitting, but he couldn't abandon his brothers in the middle of a call.

But when he heard the dispatch, his blood ran ice cold. "Prairie Dispatch to Station One. Holder County dispatching Station One. Please respond to a multiple alarm structure fire at the Pecan Crescent Nursing Home. Repeat—multiple alarm structure fire at 2122 Pecan Crescent Drive at Rural Route 3119. All units please respond."

The tones began to chime. Each one drilled into Jamie's head as he raced for his gear. The fire tones immediately followed the medical one. "First Responders go ahead," scratched from the radio in his hand. Charlie was surely at the nursing home now. Breakfast was long since over. She was there. They'd just dispatched all medical units from the surrounding area. And... he refused the next thoughts.

Yeager was suited up in record time. "My grandma's out there. I checked the whole place myself. How the hell did it catch fire? They have every recommended NFPA regulation. It's damn near fireproof."

"Nothing's fireproof. Let's go," Jamie growled as he grabbed his helmet and mask.

It was against regulation to answer a cell phone when you're on a dispatch. Jamie gave no fucks. When his buzzed in his pocket he yanked his headset off and answered. All he could think was that it was Charlie calling to assure him that she was fine. "Tell me you're okay," he demanded.

"We're fine, son. Gave us quite a scare, though."

"Dad? What the hell are you talking about? Where are you?"

"I'm putting the ranch fire trucks away. I would've called you, but there wasn't time."

"Called me about what?"

"The fire. The old shed between your house and Wes's went up in flames. I have no idea how long it burned before the field caught. Thank god the grass is still damp. It didn't spread as quickly as it could've. It took us some time to get it out. I had to get to Wyn to make sure he wasn't burning early and had let it get away from him. But once we got the field under control, I saw the smoldering shed."

Jamie's heart pounded out an SOS against his ribcage. "Is Charlie there with you?"

"Not that I'm aware of. I haven't seen her today. I'll check with your mother. Maybe she went up to the house. I can hear the sirens. Where are you heading?"

"The nursing home. They called in all available units. We should be there in ten. I think she might've gone there to try to get her job back. I have to find her now."

"All right. Listen to me. I'll go by Reverend Tilson's house. She's probably still there. You go do what you do. Try to keep a clear head. If she's in the nursing home, I know you'll get her out. If she's somewhere in my county, I'll find her and bring her there to meet you. I promise you that."

"Dad...what if Ed? The fire?"

"We have no proof of that, but I should've let you beat the piss out of him last night. If I find out he did this and he's anywhere near her, I'll put him behind bars and I will keep him there. You have my word. Be careful, son. You know we love you."

Jamie ended that call and touched Charlie's name on his caller list. It rang four times and then he got her voicemail.

"Get that headset back on, now," the chief barked.

———

Charlie answered her phone as she sped toward the fire station but didn't take her eyes off the road to look at the screen. "Hello?" She pulled into the empty parking lot. The engines weren't in the bays. Climbing out of her car, she walked toward the station. The uniforms that normally hung in the open shelving right beside the trucks were missing. Everyone was gone.

"Charlie, it's Trisha."

Jamie was probably back at the ranch. She tried with everything she was to believe that, but she knew the man she loved. If he'd been there when they'd gotten a call, he wouldn't have let them go without him. He was duty-bound to protect. It was in his blood. And as much as it terrified her, she loved every part of him, that one included.

"Uh, hey. I was going to stop by there today. I need to talk to Ms. Billingham." The phone filled with shouts and sirens. "Is everything okay?"

"The home is on fire. I'm so worried. We're trying to account for every resident as they're brought out, but some are missing. Do you think you could come help? The fire is spreading so quickly. We don't know how it happened. I don't think we'll ever get everyone out."

The world around Charlie slowed while her heart flew. She heard herself say, "I'll be right there," but she barely recognized her own voice. The line went dead, and she stood frozen on the gravel. *Move, Charlie. You have to move. They need you.* Every step back toward her car was just as uncertain as the one before. The ground shifted and rolled under her feet. Could she come help?

A thousand cowardly thoughts fought a sharp sense of bravery for dominance in her mind.

Sweat dewed on her forehead. Her side ached from the memories alone. She instinctively pressed her inner arm close to her ribcage to cover her scars.

That's where Jamie was. He would go without question. Without fear. Without doubt. That's who he was. He'd go because the nursing home meant so much to her.

And she was going to be his wife. If he was there, she could do this. She could stare down the smoky demons that haunted her past. She'd do it for him.

CHAPTER FORTY-ONE

"Charlie?!" Jamie bellowed as he leapt out of the engine. He scanned the gathered crowds, but she wasn't there. Chaos ruled supreme as other engines arrived on scene from Odell fire departments dispatched to help, and nurses and attendants tried desperately to keep the evacuating residents safely away.

He pulled on his turn-out coat and brought his headset to his lips. Strapping on a tank, he shouted, "Lieutenant Chief Holder, ladder truck one. We're on scene and going in."

"Godspeed, Lieutenant," chirped in his ear.

"Engine 4 three minutes out."

"EMT unit 42 on scene."

He should've waited for backup. Should've waited for a plan. For command from the chief. For every protocol he was breaking. But this was Charlie, and he couldn't lose her. How the hell was she back in another fire? Had the first one not taken enough?

Funnels of smoke billowed along the ceiling as it rained down on him. Hypnotic waves of heat and smoke encased him.

"Jamie!" Kincaid grabbed his shoulder, but Jamie shook him off. "Dammit, Holder. We don't even have hoses out yet."

"She's in here!" He didn't need anyone's help. He'd get her out on his own.

"Then we'll find her, but we aren't losing you in the process." He lifted his arm toward a room to their right, engulfed in smoke. "There's someone in there." They dropped to their knees and crawled through the wall of heat.

A patient was in the bed trying to scream for help. Her wails were consumed by the smoke. Kincaid lifted her into his arms. "Holder, you come with me," he ordered.

"No. I'll check the next room."

Jamie crawled along the melting linoleum feeling along the wall until he reached the next doorway. He felt his way around the room, but it appeared to be empty.

He moved on down the line, staying low and straining to hear above the roar. The sprinklers rained down on him constantly, but they didn't seem to be enough to quell the flames. They burst through the wall room after room.

The oxygen lines. Jamie realized as a spray of sheetrock crumbled beside him. How the hell did someone light the oxygen lines and where was the shutoff?

———

Charlie's cell rang as soon as she saw the smoke. She was still a half mile away. Her entire body trembled. "Uh...hello?"

"Charlie!" It was Jamie's dad. Oh god. Why was Barrett Holder calling her unless...no. Please, please no. Please. She prayed to God even though she'd been angry with him for years. She should never have told him she loved him. "Are you all right, sweetheart? Just tell me where you are. I'll come get you." Barrett's deep soothing voice boomed in the middle of her prayer and for a split second she wasn't certain which father was reassuring her.

"What?"

"Where are you?"

"Is Jamie okay?" The words stirred the ashes in her throat.

"He's fine." Her previously stalled heart restarted, suddenly making her woozy. "Where are you?"

"I'm almost to the nursing home. They need my help."

"Brave girl. Listen to me, if this is too much for you it's okay to tell them no."

"I want to help. Jamie's there. I know he is."

"He is there, and I'll be there in just a few minutes."

"I need to go. I'll find Jamie."

She ended the call and raced out of her car and toward the rolls of flames and smoke pouring from the western wing. Flames shot out of the roof and consumed the siding. That smell. Oh god the smell of melting carpet tiles gut punched her. She raced to the bushes and vomited out the smell, the memories, the horror.

Firefighters raced around her, some rolling out hose. "Bust out those windows," someone shouted. Two firefighters raced by her with axes.

The scream of the sirens internalized in Charlie. They echoed in her chest so loudly she wasn't certain if they were coming from her mouth or from the living, breathing monster of fear housed deep inside of her. It clawed at her vocal cords and cinched its claws around her throat. She'd been here before. How could déjà vu be so cruel?

"Ma'am, we need you to get back," another insisted but she couldn't focus on her face long enough to really see her.

Chief Riggins was opening the hydrants. Someone somewhere was screaming about the power lines and some kind of shutoff valve. Where was Jamie?

The rhythmic metallic strum of water brought the hoses to life and the scrapes of ladders on the cement clawed against her skull.

CHAPTER FORTY-TWO

Flames had eaten through the elevator shaft. The patients on the second and third floor would have to be gotten out with ladders. Charlie's office was on the first floor, so Jamie continued his crawl. He searched every inch with his hands.

Suddenly he ran into someone else crawling towards him. They gripped his shoulder. "Help. Please," wheezed from the elderly man. "My wife."

"Where is she?" Jamie shouted.

The man, with his waning strength, tried to pull Jamie farther down the hallway.

"I'm getting you out first. I'll come back for her. I promise you." He wrapped his exterior coat around him and guided him toward the entrance. When the man could no longer crawl, Jamie lifted to his knees and hoisted him into his arms. Remaining hunched forward, he cradled the man in his arms and raced for the entrance.

Brady met him a hundred feet away, gave Jamie back his jacket, and took the man from him as more search and rescue joined him in the rapidly disintegrating corridor. "We've got to shut off the oxygen lines," Jamie shouted. "That man's wife is in a room down here."

"They're working on the oxygen. The new director can't remember where the shut-off valve is located."

The director would be losing her job if Jamie had any say at all. Flames licked at the walls. He crawled back toward the inferno as the sprinklers continued to rain down water-soaked sheetrock on his helmet. He couldn't see through the visor. The flames devoured the insulation, and the fire fueled itself.

———

Charlie tried desperately to see the names on the sheets attached to the clipboard Trisha had shoved into her hands. The letters swam across the page. She was supposed to check off names as patients were brought out and then check them against the sign-out sheets families filled out when patients left the facility for any reason.

But she couldn't think. She couldn't even breathe. Kane Kincaid raced out next carrying sweet Mr. Clawson. "Kane!" Charlie all but attacked the poor man. "Is Jamie in there?"

"Yeah, but he's looking for you. I thought you were in there."

He's alive. He's alive and he's fine and he's going to come out of there and everything will be fine. Her heart thundered in her throat. "Obviously, I'm right here. I was never in there. I have to go get him."

"You're not going in there," Kane corrected her as he handed Mr. Clawson to an EMT to be loaded on a stretcher. "I'll tell him you're out here, but you stay back."

Charlie felt a steadying hand on her shoulder as she watched Kane race back into the flames. She turned to stare up at Barrett Holder with tears in her eyes. "I shouldn't have come here," she finally admitted. "I'm no help. I can't read the names on this paper," she thrust the clipboard in his face. "I can't see. I can't think. I can't get over what happened when I was little. I'll just...always be afraid."

Barrett gave her a kind fatherly hug. "Sweetheart, I promise you that you are not the only one who's afraid. You're awfully hard on your-self, did you know that?" He swayed her back and forth until she felt a little of her sanity return. "When I was a little boy, I went riding with my father. He...well, he didn't always make the best decisions when it came to me and my brothers. I was only five at the time. He told me to get my horse to follow his. I did as I was told and followed him along a river back up in Montana. He'd been planning to purchase some land up there.

"Anyway, the path between the water and the mountain beside us continued to narrow. I was terrified, but I was also afraid to say anything for fear of ridicule. So, on we rode. And the water continued to rise and rush at me until it was deep inside my boots. When we were waist deep, my father pressed on despite protests from his horse. But the next rapid that crested over a boulder cluster swept me off my horse's back. The only thing I remember is that I couldn't tell which way the air was. I'd been tossed and turned so many times. I'll spare you the most gruesome parts of the story and just say that eventually he managed to pull me out. But I've been afraid of water ever since then. I made up excuses not to swim when I was a teen. Always steered clear because that feeling that I didn't know which way was up stuck with me.

"And then Sara and I had kids, and one day I saw Jamie's horse buck and he went ass over end into our creek headfirst, and he didn't come back up. I nearly lost my mind with panic. I don't think he was in there more than ten seconds before I was neck deep in the creek with my little boy safely in my arms. Because I wasn't afraid when it mattered. I'm still afraid of water, rivers especially. Fear is always with us. It's never going to go away. It's a useful emotion at times. You don't have to master fear, sweetheart. You just have to decide when it's okay to give into it and when it's not. I've known you most of your life, and I'd bet my entire ranch on the fact that if my son needed you right now, you'd race into those flames to get him. Fear be damned. You know that fear will always saddle up with you. You just can't hand it the reins."

Ed's shouted voice slithered over Charlie. Both she and Barrett turned to stare his direction. "It's probably Mr. Graham. He's been sneaking cigarettes even while he's on his oxygen."

Ms. Billingham's voice drowned out Ed's. "I'm sorry. I just don't remember where the shut-off valve is. I don't think the old director ever told me. Do you have the blueprints yet?"

Charlie lifted her head. "What shut-off valve?"

A firefighter from Odell answered, "To the main oxygen lines. That's what's on fire and we can't put it out until we shut that down."

"I know where it is." Charlie had taken special care to learn every single safety measure the design team had installed the year before. She knew every exit strategy from every floor. "Come with me."

"You see there," Barrett smiled, "when it matters."

She accepted an extra jacket from one of the trucks and put on a mask. Then she raced toward the flames pouring out of the building.

CHAPTER FORTY-THREE

Jamie pulled off his helmet and then yanked his mask up over his head so he could lay it over the woman's face. The ceiling from the floor above splintered and fell across her bed. He lifted her up and had her in the doorway just before the entire thing collapsed.

He couldn't see a clear path to any entrance. There was nothing but smoke and flame and the putrid scent of melting plastic drenched with wet sheetrock. Unable to breathe without the mask, the entire world spun. He couldn't quite recall which way was up.

Sinking to the floor, he found it nothing but a heap of incinerated rubble. He had to get them out of there. He had to find Charlie. But he couldn't go on.

Suddenly, he was being hoisted in the air. Someone took the patient from his arms. Jamie was aware enough to detect the steady bounce of his rescuer running. "Charlie's outside. She's waiting on you," Kincaid shouted. Abject relief was the last sensation he remembered feeling before the world went black again.

He woke to the sensation of someone strapping another oxygen mask on his soot-covered face and to the steady roll of the stretcher. Water hit his face. He blinked his eyes open and there she was. Her tears washed his face clean in a steady baptism of her love.

"Stop." He pulled at the mask, but no one listened. "I'm fine."

"I'll have them strap you down," Charlie warned him in that no-nonsense tone that under any other circumstance he would've found sexy as hell. But her voice quivered, and his heart summarily shattered in response.

They weren't gentle when they loaded the stretcher onto the ambulance. He jerked and lurched as they locked it into place. He couldn't have complained if he wanted to. He swore his throat burned hotter than the flames he'd just been pulled out of. Charlie climbed on the ambulance with him. "He's going to tell you he's fine even if he isn't, and he needs a bronchodilator shot to widen his airways."

The EMT smirked. "Yeah. We've got it."

That evening two massive IV bags hung on the pole beside Jamie's hospital bed, and a nasal cannula was strapped to his nose. That was going to get old quick. At least he could talk as long as he took sips of water between every few words.

"Do you want some more hot tea?" Charlie asked for the tenth time in the last half hour. Both of his parents were seated in the room, but they were letting her run the show, which Jamie supposed he appreciated. His brothers and his cousins were in and out with frequency. Currently, Meridian and Dalton were leaned up against the wall trying to get Jamie to laugh on occasion.

"I'm fine," Jamie tried not to cringe from speaking. "I just want to hold you." He downed another slosh of water from the massive hospital cup. She was already sitting beside him on his bed, but he wanted her closer.

Charlie leaned down and brushed another kiss on his cheek, working her way around the oxygen tubes.

"How long did they say I have to keep this in again?" he asked.

"At least twenty-four hours. They'll evaluate after that. And I will not be leaving this room for even one second so I will make certain that you keep it in."

"Nurse Ratched." His cough diminished the joke somewhat.

She rolled her eyes. "I wasn't going to say this, but you leave me no choice. I have been right where you are, only about a thousand times worse, so you have no ground to stand on to complain."

"Yeah, but I'm a dude and we're basically huge-ass babies when we're sick. You're a badass. It's the nature of our DNA."

"So you take no responsibility at all?" She was trying so hard not to laugh it made him grin.

"I ain't saying that. I'll man up here in a minute. How are you with all this, by the way? I didn't mean to scare you. I was so damn convinced you were in there somewhere. I lost my head." He cleared his throat again. That was a bad idea. Hurt like a motherfucker. He corrected by drinking more water. He was gonna have to piss like a racehorse if he kept this up. One of the bags on the IV stand was nothing but saline. The other was some kind of vitamin-rich drip bag that was supposed to make this all go away and keep his lungs healthy.

Charlie gently brushed the hair off of his forehead. "I was terrified, but I did what needed to be done when it had to happen. So, I'm also proud of myself. I'm learning when it's okay to listen to my fear and when it's keeping me from living my life." She offered a tender grin to his daddy. "Even after everything that happened today, I still don't want you to quit being a firefighter for me. I don't want you to give up a love for a fear. As long as you promise me that you'll stop trying to always be the only hero."

"I'm always proud of you," he spoke with more clarity this time. Meds must've been kicking in. "And as long as I have you, I'm not giving anything up." At the moment, if he never had to race back inside a burning building that would be just fine by him. But he suspected in a week or two, when breathing didn't feel like he was inhaling the surface of Mercury, he'd want to be back at the station. "And believe me, I know I'm only here because of my team. I was an idiot. That won't happen again."

Once again, most of the Holder family clogged up the waiting room. But Chief Riggins, the rest of station one, and a host of police officers and sheriff's deputies were all mulling around outside his room. Almost the entire floor was being used to treat victims of the Pecan Crescent fire.

About the time Charlie was forcing more hot tea down Jamie and lecturing him about the cilia in his lungs, two second-shift firefighters from Odell came in along with some staff from the home. One of the firemen handed Charlie an open cardboard box. "Ms. Tilson, we brought some things we pulled out of your office during salvage and recovery. We're trying to get everything cleaned out so reconstruction can begin as soon as the arson investigation team has completed their assessment."

———

Charlie's nerves were shot so she was unable to keep the defiance from her tone as she commented to no one in particular even though Ms. Billingham was standing nearby. "It's not really my office anymore."

Ms. Billingham entered the room just then and sighed. "I might've been hasty in my decision on your job."

Jamie squeezed her hand bolstering Charlie's hope further. "What made you decide that?"

"I was just speaking with your father," she gestured outside Jamie's room where her father and Louann were stationed. They'd come to check on Jamie and to apologize to Barrett. Charlie was very pleased. "It seems...perhaps...that I might've given Chaplain Weaver more credit than he deserved."

Setting the box down on one of the guest chairs in Jamie's room, Charlie gave herself a moment to process being back on the receiving end of things given to her during a fire salvage and recovery. How had this happened again?

She mentally scanned the items in the box. She'd slowly cleaned out some of her office last week so there wasn't much in the box.

A flood of memories filled Charlie's mind as she lifted her old laptop out of the box. "I thought you said this wasn't in my office."

The director attempted to smooth her skirt and refused to meet Charlie's eyes. "I...must've been mistaken...again."

The events of the day tallied in her mind. A few key moments stood out above all the rest. "You weren't mistaken," she whispered.

Jamie's brow furrowed.

"What?" Ms. Billingham looked just as offended that Charlie agreed with her as she did when she was having to apologize.

Charlie turned back to face everyone in the room. "You weren't mistaken. It wasn't in my office. Ed had it." She raced toward the door. "He shouldn't have known about Mr. Graham. He was bringing my laptop back. That's why he was there."

"Where are you going?" Jamie asked through another storm of coughs.

"To find Ed."

"The hell you are." He tossed the sheet and blanket off of his legs and stood, while trying to keep the parts Charlie rather liked thinking of as only hers covered with the loose hospital gown.

Chief Riggins halted her at the door. "Holder, get back in that bed. No one wants to see all that, and you're already in trouble with me. And are you talking about Ed Weaver?" he asked Charlie.

"Yes, sir. I have to find him. I think he might've set the fire at the nursing home."

"If that's the case, you aren't the one who needs to find him, I am. And he's down being checked out in the ER. He sustained a minor burn to his inner arm. I'll bring him up here when he's released. You stay in here with him." He pointed to Jamie. "Stubborn goat. If I ever hear of you taking off that mask when you're on scene again, I'll whip your ass. How many times do I have to tell you you're not Superman? You're on twelve-week suspension for going in without orders too."

Charlie glanced Jamie's way and gave him a sorrowful expression. She couldn't believe Ed had done this, and now Jamie was in trouble because of it. She felt at least partially responsible for making Ed so angry he'd even contemplated something so cruel.

She reminded herself that his actions were not her responsibility, but he'd hurt her Jamie. He had to answer for his crimes.

"All right, here, I'll say it—I screwed up. I thought I could get my mask on her and get us both out of there. If it weren't for my team, I wouldn't be here. So, thank you to all of you standing out in the hallway talking about me like I'm not right here." He downed a long sip of water. "Damn, that hurts."

Chief Riggins seemed somewhat pleased by that announcement. "Somebody record him saying that. I'll be right back."

"I can't believe he did this," Charlie slunk back down on Jamie's bed. "I know I shouldn't, but I feel responsible. You were able to save Mrs. Trammel, but other people weren't so lucky."

"What did he do, honey?" Jamie was unable to whisper so most of the room heard his question.

"He had my laptop. I bet he went and took it out of my office when the bank wouldn't give him access to my accounts. He wanted to track everything. So, he went and stole it. That's why they couldn't find it. The only place there was any information about Mr. Graham sneaking cigarettes, even when he was on his oxygen tank, was in my patient notes on my laptop. I took the cigarettes from his room after I saw him on Friday. I told Trisha to check on him constantly. But she was the only other person who knew about the cigarettes. Ed tried to blame the fire on Mr. Graham. I heard him. Why would he blame someone else unless it was to take suspicion off of himself?" She shook her head. "I don't want to believe that, but it's the only explanation as to why he was there at all."

"I did pass him heading that direction when I was on my way to the firehouse. That would put him there at about the right time."

A few minutes later, Chief Riggins shoved Ed into Jamie's room along with two sheriff's deputies. Jamie looked supremely annoyed, probably because he was in a gown, but Charlie would deal with him later.

"You had my laptop," Charlie launched in as soon as one of the deputies closed the door. "That's how you knew about Mr. Graham and the cigarettes. You had to have seen that on my laptop. Why were you even at the home today? You start your new job on Monday."

"That's a good question," Chief Riggins said, "and I'd like an answer."

Ed cleared his throat. "I came up there to help. They called me."

"Who called you?" Ms. Billingham asked. "I was in charge of calling extra help, and I never phoned you."

"I don't know who it was. I came as soon as I heard."

Riggins nodded. "And I'm sure you wouldn't mind me taking a look at your phone to prove that?"

Ed shifted uncomfortably. "I didn't have anything to do with the fire."

Barrett Holder stood. "Correction," he countered, "you didn't have anything to do with *that* fire." No one spoke. No one even moved when Barrett Holder held court, but Charlie noted the growing fear in Ed's eyes. "I've talked to almost everyone involved in my son's and Charlie's day, and I think I've got it mostly put together. The burn on your arm didn't come from the nursing home. You never got close enough to have been burned. I had my eye on you the whole time. You didn't start the fire at Pecan Crescent because you were too busy setting fire to one of my sheds."

"What?!" Charlie leapt off of Jamie's bed. "Wait. What?"

Barrett pulled something from his back pocket. "After Jamie left this morning, the old shed between Jamie's land and Wes's caught fire and took out about seventy-five acres of land. Now, it is a field we'd planned to burn back in a few weeks, so it's not a big loss, but Wes and Hallie found this after we'd gotten the fire out." He held up something Charlie immediately recognized the red cording on. But it had been badly burned.

"That's the menu from the Three Squares diner, where Jamie and I ate on our way to Nebraska."

Jamie sat up in bed. "If I'm about to find out you were in my house, fucker, I'll find a way to whip your ass, oxygen or not."

"Son," Barrett pled with him. "Simmer down. I didn't have any idea what it was until I stopped by Jamie's house to get his toothbrush and some clothes since he's staying here tonight. I saw a duplicate menu on his kitchen table."

"I really want to slap you again," Charlie informed Ed.

Jamie's cousin Meridian was also the Holder County assistant district attorney and the ball had just been rolled into her court. "Second degree arson," she slid a low whistle between her teeth, "that's a twenty-thousand-dollar fine and up to twenty-five in prison if Jamie or Wes decides to press charges." She narrowed her eyes. "Of course, if you didn't set the one on the ranch, we'll launch an investigation into just how that fire got started. It's a long dirt road to Jamie's house and tire tracks are very, very car specific. And then there's the fact that if we can't prove you started the prairie fire, but we do prove that you had something to do with the Pecan Crescent fire, you're going away for life. Because I'll try you not only for first degree arson but for murder as well."

Jamie's eyes narrowed. "Hey, somebody grab Nate from out in the hall."

CHAPTER FORTY-FOUR

Nate Wilcox joined the crowded room. "Isn't there like some kind of number of visitors rule or something?"

Chief Riggins brushed him off. "We'll get everyone out of here in just few. Jamie has a question for you."

"That tip I gave you this morning. Did it pay off?"

Nate shook his head. "Nope. Channing never saw him before he left up there and headed back to the station an hour later."

Jamie nodded. "So, that means either you spun your car out in the ditch on 5290 or you stopped by the ranch. I saw you flying that way. There isn't anything between where you were when I passed you but our property and the trap."

"That doesn't prove anything," Ed huffed.

Meridian laughed. "It will prove a lot of things when I present it in a courtroom."

Barrett interrupted his niece. "So, you went by my son's home. We leave most of our doors unlocked so I won't quite call it breaking in, but it sure wasn't legal. Grabbed this." He held up the remnants of the menu. "And then what? What made you decide to burn down the shed?"

But Jamie had his number. "Well, he wouldn't have burned down my house. That would've been too obvious. He knew it wouldn't take long for either me or Chief to have him. But I'd bet money on a thousand head that he was hoping the fire would go unnoticed for longer than it did."

"No," Charlie shook her head. "No, that's not what he wanted. He wanted to scare me." She stalked closer to Ed. "He wanted to take away the one place where I always feel safe. It didn't have to be a big fire. Just one that I couldn't help but see. You got mad after our argument this morning. You told my father there would be payback."

"We call that premeditation," Meridian explained.

Ed's temper finally loosed his tongue. "Do you have any idea what it's like to be in a relationship with someone who saves every single memento from when she's out with another man?" he snapped.

Sara Holder had clearly had enough at that point. "Then do you know what you do about that? You end the relationship with her. You don't burn my son's land, you mo-ron."

"Sara," Barrett took his wife's hand and shook his head. "Take him down to the county jail for the night. I find that gives people some good time to think on their actions. If Jamie's up to it, we'll stop by down there tomorrow and decide if we're going to press charges."

"Yes sir," Nate pinned Ed's hands behind his back and clicked the handcuffs around his wrists.

"But we still don't know that he didn't start the fire at the nursing home," Charlie fussed.

"He wouldn't have been there at the right time, angel," Jamie reminded her.

"So, what did start it?"

"We'll figure that out. I promise you," Chief Riggins vowed. "For now, we're all going to get out of your hair.

As everyone but his parents and Charlie left the room, the Tilsons entered.

The Reverend cleared his throat, "Jamie, I owe you and your family an apology for the way I've treated you...ever since we moved here, honestly. I am very sorry."

"Daddy, thank you." Charlie threw her arms around her father. Jamie could just make out what he said in return.

"You're welcome. It finally occurred to me that there were other people involved in what happened to me and your mother. If her parents had forgiven and wanted a relationship with her, we would never have moved away. And even if we had, we would've visited as often as we could. I'm hoping if I don't continue to push you away, that you'll come around and see me more often."

"Definitely," she assured him.

"Jamie, I hope you feel better. Please let me or Louann know if we can do anything to help with your recovery. Takes a brave man to be willing to lay down his life for others. I appreciate that my daughter wants to be with someone like that."

Jamie cleared his throat of emotion this time. "Uh, thank you, sir. I'll always take care of her."

"I have no doubt." Reverend Tilson offered everyone a wave as he and his wife left.

———

Early the next morning when his bloodwork had returned to normal, Jamie was released from the hospital. Since Charlie had dealt with her own smoke inhalation issues, she felt confident in being his caretaker.

"I made you soup," she announced as she carefully carried a bowl in from the kitchen.

"Baby, you don't have to fuss over me," he urged. "I'm fine. I'm suspended for twelve weeks anyway, so by the time I go back to work my lungs will have forgotten all about this."

"I hope so, but I'm still going to fuss. I had to endure it for months, so you can give me a few days."

"Fine." He accepted the soup. "I just don't want you to get annoyed taking care of me. I'm supposed to take care of you."

"We take care of each other, remember? That's the deal. That's how this works."

"I remember. Thanks for putting up with me even when I'm being stubborn."

"Sometimes I like your stubborn side," she beamed, "but everyone needs other people to look after them. If we all took better care of each other, the world would be a much better place."

"Says the preacher's daughter." Jamie winked at her.

Charlie considered for a minute before asking, "Have you decided what to do about Ed?"

"I wanted to talk to you about that. Wes is leaving it up to me and Dad. If you want me to press charges, I will. But be aware if Meridian takes him to court, he's gonna go to jail. That girl is ruthless. If you're okay with me dropping the charges, I'm fine with it as long as he never sets foot near you ever again."

"I can't believe he burned that menu. I wanted to put both of them in my scrapbook." She knew that was such a ridiculous thing to be upset about, but she'd found after the first fire that it's the little things that cut you to the core. It's not about the wedding album. It's the blurry, bent snapshot pic from when you were dating and both laughing together. Those are the things that hurt the most. Most importantly, she'd learned to make memories and to treasure them.

"I tell you what," Jamie offered. "How about after we get married, I'll drive you back up to that little diner and get you another menu. Only that time, it would be legit."

Charlie loved that he would really do that for her, even though it wasn't necessary. "Are you asking me to marry you, Jamie Holder?"

"I'm not gonna do it while I'm in sweats after spending the night in a hospital. But if I did, would you say yes?"

She smirked. "I guess you'll have to wait and see."

"Brat."

"Your brat."

"Damn straight."

They went down to the Holder County jail together. Charlie wanted to show Ed that this wasn't just Jamie's decision. He signed the papers for Ed's release, agreeing not to press charges for the damages to the land.

But as Ed was making his way toward the door, Jamie stopped him. "You ever come near her or even think of darkening the gates of

Holder Ranch again, I can promise you I'll see to it that your ass stays in jail."

He laced his fingers through Charlie's and guided her out to his truck.

They ate dinner with her father and Louann. She brought all of her scrapbooks with her and showed them to Jamie and her father.

CHAPTER FORTY-FIVE

Charlie returned to work as the lead occupational therapist at Pecan Crescent Nursing Home. The arson investigator had determined that it was a patient who'd caught his cannula line on fire while sneaking cigarettes, but it was not Mr. Graham.

Construction was underway on the north wing and was expected to be finished soon. Some of her patients had been moved temporarily to other facilities. Others had gone home for the time being. But most of the ones she'd been working with the longest, like Mrs. Garcia, were still there.

"You can't dance unless you put on your dress," Charlie gently reminded her. Continuing to work on the activities of daily living was important for early onset Alzheimer patients. Besides, she knew Mrs. Garcia could do it. She always wanted to dance. It was one of the many things Charlie adored about her.

"I'm just picking the right one." Mrs. Garcia stood at her small closet touching each of her four dressier dresses. Charlie wondered if she was lost in the moment, perhaps retrieving a lost memory of dancing as a young woman or if she really was just picking one.

"The pink one is my favorite. It makes your beautiful skin sparkle."

Mrs. Garcia tsked. "Pond's makes my skin sparkle, dear, and if you like the pink then the pink it shall be. It's a special day."

That was the fourth time she'd said something like that. As far as Charlie knew it was just a regular Monday kind of day, but she appreciated that Mrs. Garcia was excited to see her.

She was so thankful to have her job back she'd wanted to hug all of her patients every time she saw them for the last several weeks.

"Do these have a runner?" She held up a pair of knee-high hose that didn't really match the dress, but that didn't matter. It was helping her work through the process of getting into them that mattered to Charlie.

"I don't see one. I think they're perfect." She watched carefully as Mrs. Garcia eased the hose onto her feet. Charlie helped some, but she did it almost entirely on her own. Pride welled in Charlie.

"Okay," she held up the gait belt and wrinkled her nose. She knew what was coming. "You know the drill."

"It ruins my outfit," she fussed.

"It keeps you safe and wearing a belt is slimming."

"Not a belt like that," Mrs. Garcia fussed but she let Charlie attach the safety belt around her waist.

"Trust me, I understand having to wear stuff like this. I've been in your dancing shoes before."

"I know you have. Let's go. We don't want to be late."

Charlie wasn't sure what they might be late for, but she went along. They ambled down to one of the larger activity rooms, since most of the smaller ones had been destroyed in the fire. She'd already put away most of the tables to make room for the dancing lesson.

"I downloaded us some new music," she announced as she plugged her phone into the speaker system.

"I hope it's good for dancing."

"It'll be perfect." She switched on the Andrews Sisters and watched Mrs. Garcia's eyes light. "Okay, are you still teaching me the step ball change or are we doing a different step today?"

Her weekly dance "lessons" had become some of her most treasured time. "We don't move onto the next step until we've mastered the basics."

"Got it." Charlie braced her left hand behind Mrs. Garcia's back and took the other in her right. She let her patient lead. "Remember to roll your shoulders back, open your chest," she gently reminded as they moved.

"Glenn used to take me dancing on his off days," she commented with a dreamy look in her eyes.

Charlie beamed. "Tell me about him." Keeping her talking while moving was so good for her lungs.

"He was a firefighter." Charlie almost missed the next step and tripped over her own two feet.

"You never told me that before."

"Well," she shrugged, "I'd rather talk about me."

Chuckling at that, Charlie continued to ask questions. "Today is Jamie's first day back at the station." He'd already called a dozen times to check on her, but she was doing okay with it all, for the most part. "Were you ever afraid when he was at work?" she couldn't help but ask.

"Sometimes. Of course I was. But honey, I came up at the end of one war and then we were in another. Recession. More war. I finally decided one day there were always gonna be things to worry over. I was tired of letting the worry have my good days, though. So, I was gonna collect all the good days that I could. I wrote 'em down too. Had a little book where I recorded everything. When my babies were born. When my grandbabies were born. And little things too. I liked to have a record of when Glenn did something stupid so I could remind him of it from time to time."

Charlie shook her head at that. "I bet he didn't like that too much."

"Oh well," Mrs. Garcia's smile was bright enough to shame the sun, "he knew I was a firecracker when he married me. He liked my naughty side."

"Oh, I bet he did."

"But I'll tell you, in all those tiny notebooks I kept, whenever I'd go back and look at all the days there were always so many more good ones than bad ones. I think if you look back on life and have that then you can't complain too much. Worry robs too many days of their good and turns them bad."

"I think you're pretty smart and quite the dancer."

Mrs. Garcia let go of Charlie's hands and did a turn all on her own.

Trisha stepped into the room with a smile. "Can I help for a minute?"

Charlie's brow furrowed. "We've got it."

Trisha nodded and then pointed to the back of the room. Making certain Mrs. Garcia was stable, Charlie turned to see Jamie standing with a crowd of his family, her patients, the entire Holder County Fire Department, and her father, sister, and stepmom.

Her hand flew to her mouth to try to catch the gasp before it escaped. Jamie met her in the middle of the makeshift dance floor. "I wanted everyone we love to be here for this." He dropped down on one knee and tears sprang to Charlie's eyes.

"I know I shoulda done this years ago. I'm not willing to waste any more time. Charlie, will you make me the happiest guy on this planet and marry me?"

"Yes," she choked out and bounced on her toes. He slipped the most beautiful vintage diamond band she'd ever seen on her finger.

"You must dance," Mrs. Garcia called.

Jamie stood and gathered her in his arms. "Can I have this dance?"

She managed a nod this time while crying and trying to hug him and look at the ring and beam at their families all at once.

"Uh, may I?" Barrett Holder asked as he headed toward the speakers.

He switched his phone for Charlie's, and Harry James's *It's Been a Long, Long Time* belted out from the speakers.

Laughing and crying all at once, she let Jamie spin her around the nursing home activity room. She couldn't think of a more perfect way to have asked her, even if she was in her scrubs. Or a more perfect guy to marry.

"Kiss her," Mrs. Garcia ordered.

"I like her," Jamie teased just before he leaned in and mated their mouths in slow, decadent kiss.

CHAPTER FORTY-SIX

Wearing a black tux with a white tie, per Charlie's orders, Jamie headed up the stairs at the church to the bridal room. His parents were at the church, but the rest of his family was setting up the reception down on the low creek of Holder Ranch, right where it needed to be. They'd be there in time for the ceremony.

He smiled at Clint Masterson, just one of the surprises he had up his sleeve that day. Becca was stationed outside the door. She laughed. "I knew you wouldn't wait on her to walk down."

"She has a habit of running from these things, you know?"

"I know, but I don't think that's going to happen this time. All she's been doing all morning is swooning and getting teary-eyed. I had to get out of there. She's driving me slightly insane with all the tears."

Jamie chuckled at that. There was a very tiny and also absolutely huge reason that his baby was so emotional. And in about seven and a half months, when their first little one made an appearance, it would all make sense to Becca. He gestured to Clint. "There's someone I think you might want to meet. This is Lieutenant Clint Masterson from the Oklahoma City fire department. You've, uh, met him before, but I doubt you remember."

Becca's face fell and all of a sudden it wasn't only her sister who was emotional. "Oh wow." She scrubbed away the mere appearance of tears. "So...you're...him?" She shook her head. "Sorry. I'm Becca Tilson. Thanks for saving me. I'm really sorry I tried to bite you." She cringed.

Clint laughed. "It was a rough night for all of us, and I'm thrilled to meet you. This whole day makes my job worth it."

Jamie smirked at his soon-to-be sister-in-law. "I was checking cattle early this morning and noticed a car that looked just like yours killing the grass down at Boone's house."

Becca's eyes widened. "Don't tell Daddy," she pled.

"Daddy?" Jamie chuckled. "You need to be worried about telling Charlie."

"Don't tell her either."

"I don't keep things from her, so get it figured out."

"It's nothing. I'm not my sister. I'm never meeting anyone at the end of an aisle, so it doesn't matter enough to tell Charlie."

"Uh huh. Sure." He gestured to the door. "I hate to make her cry harder, but I wanted to introduce them before I give her the gift."

Becca seemed relieved Jamie had dropped his line of questioning for the moment. "Everything makes her cry today. Hang on, let me make sure she's dressed."

He stopped her. "He's staying out here, so even better if she ain't." He waggled his eyebrows and let himself inside.

Charlie laughed but Louann and his own mama gave him disapproving head shakes. "I had to make sure she hadn't made a break for it."

She raced into his arms. "Never. I've always been looking for you, remember?"

"And I'll always be right here. You ready to get this show on the road?" She was beautiful. He smiled at her hair done up in one of those intricate braids that her OT had taught her to do back in the burn unit.

"It's still another two hours until I'm supposed to walk down."

"But I'm ready now. You're in...this thing." He gestured to the gown she'd picked for this wedding, very different than the last. It was off the shoulder and if a person knew where to look when she moved her arms you could see the scars. He was thrilled she didn't care. She'd gotten the gown she'd dreamed of. "Let's get this show on the road. Wait, why are there so many hooks?" he asked as he took in the back.

"I like to be a challenge."

"Don't I know it." He discreetly slipped his hand over her pearl and satin covered belly. She beamed at him.

"The guests aren't here yet, babe. We can't get married yet."

"Shoulda done it at dawn like I suggested."

His mother came to rescue Charlie. "Jamie, honey, where is your father? He was supposed to keep you in the rec room downstairs."

"I like how you seem to think anyone could keep me from her."

"Go back downstairs and let her finish getting ready."

"In a minute." He turned back to Charlie, "I got you something and I wanted to give it to you now, and then there's someone I want you to meet before we get to the marrying."

"Please tell me it's not lilies."

"You hate lilies. Why the hell would I get you something you hate?"

"I love you." She hugged him tight again.

"I love you too, sugar. Here." He pulled a small box from his back pocket and handed it to her. The wrapping paper he'd used was a little masculine and a little worn, perfect by her estimations.

She carefully opened the package, planning to save the paper for the wedding scrapbook. But when she saw the box, she almost dropped it all. "Jamie," she gasped.

He helped her remove the delicate bottle from the box. "I called around a bunch of places and looked online. Becca helped me. It's a vintage bottle of the perfume your mom wore. I found an old supplier who had a lot of stock left, so I bought them all. You don't have to save it if you want to wear it today. I've got fifty bottles."

"I can't believe you did this." She was going to cry off all of her makeup long before she ever got down the aisle. "Thank you so much. I don't deserve you."

They cradled the bottle between them as he hugged her. "Same goes, angel. Can you come out in the hallway for a minute?"

"For another surprise?" she choked.

"Kinda."

Jamie introduced Charlie to Clint. She did indeed sob, but when she instinctively rubbed her hand over her womb while she continually thanked him, Clint caught on.

He hid a grin. "Nice work," he whispered to Jamie.

"I do what I can."

"All right, ladies," Clint tipped his hat to the Tilson girls, "I'm going to go take my wife and kids out for a little lunch before we come back for the wedding. I can't wait to see it, and my wife can't wait to meet you, Charlie."

"I'm so honored you're here. I can't wait to meet her either," Charlie assured him.

After he headed back down the stairs, Jamie sighed. "So, I guess I have to go back to the basement holding area until you're ready."

She lifted her head and grinned at him. "You don't have to. I'm the bride so if I say you can stay up here with me then everyone has to go along."

"Sounds like a plan."

One hour and forty-five minutes later, Jamie made his way to the altar. Ford was already there waiting on him along with her father. They watched Becca make her way down the aisle. And then the music swelled and there she was—on his daddy's arm since her dad couldn't be in both places at once.

And the relatively short aisle of the church seemed like it was a mile long as he watched her walk. He didn't want one more minute for her to be his wife. He wanted it all right now. Patience still wasn't his virtue, but she seemed okay with it.

This time Charlie couldn't wait to get down the aisle, and she was marrying her best friend. It was just the way it should always be and should always have been. She lifted her wrist to her nose gently just before Barrett gave her hands to Jamie to catch the scent she'd sprayed there. She cemented her mother's memory in that church right then.

Even more than vowing to love and honor and cherish Jamie for the rest of their lives, she vowed to make as many good memories with him as she possibly could. Because nothing is guaranteed except that love always wins in the end.

Bestselling author Jillian Neal likes her coffee strong and sweet with a shot of sinful spice, the same way she likes her cowboys. In fact, her caffeine addiction is quite possibly considered illicit in several states as are a few of the things her characters do. When she's not writing or reading, you'll find her in the kitchen trying out new recipes or coming up with ~~excuses~~ reasons to purchase yet another handbag or make an additional trip to Sephora. Though she'll always be a Bama girl at heart, Jillian hangs up her hat and kicks up her boots outside of Atlanta with her hunk-of-a-husband and her teenage sons.

For more information...
jillianneal.com
jillian@jillianneal.com

ALSO BY JILLIAN NEAL

HOLDER COUNTY

Oklahoma Sky

BROKEN H.A.L.O

H.A.L.O. Undone

H.A.L.O. Redeemed

Fractured H.A.L.O.

CAMDEN RANCH

Rodeo Summer

Forever Wild

Cowgirl Education

Un-hitched

Last Call

Wayward Son

BOHO BEACH TO CAMDEN RANCH

Boho Cowgirl

Coincidental Cowgirl

www.ingramcontent.com/pod-product-compliance
Lightning Source LLC
Chambersburg PA
CBHW030348200726
48286CB00013B/515